PLAY PRETEND

EMILY ALTER

Copyright © 2024 by Emily Alter

All rights reserved.

No part of this book may be reproduced in any form or by any electronic or mechanical means, including information storage and retrieval systems, without written permission from the author, except for the use of brief quotations in a book review.

Edited by R. Phoenix.

Cover Design by Jo Clement.

PLAY PRETEND

Kara

When I put an ocean between my ex and me, I made myself a promise. No getting closer to Dommes again. Ever. There was no way I'd put myself back in the same situation.

So of course my new boss is the epitome of one, and of course I find that out when I was having a panic attack in a BDSM club. I should've run away then, but… I couldn't, not when I'd just gotten a glimpse of what my life could be.

Mónica

I liked to keep my life as headache-free as possible. Which wasn't always easy when working in a male-dominated field with my four brothers. Still, dealing with my brothers was nothing in comparison to having to talk my new secretary through a panic attack in the BDSM club I helped fund.

I tried to reason, to negotiate how to keep my two worlds separate—the way I liked them. The last thing I'd ever do was put her in a situation where she was even more vulnerable but… I was going to become the cliché boss who fell for her secretary.

Play Pretend includes a Little reconnecting with kink through group play, an ice queen by day/soft Domme by night, an office romance, hurt/comfort, queer chaos, and a kink community to die for.

KINKS INCLUDED IN PLAY PRETEND

- Age play (diapers mentioned)
- Bastinado
- Boot worship
- CNC (mentioned)
- D/s
- DP (mentioned)
- Exhibitionism
- Fisting
- Group play
- (Other forms of) Impact play (mentioned)
- Leather
- Objectification
- (Medium to high) Protocol
- Praise
- Primal play (mentioned)
- Puppy play
- Rubber
- Sex toys (dildos, vibrators, strap-ons)
- Sharing

KINKS INCLUDED IN PLAY PRETEND

- Voyeurism
- Worshipping

CONTENT WARNINGS

- Play Pretend is, first and foremost, about Kara's healing journey from an abusive relationship. However, this means that, throughout the book, there are references to this abusive relationship, and the aftermath of it (such as panic attacks, low self-esteem, and dissociation).
- **Family rejection** (mentioned).

GLOSSARY

- **Plumas:** feathers. Pluma is also used to say someone "looks gay/fem" (mostly used when referring to queer men). For reference, plumo-fobia means fem-phobia.
- **Unicornio**: unicorn
- **Botas de cuero**: leather boots

1

KARA

This was supposed to be a new beginning.

"Supposed to be" was the key phrase in that sentence.

I scrunched up my nose. I'd been chilling at home, sitting on the arm of the couch for the past hour, staring at my phone. I should have moved to my room to do this, but once I started something, it was hard to take a break.

Stupid ad.

A voice inside my head said it was too soon. I was still hurting, still licking all those invisible wounds I'd promised I'd talk about with someone. If I closed my eyes and tried to imagine myself in any kind of scene… I shuddered.

I just—

I used to be good at visualizing things, but not that. I got goosebumps, and just pictured myself running away. Crying, too, to be honest.

The distance was supposed to help.

"Supposed to" was the key phrase here, again.

It didn't.

I read somewhere that mourning a relationship should take a month per year of that relationship.

I didn't think that held true. Maybe it worked for vanilla, trauma-free relationships, because according to that statement, I should be way over it and moving on by now.

I was so far from it, it wasn't even funny.

It was why it didn't make sense that I was so frozen, staring at the ad for yet another fetish app.

I used to have all the mainstream apps, but I'd deleted all my accounts. It wasn't even about not wanting Her to find me—I could've blocked Her and all of our common friends.

I would've just never been able to relax. There was no way I could've signed up for any event, or done anything without checking every five minutes to see if She was signing up, too. Or someone else who would eventually become another person we had in common.

Even after moving all the way to the north of Spain, I hadn't dared to open another account. A voice inside my head kept telling me She'd find me. Another voice, instead of offering the opposite argument, chipped in to point out I'd never feel comfortable in a kinky setting again.

I couldn't fight that voice.

The mere thought of submitting, of kneeling or lowering my guard in any way, made me sick.

My stomach clenched with unease, and I hadn't even clicked on the ad yet.

I should've just closed it the second the option to do it popped up.

There was just a teeny tiny problem—a third voice that lived rent free in my head. It whispered, begged, pleaded. It reminded me of the things, the truths, I so wanted and didn't want to forget.

Kink was a big part of me, always had been. I *could* function without it, I supposed, but it felt hollow, like a big part was missing, a key to actually reaching full happiness. I'd only gotten a few glimpses of it.

I didn't want to lose it, to have to accept that I'd never experience anything like it again.

My eyes watered. It happened every time. I didn't bother doing anything about it. My roommates wouldn't be in the apartment until later at night. I didn't really know them yet, but I knew they worked late at the hospital. I didn't know why they'd thought we'd be a good match.

I was just a secretary for a construction firm, and I hadn't even started working yet. I'd just gotten my visa early and wanted to move in as soon as possible. Staying one more day in the same city She was in had made no sense. I'd made myself promise I was going to move on and turn over a new leaf, and I was intent on doing exactly that.

Which was why the ad gave me pause.

It was a fetish site, but it was for a local community. She wouldn't be there. No one who could possibly get back to Her would be there. There was a whole ocean between us now, and I'd made sure no one learned about my plans to move countries. Only my previous boss had, and that had only been because I needed a referral.

My old boss was the most stereotypical, vanilla cishet man there was, though. I'd panicked about it at the time— paranoid much?—but there was no way they'd cross paths.

A beep broke me out of my thoughts.

I didn't used to get so deep in my head. I hated it.

I hated the extra seconds it took me to recognize the sound, too. Before coming to the couch, I'd put a casserole in the oven and set the timer. My roommates hadn't said anything about doing things for each other, but I'd wanted to make a good impression. They still wouldn't be here for hours, but I'd already written down instructions on how to reheat it.

Ideally, I would've waited to pop it in the oven for when they'd be back, but so far, they'd been making it home by the time I was already in bed.

I didn't want them to think I was a hermit, or tiptoe around me. I could be social and make friends and care for them.

Baking them a meal should be a good start until they had a day off so they could see I'm not weird.

Not too weird, at least.

I grabbed the mittens from the cupboard drawer, even if I still didn't understand why they were *there* of all places, and placed the baking dish on the granite counter.

My anxiety usually meant I wasn't too hungry, but my stomach still rumbled as the smell hit me. I'd found a place that sold all the good spices two days before, and now the mix of them transported me back to my grandma's backyard. She'd always insisted on having big family meals outside. There had even been times when she made the whole family reschedule if it was raining or the weather was too rough.

I didn't miss the big family dinners—I'd been cut off from them years ago—but I missed the warmth her food provided.

The plates were still in the dishwasher, so I grabbed one from there, and cut myself a piece. I double checked the note was legible, then took the plate and a fork to my spot on the couch.

The screen on my phone had turned off, but I was still aware of the local site I should probably check out.

Food first, though.

At least cooking was something I was genuinely good at. My grandma always joked about how her genes had skipped a generation.

Cooking was just so underrated. It was soothing.

When everything spun out of control, I knew I could go in the kitchen and create something good. It helped.

A friend had said once cooking was how I expressed love.

I thought I expressed it in many other ways, thank you very much, but I hadn't known how to argue their point back then.

Verbalizing things wasn't my strongest point. It hadn't been so bad, but then… Yeah. Ex who shall not be named.

I sighed.

I'd eaten about half of my plate already, but I didn't think I'd be able to finish. The whole thing with the site was going to nag at me until I actually did something about it. I wasn't good at functioning with things hanging in the background like that.

Sitting up properly on the couch—instead of on the arguably much more comfortable arm—I placed the plate on the coffee table and grabbed my phone again.

Nerves swarmed through my belly as I clicked on the link to the site. There wasn't a sound as the link loaded, and I was pretty sure I wasn't breathing, either.

Huh.

What popped up was surprising.

I'd been expecting the theme every fetish site seemed to have—black and dark red backgrounds, sometimes with a smidge of purple, or even yellow. It was a thing, and it was ridiculous, and I'd heard many Littles complain about it. How were people expected to believe kink wasn't scary, when the sites all screamed darkness and gore?

This site, though, had a pastel blue background with a few accents in red. It wasn't the typical dark, blood red, either.

It was nice.

It helped give me the boost of confidence to actually click on the button to create an account.

Thankfully, it wasn't as clunky as fetish apps tended to be, either. I usually didn't even bother using them on my phone, but my laptop was all the way up the stairs in my room.

I was avoiding spending too much time in there—mostly because I hadn't brought myself to unpack everything yet, and seeing all the cardboard boxes was depressing.

After asking for an email address and a password, the site asked me for a nickname. I chewed on my bottom lip. For the longest time, I'd used the same nickname in all the apps. It had been easy.

I could still do that—no one was going to recognize me—but it didn't feel right. How could it be a new beginning, if I was still clinging to the past?

Choosing nicknames was hard, though. Some people simply wrote their main role and their name or a shortened version of it. It worked for them, but I always thought that was lazy. I liked it when nicknames gave a peek into the person behind the screen. For example, one of the first kinksters I'd met online had *waffles_and_whips* as a nickname. I wasn't sure I would've replied to his DM if he'd just been *maso_Cam*.

My fingers drummed against the back of my phone as I tried to come up with something. I'd never been the most imaginative person out there—hence recycling my nickname everywhere I possibly could.

In another lifetime, I'd text Cam to ask for ideas. He had always been good at those kinds of catchy names. The problem was that we hadn't spoken in years now. I'd abused our friendship, used him to unleash all the trauma that came from staying with Her. He'd ended up building a distance between us that grew larger and larger.

I got it.

Just another consequence of a shitty relationship.

It just sucked.

I missed him, but I wasn't sure there would ever be an excuse for us to reconnect. I'd ruined things.

I tried typing a couple of things until one stuck a chord.

soft_and_sweet

I wasn't—hadn't been in a long time—but I wanted to be. Even if no one would know, it was an homage to him. It felt right.

The labels section came next. That was easy. Cis woman, 28, she/her pronouns, bisexual, single, Little. I didn't add any more roles or fill in what I was looking for. Both casual and long term options sounded dreadful.

The about section came next.

I took a few swigs of water before I tackled it. My about sections had always made me cringe, always too long or too short or too plain.

> i am a little, and i've just moved in from the US (i speak Spanish too; my father was from here). i'm only looking for other little friends, maybe playdates with them, but absolutely no Domms.
>
> i don't accept friend requests unless we've met in person, but you can DM or follow me if you're not a creep.

Ugh.

Too plain.

Cam would've made it much better.

Whatever. It was done, and it was a big step. I still had to find a new therapist here, but the one I'd gone to for a few months back home used to drill it into me that I had to acknowledge my accomplishments and celebrate them.

I'd made the profile, and even if I hadn't added any pictures, I'd made it. I'd even written that I wanted to meet Littles and have playdates. Playdates had been fun when they weren't too closely monitored by Domms too interested in turning them sexual.

They were also the one thing that I could picture myself doing without wanting to throw up. And the thing I was craving, if I was honest with myself.

I looked around the living room. I'd been stress cleaning the day before, unsure of what to do with all the energy that sometimes overtook my senses. It hadn't taken long, though. The TV was framed by big oak furniture with different drawers and open shelves. That had taken a bit longer, making sure I didn't throw anything away while dusting it to perfection. The rest of the living room was rather bare, though. There was the big sectional couch, the coffee table in front of it, and a table in a mismatched shade of brown where they never ate or did anything.

The house wasn't the most homey, but it had been within my budget, they hadn't turned me down the second they realized I was American, and it wasn't a cramped apartment.

I hadn't lived in anything other than cramped apartments ever since my family decided I was no longer welcome at their house. A combination of "it's important that you figure out how to live on your own" and "we're more conservative than we're willing to admit" I tried not to think too much about.

Turning on the TV was almost a reflex. My roommates had set up a profile for me on their Netflix account earlier that week. I'd tried to say I could cover part of the monthly fee, but they'd insisted we'd talk about it once I'd made my first paycheck.

Thinking about that paycheck and the new job I kept wondering if I was really qualified for was not going to take me anywhere. Instead, I scrolled until I found the new *Matilda* musical. It was my go-to when I was feeling small or in Little space.

2

MÓNICA

"Mónica!" My brother ran up to me, waving his arm.

I fought the urge to roll my eyes. I'd tried to point out to him that I didn't have any hearing problems, and the building we were at was a monstrosity of glass and wide hallways with nothing blocking the view.

It was a lost cause at this point, one of those things that just were the way they were.

"Yeah?"

I hadn't bothered speaking until he was close enough. My nose wrinkled, but I stilled the movement. One would think a man in his late thirties would know about *daily* personal hygiene by now. It wasn't as if he spent every day outside doing actual labor. We might work in the construction business, but he'd never gotten his hands dirty in any sense of the word.

"Come meet the new secretary. I was just telling her she'll be mostly helping you."

Again, I had to fight not to roll my eyes. Noel made it sound as if she'd be *mostly helping me* because I was lesser than the rest of them. Not because I was the one in charge of the international client base we were trying to grow.

"Lovely."

I might be able to control my facial features, but I couldn't keep the sarcasm from my voice.

I wasn't sorry about it, either.

Noel barely noticed, anyway. None of the men in our family were known for their emotional intelligence.

"I put her in the office next to yours, but maybe we can set a desk in your office so she can shadow you the first weeks or so."

I ignored it. It angered me that he'd already given her an office and taken over when she'd be *mostly helping me*, but I took a deep breath and upped my pace so I was entering the office first. There was only one empty office next to mine, so it hadn't been too hard to figure out.

"Hello, I'm Mónica Boján, and I believe you already met my brother Noel."

"Kara Steuber." Kara met my extended hand and shook it. It was a nervous shake, but not so weak that it would raise alarms about her ability to perform. "Nice to meet you, Mónica. Noel was just showing me around."

"Right." I'd only met Kara once during a video call. HR had already cleared her, and my father had sent me a Word document with three pages of reasons why she was his first choice. The call had only been a formality, and we'd both known it. "Did you want some coffee? I was going to get some from the break room before I logged in."

"Uh, okay."

I almost smiled. Kara looked like a deer caught in headlights, stormy blue eyes looking up in clear confusion. It was easy to forget that American work culture differed quite a lot from us here—even if my brothers kept insisting on turning this building into corporate Hell.

"Come with me, then."

"I'll leave you two to it." Noel had to, of course, have the last word. "It's been great meeting you, Kara."

"Thanks."

Kara was subdued now, but I ignored it. First days could be overwhelming, and I hadn't gotten the impression during our video call that she was the most confident candidate.

"Have you had time to settle in yet?"

"Yeah." Kara gave me a soft smile. I ignored how angelic it made her look. "I arrived about two weeks ago, and I'd already found a place to share."

"That's nice." I hadn't been in close quarters with a native English speaker in a while. The faint throb in my temples reminded me of that fact. Video calls were less demanding. I liked her voice, though—it was gentle and clear and delicate, for lack of a better word. "I must say, we were surprised you could move so quickly. We've been trying to fill this position for months now."

"Does that mean I'm gonna have to catch up fast?" Kara's eyes widened as she placed the question—probably because she realized the way it could've come across. "It's not a problem! I'm just trying to figure out what my first days are going to look like."

"Don't worry about it." There had been pure panic in the way she rambled through her excuses, though, and I didn't like it. Thankfully, the break room was right around the corner. "How do you like your coffee? We can talk about your first weeks once we're sitting down."

Kara looked relieved. Her steps didn't falter as she followed me into the empty break room. My brothers all got their interns to bring them their coffee to their office, but I'd prided myself in never doing that. I also prided myself in not trying to fool my father into thinking I was working more hours than I actually was.

The numbers always spoke for themselves, anyway. I'd leave the idiots to keep believing that not leaving their office made everyone think they were hard at work.

"With lots of flavored creamers."

"I think we have hazelnut and normal creamer." I was already opening the cupboard where the bottles of creamer were as I spoke. "Talk with the building manager if you want other flavors."

Kara nodded. She'd moved too close. I knew she was trying to get a look at the cupboard, but my body reacted to the proximity regardless.

It was only a second, but enough to keep me on edge as I added the pods to the Keurig machine and grabbed two cups from another cupboard. When I'd turned around, Kara was reading through the label for the hazelnut creamer. There was a slight frown on her face.

"Is there a problem with the brand?"

As far as I knew, none of my brothers used the creamers. They were only there to impress interns and prospective clients who asked for a visit to the main offices. If one of our employees was actually going to use them, they had a right to say which brand or whatever we got as far as I was concerned.

"No, sorry. I was just curious. My roommates only have the creamers that come in tiny packets. I thought maybe these weren't a thing here."

"You have to order them online, I believe."

Kara nodded. The Keurig beeped once it was done, so I grabbed both cups and slid hers closer. I made sure our arms didn't touch, but I noticed the goosebumps in hers. I wouldn't be inferring anything yet, but reading body language was second nature.

"Thanks."

"Of course."

I watched Kara doctor her coffee with enough creamer to make me worry about her arteries. Most people would've hidden that in their first day, postured as the cool type who drank their coffee black or almost black. I respected that she didn't.

"This is good."

She'd only taken the slightest sip, but I wouldn't call her out on it.

"Have a seat. Did Noel give you your work ID yet?"

"He said someone from HR would come either later today or sometime this week, and I could use my laptop to clock in and out in the meantime."

"We'll go downstairs after this, then. It'll only take them two minutes."

I had nothing against the human resources department, but they could take their sweet time if left unattended. Plus, even if clocking in and out from one of the office laptops was easy enough, Kara would still need her ID to get inside the building. Otherwise she'd have to wait outside for one of my brothers to let her in.

There was no way I'd subject anyone to that.

"Sure." Kara bobbed her head up and down. She took a larger sip of her coffee before sitting down in front of me. The chairs weren't the most comfortable, but my father had only cared about how sleek and modern they looked. "So I'm going to be your secretary? Or the floor's secretary, but mostly yours? Sorry, I just wanted to ask since Noel said—"

"There is another secretary on the floor," I explained. I didn't want to wait and see what it was that my dear brother had said exactly. "She's on holiday right now, but I'll introduce you when she comes back next week. You're going to be working with me, though, unless my brothers need you for something, and I'd be approving it first."

"Oh, okay."

I frowned as I watched her fingers fidget against the coffee cup. "I thought they would've explained this to you in the interviews?"

"I don't know. Maybe they did and I didn't quite catch it." A blush spread through Kara's cheeks and down her neck as she put the blame on her shoulders. "They just said that the company was taking more international clients, so they needed a secretary that was a native English speaker too."

I nodded. "That's pretty much it. What they didn't say was that I'm in charge of all the international accounts."

"Ohhh. So, I'm with you, unless they start taking international accounts as well?"

"Pretty much."

That wasn't likely to happen anytime soon, though. Noel's English was good enough to greet someone at the door, but that was about it. The rest of them weren't any better. I was the one who'd chosen to study my MBA in English to push myself.

"Okay." Kara licked her lips.

She looked jittery, her legs bouncing slightly. I tried to look as if I hadn't noticed. Instead, I took a sip of my own cup of coffee. I was almost done with it, but I didn't want to rush her. I had nowhere to be this morning because I'd wanted to have time to go over everything with her.

"You said you were from Rhode Island, right?"

"Yeah." Kara's smile was stilted. "My mother is from there, and then my father is half Spanish, half German."

"So you're trilingual?"

"Mostly bilingual," Kara admitted. There had to be a story there, in the way her lips curled up into a teasing smile. "My father was born here—well, in Galicia, so he mostly spoke Spanish unless he was talking with his grandparents in Germany or something. But when I was born, they were already dead, and his German was rusty anyway from what he said, so it was never a priority."

"That sucks."

Kara just shrugged. "I mean, it did for a while, but it is what it is. I do want to visit though, now that I'm here."

"I go to Berlin most years," I said. "I always try to visit the towns and parks outside of the big cities, too. Some of them are really stunning."

"I'll have to ask for your recommendations then."

Another blush made it to Kara's cheeks, but I supposed it was understandable.

"I'll be happy to help."

"Uh…" Kara took a larger sip of her coffee. I was pretty sure she'd finished, but I couldn't tell for sure while she was holding the cup so close to her mouth. "I'm sorry, I've just realized we've been talking in English nonstop. Your brother just greeted me in English, and got the ball rolling. But we can switch? I'm really perfectly fluent."

"I know." It was one of the big points my father had made about hiring Kara. He said she could help if we needed to unload the local contracts, and he'd be able to talk to her, too. He'd seemed to have made up his mind that we would use a secretary to hide things from him, or… Who knew what that man thought? "But it's good. As I said, I'm in charge of all the international accounts, so it's good practice."

"Right."

Kara placed the cup on the table, then, and I confirmed it was empty.

"Let's put this in the dishwasher and head to my office. We can talk business there."

"Fun," she joked.

I hummed. I wasn't sure how to read her yet, but I got a good feeling, and I trusted my instincts.

FOR THE NEXT THREE HOURS, I went through every slideshow we had with her, and through every account she should start getting familiar with. I promised she wouldn't be answering any calls or doing anything else other than familiarizing herself with them this week. She breathed out in relief, and I pretended not to see it.

After that, we came up with a plan of action. I spent about half of my day, if not more, outside, driving to the building sites and putting out the fires that needed to be put out. I went through the numbers with my crew, too, to minimize last minute surprises.

I loved it, but it made training someone difficult. It made no sense that she came with me, either. After all, none of her job functions had to do with the actual work that was going on in the sites.

So I shared my calendar with her, and we set up one hour a day—in the mornings, mostly—where she'd come to me with questions about any of the accounts or any of the files I sent her. I wasn't presuming she'd be full of questions, but I knew we worked differently than the companies she was used to. I also suggested that she study construction in general and came to me with her questions. The main reason why I hadn't been convinced about hiring her was her lack of knowledge in it. Even if she mostly handled schedules and meetings and logistic stuff, knowledge never hurt anybody.

"Do you really visit all sites this often?"

I shrugged. "My brothers aren't as hands-on as I am, but yeah. Most of the clients ask for weekly or biweekly reports, and I don't wanna rely on what someone else thinks I want to hear."

Another reason was that construction sites were what I knew. I'd started working as another layman when I was sixteen. Even when I was studying, I'd work the weekends, all day long. Some of the workers we still employed had taught me everything I know when I was still a teenager wearing braces and oversized shirts.

A part of me missed the manual labor, even if another part enjoyed my current salary and schedule more.

"I bet the clients appreciate how involved you are."

I smiled. It might've felt like kissing ass from someone else, but Kara made it sound sincere. "They do."

For the rest of the day, I focused on reports and budget planning. Well, I tried. My gaze kept drifting to Kara's makeshift desk in my office. I hated that Noel would come by and think his idea was genius, but we were going with what he said—even though neither of us had phrased it that way.

She was laser focused on the screen before her. I'd moved earlier to take a bathroom break and noticed it was one of the accounts I'd mentioned we were trying to get. It was smart—prioritizing the accounts she'd be needed the most for. After all, the others we'd secured earlier already knew us and how we worked. It was the new ones we needed to woo more.

I'd say she was still going through the same one, but couldn't tell for sure.

There was something about her I couldn't help but notice, like she was trying too hard to appear confident, but there were cracks in that facade.

It was hard to read people in the office, though. Maybe it was just me, but I knew I dressed and even acted differently outside of this building, and I'd like to think most people did. For instance, Kara was now wearing her long blonde hair in a tight, gelled ponytail. But was she one of those people who hated when even a strand of hair fell out of place, or was this just an attempt to look professional?

Her clothes, too. She was wearing checkered slacks and a white thin sweater. But was that her style, or something she'd put together after Googling appropriate office outfits?

I would probably never know, but it didn't keep me from wondering.

"So…" I checked the time. One thing I didn't like about this building was my family's insistence on having all this artificial light that tricked your brain into thinking it was daytime. I could never tell when it was time to start heading out. "How was your first day?"

"Good!" Kara rushed in to answer, almost jumping on her seat. "It's good. I wanna read some more on a few things, but I'm good."

"Not too much of a headache?"

If anything, Kara's smile only got brighter. "Not at all."

It had to be a lie.

I didn't call her out on it.

3

KARA

Was it too dramatic if I said I wanted to carve my eyes out?

It probably was, wasn't it?

I didn't care.

It was Friday, and I'd just arrived home, and the only thing I wanted to do was curl up in bed with a million blankets.

Fine, so that number wasn't realistic. A dozen, maybe? I didn't know if I had that many, but maybe my roommates did and would let me share.

Then again, they probably needed the blankets more than I did.

"Hey, Kara." Lucas grinned when he spotted me from the kitchen. "Long day?"

"Yeah."

It wasn't Mónica's fault. She was just so competent. She was so in control of every single thing, knew the clients and the construction sites inside out, and I was just beginning to figure out what each person in a site was doing. At least I had a good memory, so I could parrot back names and numbers and deadlines to projects.

To be fair, Mónica hadn't complained when she quizzed me on things I didn't know, or I said something that wasn't quite it.

I just didn't want to disappoint her. I couldn't afford to, either. Why on Earth had I thought a six month probationary period would be fine? I was going to lose all my hair before it was over.

Mónica was a good boss, though.

She seemed to trust me, too. She'd just let me know on Monday I was supposed to start working from my own office. I'd start answering calls and handling things, too.

I didn't know if I could do it.

Here I was, sure that I'd gotten over my imposter syndrome after I passed the third round of interviews.

Apparently not.

Story of my life, really.

"I got blueberry muffins if you want some?"

Aw.

Lucas had been offering me sweets and treats ever since I left the casserole for him and Alex last week, but I shook my head. I didn't have much of a sweet tooth—unless we were talking milkshakes and drinks—and I wasn't hungry anyway. Mónica had gotten me a sandwich about an hour before we clocked out when she realized I'd missed my lunch break, and I was still full.

It wasn't fair that she was such a good boss. I got a vibe that she was a bit of an ice queen, especially when she interacted with her brothers—who had been easy to avoid all week—but she was also thoughtful and kept smiling at me and being *patient*.

Ugh.

"Oh, no, thanks, I was just gonna go to bed."

"Already?" Lucas frowned.

In my defense, it was seven because I'd missed the bus, and as much as I'd been trying to stick to a Spanish schedule where going to bed around midnight was the norm, it had been a long week. I had to give up on some battles.

"I'm just so exhausted." My phone buzzed as I spoke, but I ignored the itch to check who it was. Not many people had my number. "But we can maybe have dinner together sometime next week?"

"Sure," Lucas drawled out the word. He probably had something to say, but he must've thought better of it. "I don't know what Alex's shifts look like for next week, so text it in the group chat?"

"Will do."

I'd just wait until the next day, when my brain didn't hurt with numbers and names and random facts about mortar and sustainable materials.

I did check my phone before just plopping into bed. I wasn't a heathen, after all.

Maybe I shouldn't have.

It was a notification from the local kink app. Someone had messaged me. To be fair, I'd found it strange no one had yet. It might be that my bio had dissuaded people, but in my experience, online Domms weren't the best at respecting what was written there. I had edited it the following day to add a Spanish translation underneath, but that had been all my activity in the app. I didn't even have a profile picture.

> UNICORNIOXX
>
> hi, how are you? a friend and i are trying to set up a Little playdate on Sunday. do you wanna come?
>
> SOFT_AND_SWEET
>
> i don't know. will there be any Domms?

I placed my phone on the nightstand. There was a green dot next to Unicornio's profile picture that said they were online, but I'd only feel queasier if I held on to my phone while waiting for a reply.

I hadn't expected to be invited to a playdate this soon, either. That took some processing.

My phone buzzed again before I could start figuring out how to go about it.

> **UNICORNIOXX**
>
> well, the playdate is in the kink club here, Plumas, so there will be DMs, but i don't think they'd bother us much
>
> Some littles have Daddies and stuff, but they usually just hang out at the bar while we're in the Little room
>
> it's really cool if you've never been

> **SOFT_AND_SWEET**
>
> i've never been, i just moved here
>
> i just feel very anxious?
>
> is this something you do weekly, or monthly, or…?

> **UNICORNIOXX**
>
> no need to feel anxious! i promise we're nice
>
> but yeah, we try to make it a monthly thing at least. some months it's just me and another Little though *sad emoji*

My phone hated me. The keyboard glared at me, the brightness still too bright even though I had it set to the minimum. I kept trying to type something, but nothing sounded quite right. I hated it, all the doubt and anxiety and insecurity crawling deep within.

I clicked on his profile picture to distract myself. He was

25, gay, and a Little like me. Some of the ways he posed in his pictures reminded me of Cam. He was into ABDL, too. I wasn't, but I'd played with many Littles who were; that was fine.

My indecision was the only thing that wasn't fine.

SOFT_AND_SWEET

would it be okay if i don't talk a lot?

UNICORNIOXX

sure! no worries, we can just color or watch cartoons, or maybe cuddle? if you're comfortable with that, of course

SOFT_AND_SWEET

yeah, i like all those things

THIS WAS A MONUMENTALLY BAD IDEA. I'd already sent the text to let Unicornio know I was waiting outside—to enter, one needed to be a member or be accompanied by one —though. There was no going back, as they said. Plus, there was someone by what I assumed were lockers or a coat rack who had already spotted me here. If I ghosted Unicornio, but later on decided to join the club, I didn't want people to think of me as the awkward person who flunked on a simple playdate.

And I was supposed to push against my comfort zones— my therapist had said something like that. Getting stuck was no fun. Neither was feeling my whole body draw taut as if the gallows waited for me behind the dark doors to the club.

Just saying.

It was cold, too, which didn't help. It had been raining all morning, which I'd thought would be a good excuse to cancel, but it had stopped about two hours ago. So I was left without an excuse, but with a sad looking sky and puddles and humidity that clung to the skin and pushed the cold further in. I was wearing layers, but I knew I looked miserable.

Thankfully, Unicornio didn't take long to come out of the building.

"You're soft_and_sweet?" He had a nice voice, lower than I'd expected from his profile, but he wasn't a catfisher. I forced a smile and nodded. "Great! I'm Sergio. Come on in. It's freezing outside."

It wasn't *freezing* per se, but I made myself move. Sergio—whose name didn't quite fit him—hadn't moved from inside the club. He was wearing sweatpants and a hoodie, but I thought maybe he'd just put them on to open the door. His buzz cut was a bit longer than in the pictures, but he must've touched up his eyebrows. One of my old friends had a slit like he had and I'd heard a lot about how often she had to shave it.

"Hi."

"Hi!" Sergio half-laughed, half-giggled. I supposed he'd been playing when I texted him. I really hadn't meant to be late for once. "Oh my god, I love your hair. It's so blonde and long and pretty!"

With the exception of Mónica, every person I'd met in Spain had had something to say about my hair.

I tried to smile, but I knew it came out forced. Terrified, maybe. I'd gotten a vibe that he was energetic when we texted on Friday, but I hadn't counted on my reaction to that kind of energy.

I clearly was out of practice.

"Thanks."

"So we have the locker room here if you wanna change or

just drop your phone and stuff. I had my phone with me because I had to let you in, but we don't usually allow phones or anything that can record or take pictures upstairs." He talked fast, that was for sure, but at least he was moving while he did, so I didn't have to stand there feeling self-conscious about catching up. "It's just the bar and the locker room here, but all the playrooms and everything is upstairs. They told me I had to offer to give you a tour before I took you to the Little room, so…"

"It's okay."

I grabbed the bracelet Sergio offered me. It was one of those you pressed against a lock to open it, and it had the locker's number engraved on the side. Clunky, but it was bright orange, and bright colors always made everything better. My hands were shaking, but I put my phone inside the locker he'd taken me to, and I started to take off my coat as well. I hadn't brought a change of clothes, but I was wearing my lucky hoodie and white leggings with glittery drawings on them, so I hoped that was enough.

Sergio, of course, was the kind of Little who played wearing a T-shirt with one of the Paw Patrols dogs in it and nothing else. Flaccid penises always made me giggle when I was in Little space, but that would mean I was more relaxed. Instead, I just pretended not to notice or care. To be fair, I didn't—not in that way.

"I'm, uh, ready if you are."

"Yeah!" Sergio had been quiet for a whole minute, maybe, and he perked up the second he got a chance to talk again. "So you didn't wanna have the tour?"

"Maybe another day." My lips felt too parched, my mouth completely dry. I knew I'd drunk plenty of water before coming here, and it was in my head, but that didn't fix the building discomfort. "Can I get some water, at the bar?"

"Yeah, of course. Let me get it," Sergio ran on another

explanation. "We work with a tab system here, so the person behind the bar just adds whatever to your tab and you pay when you're going to leave after you grab your things and wallet and stuff."

"Okay."

I'd been in clubs that worked with similar systems, but they were usually the more exclusive ones where all members knew each other—sometimes in a biblical sense.

"And if you forget to stop by to cover your tab, that's fine. I do it all the time, but they just charge my card the next day and we're good." Sergio shrugged, but he must've remembered something because he grimaced and halted. "Well, I do get scolded a bit, which is *no* fun, but it's not like I do it on purpose."

I chortled. It wasn't a full belly laugh—I was too on edge still for those—but I counted it as progress. I let him order my water and lead the way upstairs.

Downstairs had looked pretty standard. Dark and rather bare, with an industrial feel to it. I hadn't been sure what to expect after their website had looked so different, but I couldn't say I was too surprised.

Upstairs was different, less industrial-like with the cement walls and bare pillars, and more woody, with a few accents in red. Not what I was expecting, either.

The floor opened to a large area to the left, where I could see another bar and a few seating areas. There were some people on the couches, but their backs were to me.

It was for the better. The hints of leather I caught in their gear screamed Domm.

Sergio didn't stop there, thankfully, so I just followed him to one of the doors on the opposite side.

"So this is the Little room," he said with a flourish before opening the door. I had to say, I probably would've found it easily thanks to the plaque filled with stickers and glitter. "I got all these stickers to decorate it, but the Big Domms only let me do the plaque there."

"That's too bad," I hummed.

Stickers were cool, but not my favorite thing in the whole wide world. Stuffies, on the other hand… It would make sense, too, to add stuffies to the door. Not stapled, though, obviously, but maybe bound with some cute rope or something. I'd seen it done online, but we'd need to find someone who was good with rope. I liked it, but the one time I tried to do the most basic of knots, I'd somehow gotten us both tied together.

It was a good thing it had been a demo class, and the rope master had noticed my fuckup right away.

No harm done, and all that.

"You good?"

Shit.

I blinked.

I really didn't used to get so lost in my head.

"Yeah, sorry."

Sergio just beamed at me. I supposed there was a possibility that he was faking it. For all I knew, he could be thinking I was a weirdo and regretting that he invited me today. I didn't know him enough to really read him.

If I followed my gut instinct, though—something I had to get used to doing again—I didn't think he was the kind of person with a hidden agenda. He had that vibe, the "this is what you get" kind of look.

It was a look I could trust, so I stuck to his side and took a deep breath as he led us inside the room.

4

KARA

Sergio was even sillier than I thought. I kept getting an eyeful of his dick from where I was lying on my stomach, too. He was sitting cross legged, but lying down was comfier. I didn't make the rules, and the other two Littles agreed with me. I didn't catch their names because nerves had built up in my stomach the closer I got to them, and after a while, it had been embarrassing to ask.

But it didn't matter. They laughed at Sergio for not covering up more when it was so cold outside—they both had the same Daddy and they were wearing matching onesies—then they offered me one of their coloring books.

It was full of mermaids, too, which were really cool, and they shared their crayons too, so I could add rainbow tails. Rainbow tails were fun to make, and they all oohed and ahhed when they saw them. I barely spoke, but Sergio had been right in saying it was okay if I didn't.

I lost track of time the longer I spent drawing and doodling and listening to the two Littles teasing Sergio and Sergio going on and on about every ridiculous thing ever. Like now, he was starting a story about a Sadist they all seemed to know. Apparently, he had tried to get him to say Sadists knew better, which was never going to happen—his words.

I wanted these three to be my friends.

I hadn't looked at a person and said I wanted to be closer to them in months. Years, maybe.

My heart raced at the thought, fear still lingering behind everything I did, but there was warmth too. I clung to that, focused on the way it spread through my core and filled all the empty spots in my body.

My gaze slid around the room. It was cozy and full of shelves with colors and books and stuffies. I kind of wanted to grab one, but I didn't quite dare.

Yet.

I told myself I would one day. Maybe I could message Sergio later, and he could help me choose when we met up next time. As insecure as I was about everything, I wanted to keep meeting with him. I thought he did, too, even if I wasn't sure what I had to offer other than my blonde hair. He'd said he was going to watch tutorials on how to braid hair like Elsa's, and I'd said I was okay with it. I didn't have the heart to tell him I was pretty sure my hair wasn't long enough to achieve an Elsa look, even if it was pretty long.

"It's eight!"

"What?" the quieter one of the two Littles in onesies shrieked, sitting up. "Come on, we have to pick up fast, fast."

"Oh?"

"Their Daddy said he'll be here at eight thirty," Sergio explained. "Jen always feels bad if he has to wait for them."

Jen. That was right. They'd said her name was Jennifer—which wasn't such an uncommon name in Spain, according to the yearbook my father had kept from his time in college.

"We'll help then."

I said the words, but as everyone started moving in a

frenzy, I was… frozen. Objectively, a voice at the back of my head told me I was overreacting and being a child, and I knew it was right. It didn't stop me, however. My eyes welled up with unshed tears before I could do anything about it.

"Kara?" It was Jennifer's partner who noticed first, but that caught Sergio's attention.

"Oh no!" he dropped the small broom he'd picked from a hidden closet and ran to me, falling onto his knees. "What's wrong? Did you pinch yourself with something? Do you need a band-aid?"

"Sergio!" No-Name Little screeched. "She's upset!"

"Ooohhh." He blinked twice before staring back at me. I wanted to shake my head, to move away, to say something, anything, but I couldn't. "Shit. What can we do? What's going on?"

Stupid. Stupid. Stupid.

I choked on air. I knew my mouth opened, words trying to come out. They were right there, but every thought battling for attention in my head was too loud. Too fucking loud. I couldn't focus on a single thing—nor my head, nor the guys who I'd wanted to be friends with and their worried glances.

"We have to tell a DM, Sergio."

"No!" Sergio voiced what I wanted to say, my eyes widening and my heartbeat beating impossibly faster as I drew back. "Marga, she said she didn't want any Domms. I promised."

"But those are the rules!" Marga talked with her arms a lot. "They let us have the Little room for ourselves under the condition that we call them if someone gets hurt or upset."

Everything was happening too fast. Marga and Sergio kept fighting about rules and bending them when they had to. I tuned them out. Tears slipped down my cheeks, and I tried to keep it quiet. I'd gotten really good at doing that. Attention on myself wasn't something I was comfortable with, or something I felt safe with. It hadn't been for years.

The voices kept growing louder, and I was just there, shaking my head.

I did not notice when Jen left, but I heard the rapping on the doorframe.

"What's going on here?"

No.

No, I couldn't recognize that voice, but I did.

"No," I whimpered, scrambling backwards until I hit one of the shelves against the wall.

It hurt, but I gritted my teeth and pushed through it. Mónica couldn't be here. It wasn't possible. My luck couldn't be running that low, could it?

But I'd recognize her anywhere, even if her clothes were different and she had no makeup on. My eyes fixated on the military boots she had on. My heart raced. *She* used to wear military boots too. I remembered... No. I forced my eyes shut, swallowed once, twice, three times. I couldn't go there. I wasn't there anymore. Mónica wasn't Her.

A whimper left my lips again. Embarrassment started to trickle in. The whole situation was too much, too overwhelming. I should've ignored my therapist talking about leaving my comfort zone. I should've just stayed home. There was no way I could talk to these people again, even if they had been nice. How did I explain—?

"Kara?" I looked up, but only for a second—enough to see Mónica had crouched down. She'd kept some distance between us, but she wasn't by the door anymore. "Can you tell me what's got you so upset?"

I couldn't describe the choked noise that came out. Suddenly, everything was spinning, too fast for me to grasp onto anything. "Please don't fire me. Please, I can't go back, I need this job, I swear I'll—"

I wasn't sure where I was going with my rambling, to be fair. It was a good thing that Mónica stopped it. She didn't touch me or talk over me, but the way she lifted her hands, palms up, was enough to cut my jumbled words short.

"Kara, I'm not going to fire you for being a Little."

"That would be silly, Ma'am," Sergio interjected. It had only been seconds, maybe a couple of minutes, but I'd forgotten he was there. "And hypocritical."

Mónica grimaced when Sergio started talking, but she chuckled as he added the last part.

"Exactly." She turned toward him, and I didn't know if it was a good or a bad thing that I didn't have all of her attention focused on me. There had been something primal about the way she'd been studying me. "Sergio, why don't you go fetch us some water? I'm sure Kara will text you later when she's feeling better."

"But," he started protesting, "she didn't want any Domms, Ma'am. It says so in her profile, too."

Mónica's gaze drifted back to me. If anything, her eyes burned hotter against my skin. "Is that so?"

I nodded. I didn't know how I was going to explain anything, but apparently, I wouldn't have to. At least, not right away.

Mónica just continued with her assessment. "Would you feel more comfortable if Sergio stayed with you?"

I nodded again. I knew I was going to regret it. Cam had left when I'd made everything about Her and my trauma, and Cam had known me for months before I spoke up about it.

If I'd had five more minutes, maybe I could've put myself together enough so I could've said no—so I could've been stronger.

"Can I hug her, Ma'am? I think she needs a hug," he spoke.

I realized he was hesitant, more subdued than he'd been all day, fidgeting on his feet.

I'd done that. The thought threatened to send me into another panic attack, but I buried it down—ignored the way my eyes watered, too.

"That's up to Kara, isn't it?" The patience in Mónica's voice contradicted the fire in her eyes. I was attuned to catching those contradictions. "Do you want a hug from Sergio?"

"Yes, please," I croaked, my voice barely more than a whisper.

Sergio threw himself at me, much like he'd done before when he noticed me "upset." I really hoped he wouldn't pull away when he realized I was more baggage than anything else.

Maybe there was some other rival community I could go to.

I would have to, anyway, since Mónica was here.

Before my thoughts could keep unraveling, Sergio's arms were around me. I noticed his dick squeezed against my thigh. It was kind of funny in a stupid way, and it made me blush, but I still giggled.

Mónica's pupils darted downward. She gave me a soft smile. Sergio just squeezed me tighter. It helped. Maybe not outwardly—my chest still heaved up and down with each beat, and I was still not sure I could speak much—but I felt my thoughts begin to slow down.

"I'm gonna go get that water, then. You two stay put, all right?"

"Yes, Ma'am," Sergio said.

I nodded, but I wasn't sure if she saw.

She still stood up and left us. I guessed she must trust him, in spite of all his goofiness.

"You know Mistress Mónica?" he whispered once we couldn't hear the soft thud of her footsteps.

"My boss," I whispered just as softly. "I'm her secretary."

"Ohhhh." There was no way he wasn't thinking about that movie from the 2000s, but to his credit, he didn't mention it. "Well, she's really nice. You don't have to worry, I promise."

Bobbing my head up and down was beginning to feel like a reflex, something to do to get people off my back.

Mónica didn't take long. Again, my eyes went to her boots, and without her face to go along with them, the panic returned, images and words I didn't want to remember resurfacing.

"Here, try to drink some."

Her arm extended to hand me the bottle of water, but she kept respecting a perimeter around me. I liked it. I liked that she crouched down again after I'd grabbed it, and she showed no discomfort or annoyance even though it couldn't be a comfortable position.

The water felt like a lifesaver. I chugged down half of the bottle, and only then did it feel like I could take a deep breath.

Sergio's hand moved to my lower back. That also helped. He didn't comment or act as if they were only theatrics. I wondered if I could bake him something. Maybe then he'd still want to deal with me, panic attacks and all.

"Feeling better?"

"I'm sorry," I gasped out, nodding at the same time. Hopefully it made sense. "I don't know what happened. I—"

"It's okay," Mónica and Sergio spoke nearly at the same time, "It's all right."

"I just got overwhelmed, I think." It was probably much more than that, but I didn't have the energy to work through everything right this moment. "I haven't been Little in a while."

It wasn't a lie, exactly. I'd teased around the edges of Little space in the privacy of my bedroom, with books and sometimes videos that pulled me in, but it was different. Some people played solo just fine, but it was never as fulfilling when I did it. Things didn't feel as intense, either.

Mónica shifted. I heard the scuffle on the floor before I saw it. Before I could tense up, ready to be berated, I noticed her attention had shifted to Sergio.

He spoke unprompted. "We'd just been coloring, and talking, and then we started cleaning up and that's when she got upset. I think."

Mónica seemed to be deep in thought, but it only lasted a couple of seconds. I only knew because I'd seen that face on her a few times at work when she was trying to figure out what someone else wasn't telling her—more often than not, one of her brothers.

I didn't like them.

"You didn't want the playdate to end?" Mónica's eyes were on me again.

I squirmed. The movement had more of Sergio's dick brushing against my thigh. I welcomed the distraction before I had to meet her gaze.

"I don't know." That didn't feel right. It felt too simplistic, but everything was still hazy around the edges. I knew I wasn't fully back yet, the remains of Little space and a panic attack confounding my senses. "I just... Sorry."

"I don't need you to apologize." Mónica's soft smile was back on her face. That was one I hadn't seen on her before. "I'm sure Sergio doesn't, either. We just want to know how we can help."

"Yes, what Mistress said." Sergio nodded enthusiastically, although it wasn't the same as before.

I believed he was in the same place as me, not quite Little anymore, but not quite Big either.

That was comforting, in a strange way.

"Hugs help," I supplied.

I knew it meant Sergio would hug me tighter, but that was fine. He was so warm, like a human furnace. That was also fine. I burrowed into it, into that heat that felt almost foreign.

Mónica didn't say anything. She didn't push me to go to her arms instead or to take over.

"I'll let you two snuggle for a bit, then." She had her focus on Sergio again. "Did you drive here?"

"Yes, Ma'am."

"Will you drive her home?"

I looked up in surprise. It took a few seconds to remember she'd know I didn't have a car. They'd asked that when I was filling the forms for my contract.

"Yes, Ma'am."

"Good boy." I shuddered, while I knew Sergio preened. I didn't fault him for it. "I'll be with the other Domms, okay?"

"Yes, Ma'am," he repeated.

I noted a hint of snark, and I thought Mónica did too, but she let it go. I let out a breath I hadn't realized I'd been holding as she turned around. Sergio ran a hand through my hair as exhaustion started to take over my now stiff joints.

We didn't stay long. I didn't want things to become awkward, or to end up dumping all my baggage on him. Not this soon, or like this, when he'd promised a DM that he'd take care of me.

5

MÓNICA

KARA S

So… I still have a job?

MÓNICA

Yes.

I expect to see you at the office, unless you need to take a sick day?

KARA S

No, I'm not sick

Just embarrassed?

MÓNICA

I don't like mixing business and pleasure, either, I get it.

KARA S

I'm really sorry, I had no idea you'd be there

Obviously

MÓNICA

Why would you have?

> It's really okay, Kara. But if it's too uncomfortable for you, we'll figure something out, okay?

KARA S

Okay

That entire exchange had happened at six in the morning. I had just gotten up, ready to hop in the shower and go through my mental checklist for the day. I wished today could be a slow day where I could stay at the office and keep an eye on Kara. Alas, I'd be in the office in the morning to catch up on a few reports, but I had to visit two sites, minimum. Three, if I found the time. One of the lead workers had texted me during the weekend about a possible issue that might delay the deadline—and possibly take us over budget.

Today was not the day to worry about a secretary who moonlit as a Little, but that was all I'd been doing since I'd stepped into the Little Room yesterday.

Tears and panic aside, Kara had looked so… different. Her hair had been down, with no product in it, flowing all the way down her chest. Her clothes had been different, too, comfortable and cozy and warm in pastel colors. Littles didn't usually stir anything in me, but my hands had been itching with the near need to bundle all that coziness and pull her close.

Kara wouldn't have welcomed that touch, though.

I beat myself up over the whole thing, too.

It was illogical, but I kept thinking that I should've seen it. There was a story there, one that went beyond her being Little. I knew there were more pieces to the puzzle, but more of our interactions had begun to make sense—the wary looks and the state of alert Kara seemed to be in more than half of the time.

I drove to my family's office building on autopilot. It was a good thing there had been no accidents or signals cutting off a road. For a province that had as much rain as Asturias did, one would think people were better prepared to drive in it. I'd heard it was worse down south—some places didn't even have a proper sewer system—but I still didn't get how so many struggled.

It was probably tourists, but this wasn't tourist season. Far from it. We only got tourists during the summer, and only the weeks of summer where agencies could more or less guarantee there would be sun and only a little rain.

My phone rang as I headed to the elevators. Of course, it was Iván. Just the person I needed to deal with today.

"What is it?"

I kept myself from adding a *now* at the end there. Iván was the youngest, and the quickest to go running to our father if he felt we weren't taking him seriously.

We didn't. None of us was too shy about the fact.

"Your secretary says you can't splurge even five minutes to see me." No *hello sis*, or asking how I was. No surprise there. "What's up with that?"

I sighed.

Kara hadn't met Iván yet. He hadn't been on holiday, but he might as well be with how little time he spent in the office.

"I have a busy day. Unless you wanna ride with me to one of the sites, I'd heed her advice."

I had instructed her to keep my brothers off my back unless it was genuinely urgent. I didn't trust her yet to explain the difference between getting energy from solar panels or wind turbines, but I trusted her to discern an emergency from sibling meddling.

"Fine," he groaned. "I'll be in the break room." He hung up.

Of course he would.

I looked up. The screen in the elevator said I was only two floors away.

Today was not only going to be a busy day, it was going to be a long day, too. I could feel it.

And I hadn't even come anywhere near close to figuring out how to approach or deal with Kara. Even before her freaking out when she saw me, I'd gathered it was important for her to move and keep a job here. I *wanted* her to keep her job. But I didn't know how to smooth out the anxiety she must be feeling when I didn't know how to manage mine, either.

I'd never considered the possibility of my two worlds colliding. Construction workers weren't precisely a target audience for kink clubs, and knowledge around BDSM wasn't that spread out or accessible here. It never had been.

Most of the people at Plumas had only first heard about it after watching *Fifty Shades of Grey*, as dreadful as that representation was.

It had always bothered me, but I hid all of that the second the doors to the office floor opened. The hallway was empty, which wasn't a surprise. I would usually head to the break room to grab my caffeine fix of the day, but I didn't want to check if Iván had been serious.

He probably had been.

Instead, I headed straight to my office.

Kara was inside. She had her hair tied in a ponytail, all strands accounted for, and wore another pair of slacks and a button-down. The outfits always looked slightly weird on her, but the effect was stronger now that I knew what kind of clothes she'd gravitate toward.

"Morning."

"Morning!" Kara smiled big, probably too big. She had a cup of takeaway coffee ready for me, too. "I brought coffee on

PLAY PRETEND

my way here. I hope it's okay. Oh, and did Iván call you? I'm sorry. I really tried to tell him you were busy, but—"

"He called, but it's fine," I stopped her before grabbing the cup of coffee. Something was going to go well today, at least. "Thanks for the coffee."

"Of course." Kara nearly bounced on her feet.

I itched to pin her with a raised eyebrow, but I was willing to bet that would just make her more anxious.

"Sit down, will you?" I sighed as I took a sip of the coffee. It was good. I recognized the logo in the cup as one of the specialty stores down the road, but I couldn't remember the last time I'd actually stepped inside. "Is there anything you wanted to discuss before we go about the schedule for today?"

"I…" Kara gaped at me for a second, but she recovered quickly. I liked that. "I shouldn't bring up yesterday again, should I?"

I gave a one shouldered shrug while I mulled over the question. A simple *no* wouldn't have sufficed, but I wondered how I could drive the point across.

"You should bring up anything that makes you anxious." I leaned down against my chair. The leather creaked, reminding me why I'd pushed for the club to have seating options that weren't made from the infamous material—me, the one whose gear was all leather. "Is there anything specific you're worried about?"

Kara licked her lips. "I don't want to get in trouble. Or to have things change."

"I'm not planning to make any changes where your job is concerned, if that's what you're asking." It would make no sense, anyway, unless I wanted to restructure all the accounts and give them to one of my brothers. That was *not* happening. "And you are not in trouble. I'll say, I've never really found myself in this situation before, but as far as I'm concerned, who we both are outside of this building stays there. Yeah?"

"Yeah." Kara's nod was hesitant, but it was there. I supposed I couldn't ask for much more. "I got here early to check on some of the accounts you had meetings with this week, and I noticed..."

I breathed out. I hadn't been sure that it wouldn't be a bigger deal, but as Kara leaned into her observations and questions about the contract we wanted to snag with a British bank moving here, I relaxed. This was familiar territory.

Having a secretary who was also a Little was not.

At all.

"SO, WE'VE AGREED?" I pinned down the site manager with a look. It wasn't quite a glare, but it would quickly become one if he kept fighting me. One thing I liked about having crews I'd learned under was that they tended to respect me. When we had to hire outsiders, though? All bets were off, and I was the office lady who didn't know right from left. "I can work around the budget, but we can't miss the deadline."

"Yeah, yeah." The man rolled his eyes.

I kept a poker face, but I was fuming inside. I understood—more than he knew—the exhaustion and short fuses that could come with working outside all day. I still refused to let it be an excuse for blatant disrespect.

"I'll come by later this week to check in."

I'd have to ask Kara to reschedule something, probably, but I wasn't risking waiting until next week. I knew how those visits went. Excuse after excuse after excuse.

Thankfully, I'd already told Kara that I was heading straight home after I finished up here. As much as I didn't mind seeing her, the drive to the opposite side of the city would've done me in.

No, I needed to head home to my cats and to have a good soak in the tub. I would worry about reschedules and meetings again tomorrow.

Not surprisingly, when I walked in, Princess was already waiting for me, perched up on the shoe rack whereas I heard Prince zooming in the opposite direction. Their names were what happened when I thought it would be cute to let my nieces name them. Maybe that was why Prince stayed a healthy distance most times—except for the few times when I fell asleep on the couch.

"Hello, gorgeous." I ran my hand through Princess's tawny fur and heard her start to purr almost immediately. "That's my girl."

Ever the clingiest cat in history, she jumped to my chest and stayed there as I took off my shoes as seamlessly as I possibly could. It wasn't as if I gave her a treat when I walked in, but she'd been like this since I'd first rescued her. Truthfully, I didn't mind the extra attention—or all the shirts and sweaters she'd torn through until she'd learned to control her claws. Wearing some sweaters was still asking for trouble.

With Princess still in my arms, and looking in no rush to get off, I headed to the kitchen. I didn't have the energy to cook anything, but after having most of my lunches outside, the idea of takeout gave me a full body shiver.

I needed to order groceries, but for now I could grab some of the salad I made yesterday and call it a day. Princess jumped down to the floor the second I started rummaging for a bowl.

Even when she got in the way, nothing had ever fallen on

her, but it had been close a couple of times, and that had been more than enough for her. She still trailed after me as I headed to the living room, though. There was a giant cat tree on one side of the wall, but I wasn't sure I'd seen her use it more than twice. At least Prince did make use of the monstrosity.

"You're gonna let me eat, right?"

Salad wasn't something that interested her a lot, but I could never trust her not to try and get a bite—especially on the days when she sat down next to me like she was doing now.

Oh, well. The life of a cat owner.

I was eating with one hand and scrolling through my phone with the other when I noticed I had a message on the app I used for all things local and kinky.

> UNICORNIOXX
>
> hello, Ma'am
>
> i, um, need some advice?

> BOTASDECUERO
>
> What is it?

I waited while Sergio typed whatever it was he wanted. I talked with him from time to time—everyone did since he was the biggest social butterfly I'd ever met—but I wouldn't have said I'd be his go-to person for advice, as he put it.

> UNICORNIOXX
>
> i wanted to ask Kara about joining us again this weekend, but i wanted to know your thoughts first

> BOTASDECUERO
>
> Neither you nor Kara need my permission to do anything, boy.

Even before Sergio said anything, I already knew I was full of shit, and not really answering his question. It was complicated, though.

I pursed my lips. In bigger cities, and in other countries—even if there weren't many clubs that catered to us kinky folk—there were different groups and communities and crowds.

Here, though? It was just us. It made us really close, but it had its cons. If there was drama between two people, one of them would literally vanish as a result most of the time. A couple of years ago, a Dom literally uprooted his whole life after his sub had broken up with him, moving to Barcelona as soon as he got a job.

Back then, I'd just thought "good riddance," and I stuck by it, but the point was... If kink was a big part of your identity, your only chance was to make it work with us. I didn't know where Kara fell in that spectrum, and I'd hate to presume, but I got the feeling that she didn't just like a spanking while making out.

BOTASDECUERO

> Let her know what to expect, and have a plan in place in case she needs heavier aftercare. And share it with one of the DMs.

UNICORNIOXX

you won't be there, Ma'am?

BOTASDECUERO

> I probably will, but not as a DM. I think Erika volunteered in the group, but double check with her.

UNICORNIOXX

but Mistress Erika is so mean!! :(

BOTASDECUERO

> Watch it.

> **UNICORNIOXX**
> i'm just saying, my ass still hurts, Ma'am!!

> **BOTASDECUERO**
> You didn't deserve it?

Sergio took a while to answer. That was fine. I knew there had been no actual bite to his words. He just liked to stir up trouble every chance he got. I was actually surprised he'd behaved with Kara on Sunday.

> **UNICORNIOXX**
> yes, Ma'am

> **BOTASDECUERO**
> Attaboy.
>
> Let me know if Kara is going to be there, will you?

> **UNICORNIOXX**
> sure thing!

It was close to sounding cringey. I didn't fully know why I'd asked. A part of me would say I wanted to respect her; if she was going to be there, I could skip the club this weekend. It was a rare thing that I did, but Kara deserved a chance to settle in with the community without having to worry about me being there. Another part of me wondered if I wanted to know for the exact opposite reason.

That would have to be a problem for future me, however.

Besides, chances were Kara already had plans, or she had no interest in the events outside of the playdates for Littles. Those only happened once a month, no matter how much Sergio pushed to have them more often.

6

KARA

"When you suggested dinner, I thought we were ordering pizza or something," Alex said from the entrance.

They'd just arrived from work, but Lucas had been home all day. I'd prepped the day before, and I'd just finished setting up the big table in the living room. Lucas had already joked about how the table had never seen any use before I arrived.

Not going to lie, I was starting to feel self-conscious, but I didn't think I'd done too much. There was just coleslaw salad, one of those rare things I didn't think I was going to miss but did, and a veggie pie. It hadn't taken that long to make, either—once I'd peeled and chopped all the things. It wasn't as if I made the dough from scratch.

"We can still do that?" I didn't mean to squeak, but I sort of did. "I don't mind. I'll just plop it in the fridge."

"No, no. I mean, it looks great."

I didn't miss the look they exchanged with Lucas, though. I couldn't help it. Had I always been so attuned to the small things like that? I didn't know for certain. What I knew was that I couldn't not see it now.

"You have to at least let us pay you for the ingredients," Lucas said before he sat down at the head of the table.

"Sure." My ears were ringing, but I smiled through it and followed his lead, sitting down. "I'll upload the bills from the grocery store to the group chat."

Alex sat down too, and they tried to smile, but it still felt wrong. I was probably overthinking it. Alex was nice. A bit quieter than Lucas, maybe, and they seemed to work more hours too, so I didn't see them as often, but…

I chewed on my lip. I'd been excited about dinner less than ten minutes ago, but my stomach was cramping now.

"Hey, Kara?"

I looked up at Lucas. There was another exchanged look. It made sense. They'd been roommates for a few years now. They seemed close, too—probably the kind of close that could have silent conversations like that.

"Yeah?"

"Please do not take this the wrong way, but Alex and I have noticed sometimes you act like people who've been in abusive situations do?" Lucas swallowed. I didn't blink, didn't move a muscle. "You don't have to tell us anything, obviously, but we both know a few therapists that specialize in trauma, and maybe you'd like to check in with one of them? No pressure. Obviously."

I swallowed. My throat was dry. My eyes widened—I'd forgotten to grab the pitcher of water. They usually had Coke with dinner, but I didn't.

"There is no shame, if something did happen to you," Alex interjected.

"No shame at all."

I swallowed again. There was a knot in my throat while I tried to rationalize. Lucas and Alex both worked in the hospital. They'd seen stuff. It was expected, that they'd recognize signs, and that they had contacts, and everything else.

I still felt small, and not in the good way.

"Right. Uh, thanks." I blinked, my vision blurry around the edges. This wasn't how I thought tonight would go, but I knew I couldn't just run to my room. That wasn't the kind of person I wanted to be. "I… I did go to therapy, in the States. I'm sorry I didn't say anything? I don't know. I just… I wanted a fresh start."

I thought if no one knew about Her, I could just be me—once I'd remembered who that was.

"We just worry about you, is all," Lucas said.

Alex nodded.

They could be so in sync sometimes, I'd first wondered if they were together or at least harbored some kind of crush.

"If it's okay… I'm not feeling too hungry. I think I'm just gonna head to bed."

Silence met my words. Alex recovered first.

"Okay. We're here if you need us."

"Yeah." I swallowed. "Thanks."

To be fair, I knew they were, and they would be, but that didn't mean that I knew *what* to do. No one had ever sat me down for an intervention like this. No one had offered support or help beyond a very vague text saying they were there if I needed them, whatever that meant.

Exhaustion clung to me as I climbed up the stairs. It was only by force of habit that I checked my phone as I hit the mattress. Maybe my roommates would help me change it once I got my first paycheck. It would be a hefty expense, but the bed really wasn't comfortable—too soft, but not in the good way that felt like being hugged by a cloud.

A red bubble caught my eye. It was the app. I'd been stuck on a loop, not sure if I should delete it or not. Sergio was nice, and I *wanted* to be friends with him for real, and maybe the others, but… Mónica.

My whole body straightened as I thought her name, images flashing of her in the club. She'd looked so different— so herself, wildly enough.

Before then, nothing about her had made me stop to take a second look. She'd just been my boss. Sure, I'd noticed her skin was smooth with only a few moles scattered around it. I'd noticed her eyes and hair seemed to be the same exact shade of chestnut brown, and her Cupid's bow was something she'd been born with. Those were normal things to notice, though. Nothing to write home about.

They hit differently when she wasn't posing as the perfect office worker.

I refused to think hard about what that meant.

UNICORNIOXX

hi Kara !!

there's a party this weekend at the club

we can meet up and go together, if you want?

My hand flew up to my mouth, quieting a choked sob. *Fuck*. Had I really fallen so low I'd forgotten what it was like when people cared about me, *wanted* me in their lives?

SOFT_AND_SWEET

what kind of party?

My fingers were trembling over the keyboard as I typed. I couldn't decide if it was a good or a bad thing that Sergio wouldn't be able to tell.

UNICORNIOXX

the kind that's basically an orgy

it's really fun!

and i know you're going to say something about Domms being there, but there are colored bands and no one would get close to you without asking first

and there are lots of snuggles afterward! that's my favorite part, tbh

SOFT_AND_SWEET

i don't know if i can

UNICORNIOXX

oh

i mean, that's okay

but you're still welcome to join, okay? i'll send you the details

and i can protect you

i wasn't planning on playing anyway

My heart rate picked up. I could hear it thudding in my chest. Minutes passed by where I stared at the screen, frozen, only touching it lightly every now and then so it didn't lock. Sergio didn't sign out, either. I struggled, the tiny keyboard mocking me.

SOFT_AND_SWEET

i'll let you know, okay?

The words felt like a lie, like lead sitting on my stomach. I hated it, hated how sick they made me feel.

There had been a time, back when I was newer to kink and there was no one to leash me in, when orgies and group play had been my jam. I'd loved the dichotomy of being both the center of attention and invisible among all the bodies. I'd craved the freedom to move, to feel, to explore.

Then orgies stopped feeling safe, started to have too many rules, too many unspoken restrictions that suffocated me. Group play started to feel like walking around land mines. The effort was not worth the reward.

> UNICORNIOXX
>
> okay, no pressure!
>
> we can also meet for a coffee or something sometime
>
> it doesn't have to be all about kink

> SOFT_AND_SWEET
>
> i'd love that

I would. That didn't mean I wasn't still stuck on the idea of group play. If I closed my eyes, I imagined it would be one of the things I'd want to reclaim back from Her and everything that went wrong. Fear stopped me, though. I didn't want to have a repeat of last weekend. I didn't want to freak out again over nothing.

"KARA," Mónica called out, her eyes squinted—assessing. I blinked. "Are you okay?"

I'd barely slept at all, and I'd missed my first three alarms, which meant I hadn't had more than a protein bar for breakfast. I was *not* okay, but I couldn't tell that to my boss. I was still on my probationary period. Hell, I hadn't even gotten my first paycheck yet. Not to mention, the thing keeping me distracted was not exactly HR-friendly.

"Yeah, sorry." I forced a smile. "I went through your

calendar for next week again, and I think it should work now."

Part of my being distracted translated into not realizing I'd overbooked her Tuesday, when she'd already told me she was going to be on the road for most of it. I knew bosses who would've fired me on the spot, but she'd just knocked on my door and asked me to take another look at it.

That had been… three hours ago, I realized with a quick glance to the computer screen. Time had just passed me by, and it was time to leave.

"I noticed." Mónica smiled. She was still by the door, leaning against the flimsy glass frame. "Were you planning to do extra hours?"

I saw as she tried not to, but she still scrunched up her nose. Mónica had one of the strongest work ethics I'd encountered on a job, but she was also big on not sucking up or doing extra time. It was one of the first things she'd drilled onto me, as she'd said it was important so I didn't fall into the American ways while I was here. I didn't complain.

"Uh, no." I gulped. "No, I'm packing up now."

"As you should." She nodded. It sounded kind of like praise, but then again, I was sleep-deprived, and I could never be trusted when that was the case. "Did I work you too hard this week?"

"No, not at all," I rushed to get out while closing all the tabs I'd kept open all day for the sake of keeping an appearance of productivity. "You're great, really. It's just been a long week. Outside of work, I mean."

It was probably too much information. I didn't like being the kind of employee who rambled nervously to her boss, but it was also not the first time it had happened. Mónica just brought it out of me, I guessed.

"Get some rest, then," she said. For a second, I thought that was going to be it, and I was ready to all but sink back down into my chair. But then Mónica glanced to the side, hesitated, and took a step inside. "Actually, is it okay if we talked for five minutes?"

"Uh, sure." I couldn't—or didn't want to—imagine what she'd need to talk about, but my mouth dried up when Mónica let the door close behind her and she sat on the chair in front of my desk. "What is it?"

"It's nothing bad," she started out by saying. It would've been soothing if she hadn't grimaced right after. "Maybe not the most appropriate, and you can feel free to toss the whole HR department my way. I just feel like we've been treading around the elephant in the room all week, and I'd rather we didn't."

"Oh." I frowned. "Okay?"

I could feel my anxiety rising, my heart picking up speed and my skin tingling. I forced myself to stay present, to not think beyond the words that were coming out of her mouth.

If she noticed the way I gripped the arms of my chair, she didn't mention it.

I was grateful.

"I'm assuming Sergio told you about this weekend at the club?" Mónica asked, and I just nodded. If I'd been processing things right, I would've balked at talking about *this* with *her* in the company building. Alas, I just stood there—well, sat. "I've been thinking about this all week. I'm obviously not going to tell you whether or not you should or shouldn't attend an event, but Plumas is literally the only kink club in all of Asturias, and I wouldn't want you to miss out on something that's important to you because we happen to have those interests in common."

I nodded. I couldn't speak, but nodding had to count for something, right? I did appreciate how she didn't beat around the bush or left things in the air. Candidness wasn't appreciated enough in the world.

"Okay."

It didn't change every other fact that made me reluctant to visit the club.

"Would you like to discuss what kind of interactions are or aren't appropriate?"

I shook my head, then backtracked, my eyes widening. "I mean, yeah, but… Not right now. Please."

My voice broke toward the end. I hated it. I looked down, but I still felt Mónica studying me. My skin broke out in goosebumps under her gaze, and my breathing sped up.

I shut my eyes. The walls were closing in around me. I needed out.

She let me go—or maybe I just left. It was hard to tell.

7

MÓNICA

UNICORNIOXX

are you really not coming to the orgy, Ma'am? Kara hasn't told me anything so i don't think she's coming

BOTASDECUERO

I'm not in the mood this weekend.

But you go and have fun.

The truth was, I hadn't been able to stop thinking about Kara. That wasn't conducive to me taking part in any kind of sex party, regardless of the role. If Kara happened to be there, I would be too focused on her. If she didn't, I'd just be searching for her, imagining a thousand scenarios and reasons for her absence.

It was better for everyone that I sat this one out while I got myself together. Sadly, what I'd thought would be a weekend of reflection and self-care was going to turn into another family-induced headache. I'd only learned of it mere minutes before Sergio texted; my mother called, saying something about an impromptu family meal because my nieces were visiting.

Last time I'd heard, they were studying in England. There weren't any bank holidays to explain their trip here, but my father was getting them from the airport as we spoke, so...

Family meal, it was. At least, it would be once Princess left my lap. There was no way I was moving her on a weekend. The drive from the airport would still take my father another half an hour anyway, and that was if there weren't any issues with the luggage or anything else.

Besides, as much as I loved my nieces, it wouldn't be too terrible if I arrived late. Sometimes I thought my family created these situations to rope me into spending time with them outside of work—as if work wasn't plenty.

I was absently running a hand down Princess's fur when my phone buzzed. Thankfully, she'd grown out of the phase where the thing made her zoom out of my sight—after leaving a few scratches to boot.

> KARA
>
> are you busy?

> MÓNICA
>
> Just chilling with my cat. Did you get some sleep?

Asking might be a bit too much, too out of place. Then again, I asked my friends if they'd slept all right if I knew they'd been struggling. I asked Sergio, too, and any of the other subs who visited the club often, and I didn't have a dynamic with them.

> KARA
>
> kinda
>
> i keep thinking about what you said
>
> and your question

and the event today

i hope it's not too much

you did say we shouldn't avoid the issue so i thought…

MÓNICA

It's okay. It's not too much.

I texted before she had a chance to keep blowing up my phone. The bubble showing she'd been typing had appeared before I'd finished reading.

I wasn't the kind of Domme who got off on interrupting or speaking over their subs, even when they were bratting out, but there were circumstances when I found it okay. One of them was when I could feel the anxiety oozing off a sub's pores, and I didn't need to have Kara in front of me to see it.

MÓNICA

How can I help?

KARA

i don't actually know how to say it without oversharing too much

i'm just worried

i don't want to ruin everything so early on

MÓNICA

What is everything here?

KARA

my job

my friends

well, not my friends yet, but i wanna make friends

which sounds very middle school of me

> but i mean, i want the Littles from the club to like me
>
> and other people there, i mean
>
> but i don't know if i'm ready

MÓNICA

> I can't speak for Jen and Marga because I barely know them, they only show up around the club once every couple of months, but I know Sergio is quite taken with you.
>
> I don't think you have to worry about him.
>
> As for being ready… You don't have to do anything. There are colored bracelets you can grab in the entrance that mean you're not available for play. You can just chill in the common areas or by the bar.

The three dots appeared and disappeared. I wished I could be with her so that I could help draw her focus. I didn't know her well enough to do that kind of thing, of course, but I'd noticed it helped when something got her overwhelmed at work.

KARA

> what about you?
>
> i don't want your opinion of me to change

MÓNICA

> Why would it?

KARA

> because i'm Little?

MÓNICA

> I know.

> My opinion of you would only change (for the worse, I mean) if you knowingly violated someone's consent or boundary. But that would apply even if it happened outside of a kink club.
>
> Are you planning on doing that?

KARA

no, of course not !!!!!

MÓNICA

> Then you have nothing to worry about.

I would've developed that more, but my screen switched to show my mother was calling.

"Yeah?"

There was some interference before my mother's voice pulled through the line. She always tried to stay hip and call through her watch or anywhere else, and then we had to wait while she struggled to make it work.

"Just wanted to let you know your father said they'll be here in ten."

Shit.

I pulled the phone away and checked the time. I'd gotten in the zone while texting, and didn't realize time was ticking.

"I'll head out in five."

"Okay. Don't drive too fast."

I snorted. "I won't."

I wasn't the one with the speeding tickets and DUIs, but my mother didn't care. She fretted about all of us equally.

"All right, Princess, Momma has to go, but I'll be back soon."

She didn't look happy about it, giving me the stink eye and everything, but there was little else I could do. I'd once tried to make up excuses to avoid the family meals, but quickly learned not to do it. I could do without having my parents in my space every couple of days under the guise of checking in to make sure I was all right. It was sweet, but I was protective of my space. I barely let friends or dates in.

Speaking of, as soon as I got in the car, I turned on the screen that connected with my phone and asked Siri to call Kara. Something about our texts wasn't sitting right with me, and I needed the reassurance.

"Uh, Mónica?" There was utter confusion in her voice as she picked up.

I grimaced. I didn't want to give her more to worry or be anxious about. "Hey, sorry, I had to get in the car, but wanted to check in on you, too."

"Check in?"

More confusion, but the background noise told me she'd made herself comfortable. I told myself that was good.

"Yeah." I cleared my throat and stayed silent while I took the roundabout down my street. There had been more than one accident in it because some people didn't understand speed limits or the order to enter them. "I don't like to leave things half finished, you know what I mean?"

A sharp intake of breath later, Kara muttered a simple, "Yeah."

"So…" I could think about the words more now that I'd entered the highway and had miles of straight road ahead of me, which was one of the perks of my parents choosing to live outside of the city. "I feel like there's more that you wanted to tell me, and I don't want you to feel like you can't."

"I…" Kara swallowed audibly enough I made note of it. "I just can't make up my mind. I'm sorry."

"Why are you apologizing?" I frowned.

I'd caught her doing that more often than I'd like—apologizing preemptively for things that just didn't require an apology.

"I don't know." She gulped again. "I'm anxious, I guess."

"Take a few deep breaths and start again, then."

I'd have to take the turn to my parents' soon, but if I had to sit in the car for a few minutes, I would. They could think I was on a business call.

The line went almost dead, but if I strained my ears enough, I could hear Kara's breathing slowing down. It did things to my core that she'd just *obeyed* like that—things it shouldn't do.

"I just keep going back and forth between… What if I go, and I panic, and everyone just thinks I'm a mess and casts me away? But then, what if I don't go, and that makes everyone think I'm not interested in them? You know?"

My jaw clenched. It happened every time something made me think back to her panic attack in the club last week. I knew there was a story there, and all my protective instincts rose up to the surface, but I also knew I couldn't push her to tell me. It just killed me.

"You can't control what others think, can you?" I tried to speak softly, not wanting her to think I was scolding her. "What would *you* think, in those scenarios?"

Kara gasped. I bet she was chewing on her bottom lip now. "I think… If I went, I'd feel proud of myself for going, but if I freaked out, I'd feel very embarrassed and little in a bad way, and I'd get lots of thoughts about how I should just stop trying. But if I don't go, I think my brain will just start berating me for being a coward, and all that stuff."

I blew out a breath slowly, my hands gripping the wheel tight. Kara was not my sub, but there was a reason why I had a rule with subs I played with—only I got to speak poorly of them, if I even chose to do that.

"So what you're saying is that one option has a possibility of a good outcome, and the other just leads to negative feelings."

Kara stayed silent, and I knew I'd got to her. "Yeah."

I took the turn to the more rickety road that led to my parents. One look at the time said I wouldn't be terribly late.

"Will you be going to the club, then?"

"I guess." Kara sighed. There was a hint of ruffling in the background—blankets, maybe. "Will you be there, too?"

"I'm afraid not." I let out a sigh of my own. "Family stuff has come up."

"Oh. Everything okay? Is it that urgent thing Iván wanted to talk about?"

Iván's urgency had been about a gala he thought Father shouldn't attend, so I'd forgotten about it as soon as he'd finished saying his piece.

"No, don't worry about it." I couldn't help but smile. Not everyone switched so easily from their own feelings to worrying about someone else. "Tell me how it goes, okay? I'll feel responsible now."

"Okay." Was that a hint of a giggle? I didn't let my brain get caught up on it. "But, uh, if you could leave early and attend? I think I'd be okay with it."

My eyes widened, my heart beating faster. Sadly, before I could grill her about what she meant, or process how her shy statement made me feel to begin with, Kara hung up.

She hung up on me.

Needless to say, that wasn't a thing that happened.

It was only her luck that I could already see my parents' house, and my mother watching from the kitchen window.

"YOU'RE NOT STAYING FOR DINNER?" Father asked, stealing a glance in the kitchen's direction.

Mother had gone there to get my niece's favorite cookies out of the oven. I understood the implication—she was going to be sad about it—but it had been years since I last let it sway me.

My relationship with my parents was complicated, to say the least.

"I'd made plans before Mom called." It was only a half lie. Just because I'd thought I'd skip them didn't mean those plans hadn't been made beforehand. "I'll stop by next week and take her out somewhere."

I was visiting a site not too far from here Wednesday morning, so I could make it work.

Potentially.

"I'll hold you to that."

He wouldn't. He was an even worse husband and father than I was a daughter. I didn't need to say it out loud, though. Instead, I turned around and headed to the kitchen to say Mother goodbye. She looked frailer and frailer. I didn't like it, but no matter how much I tried to get her to see a doctor, she wouldn't budge. She dismissed it as normal aging, but I wasn't so sure.

At least I'd gotten her to agree to hire someone to help her with the housework around the place.

BOTASDECUERO

> Guess what, little one? We'll be seeing each other tonight in the end.

UNICORNIOXX

really?? *starry-eyed emoji*

BOTASDECUERO

> Should I be worried?

UNICORNIOXX

no, Ma'am

> i'm going to be the best behaved boy ever, you'll see
>
> i have to look out for Kara, and i can't do that if one of you is flogging me hard

> BOTASDECUERO
>
> That's the spirit.

I started the car after sending that last text message. It was more than likely that I would arrive when things had already started, but as chaotic as Sergio could be, I trusted him.

He wouldn't have carved his spot in the community if we couldn't do that.

8

KARA

Deep breaths.

It shouldn't be hard.

Sergio had agreed to meet me outside, so I just had to wait by the tinted doors, then everything would be all right. I checked the page for the event, and I didn't know anyone other than him, but that was fine, too. Mónica had said that Jen and Marga weren't super active in the community, so it made sense.

A part of me was disappointed Mónica wouldn't be there —a part of me I buried deep down. I highly doubted she'd ever act on anything, even if she was interested—and there was no way on Earth I'd take that proverbial first step. The last thing I needed was a HR nightmare on my hands when everything was still so new and I still felt like I was on the edge of a cliff half of the time.

Besides, there was a world of difference between joining a community and playing with a Domme. I might have been fantasizing a bit—I was human, okay?—but just thinking about genuinely doing anything about it gave me the shivers.

Littles were safe.

Domms weren't.

I almost whined out loud, images flashing through my head, but I pushed them back. I was an ocean away, and I was safe. Sergio would be here, and he'd promised he'd let everyone know they couldn't play with me, and he'd keep me safe. I hadn't had to explain why, either, and… Fuck, that had made me tear up for real.

"Kara, over here!"

I turned toward the sound of the voice before I could start tearing up again. Sergio was running in my direction and sweeping me up in a hug before I could react.

I needed a second, but I hugged him back. It was chilly outside, and he was running so hot. I might have breathed him in, too. I didn't get the feeling that he'd complain.

"Ready to go in?"

"Yeah." I nodded, blinking a couple of times to will all those emotions away. It was going to be fine. "Thanks for… you know, being with me."

"Of course, boo," he joked, twisting his arm with mine before leading the way to the club.

They gave me a couple wristbands at the entrance, and I put them on right away. I didn't quite catch what they'd said, but Sergio had answered for me when I didn't, and I trusted him. It was kind of wild—the way I trusted him so easily when I'd struggled to do that with anyone for years, but I didn't question it.

I just followed him to the locker room. There were three other people there, but they were on the opposite end of the lockers Sergio led me to.

"Could you help me?" I bit my lip. I knew he liked to watch, but I didn't know how comfortable he was with touching or anything else. I didn't want to make him uncomfortable. "I brought one of those body harnesses, but all the clasps are in the back."

"Sure, I've got you."

He didn't even have to think about it, which was more soothing than he probably realized. I just started disrobing after a cursory glance confirmed the other three people were paying us no attention. I'd put on quite a few layers, and carried a duffel bag Lucas had let me borrow with everything else inside.

It didn't smell, and I'd been surprised—until he explained it was a Christmas gift he'd never gotten to use.

Now, it was used to store a pink mesh bodysuit that was half see-through and my harness. I hadn't put any of those on in a long time. I shook my head. Thinking about that wouldn't lead me anywhere good.

Deep breath in and out, I reminded myself.

The bodysuit reminded me of one of those swimming suits with a higher neck that made everyone's asses pop and left little to the imagination in the nether area. I'd once loved how sensual it made me feel. The harness would help make everything else pop, too, once Sergio helped me adjust all the straps.

"Damn," he said, "you have a killer body."

I turned around to watch him fanning himself. He winked at me, and it made me laugh, but I knew I was blushing, too. I liked wearing things that made me feel good about my body, but I didn't like focusing on it too much, either.

"Help?" I ignored his compliment in deference to dangling the straps between us.

They were holographic pink, a few shades lighter than the bodysuit. The way his eyes glinted made me think he approved.

"You're lucky you're not a gay boy or I'd totally be thinking you're competition."

"That's silly," I spluttered.

He just hummed.

"Let me know if it's too tight, okay?"

I nodded, but I knew I wouldn't need to tell him anything. He was the most careful person I'd ever met in a kink setting, and that was saying something.

"Should we go up?"

"Yeah."

If I thought too much about it, I'd just panic, so, instead, I followed him out of the locker room and prayed that there wasn't a draft from the outside gates. I hadn't considered the weather here would be something I'd struggle with.

"Did you want something to drink?"

"Just water."

We shared a smile as Sergio led us to the bar. Rule number one of going to an orgy was that dehydration was not sexy. I remembered that much.

He'd just ordered us two bottles when he turned to me. His eyes were slightly wide, as if he'd forgotten to do something.

"I didn't tell you Mónica was coming in the end, did I?"

I was going to need that water sooner rather than later. I could just feel my mouth drying. "She is?"

"Yeah." Sergio must've noticed too, his hand quickly wrapping around my arm. "But hey, it's okay. She knows you're off limits, and I told you I'll be watching over you."

"It's not that," I managed to say. I'd been blushing before, but that had to be nothing in comparison with how my cheeks burned now. "I told her I'd be okay with her being here earlier."

A groan left my lips as I hid against Sergio's neck. I could do without the shock in his face, or the mirth. The arm around my midsection felt nice, though.

"Aw, but that's good! Mónica is fun, well, when she isn't your boss, I guess."

"Don't remind me."

Sergio held me for a bit longer. It was a bit awkward with the bottles of water between us, and him naked, but I had no intention of pulling away.

"We're still moving upstairs, right?" he asked after a while.

"Yeah."

I just needed a second. It was going to be fine. Mónica being here didn't change anything. I was just going to have fun with other subs, and that was it. Or I'd hang out with Sergio on the sidelines, which felt more and more tempting as the seconds passed by. Regardless, it was going to be fine, and her being here didn't change anything—one phone conversation where it felt like she'd flayed me open notwithstanding.

Sergio led to a room farther down the hallway than the one we'd been in last week. There were more people than there had been last week, but I'd prepared myself for that.

The room still looked much larger, anyway. There were a few mattresses around the floor where some people were already lying down. Lots of fixings for rope and restraints, too, pretty much everywhere. My eyes focused on the two St. Andrew crosses and the three benches in different styles. Those were all toward one side of the room, so I guessed we —I—were steering clear of it.

Even if it was with another sub, there was no way I'd get near anything involving pain.

"Hello, Mistress Erika." I tensed, but Sergio just squeezed my hand as he bounced on his feet and waved to a woman in full body latex that clung to her skin.

Only her face and hair were visible. She was striking, with dark skin and black hair styled in long braids that reached just above her waist. I still couldn't move, not until she was smiling indulgently at Sergio.

"Already getting into trouble, little one?"

"N-no!" Sergio balked, affronted. I got it. I'd be affronted too. It was silly, really, Domms' obsession with assuming we were up to no good all the time. "Just being polite, Ma'am. I'm on protection duty today."

"I see." Mistress Erika nodded. Her eyes shifted to me for less than a second, but she didn't acknowledge me. "I'm sure you'll do a good job, but you know I'm on DM duty if you need me, yeah?"

I knew that she'd said that for my benefit more than his, but Sergio just nodded and tugged at my hand. He must've recognized the people chilling on one of the mattresses because he took me straight there.

I was proved right when they all waved and he let go of my hand to hug each of them. I smiled and hovered slightly while they finished greeting each other.

"Hi, I'm Kara."

Deep breaths, I remembered. No one had started doing anything other than talk among themselves, but there were still enough people to make me feel goosebumps.

"She's with me," Sergio interjected, moving back to my side. "She just moved in, so I'm showing her around."

"Are you a Little like him?" one of the four people Sergio had just hugged asked. They were a curvy redhead with too many freckles to count, wearing a bodice in baby blue. "I'm María. I use she/her pronouns."

"Nice to meet you."

One by one, the other three took María's lead and introduced themselves as well.

"Jaime, he/they."

Jaime was one of the two wearing a puppy suit with a hood in yellow.

"Cece, she/they." Cece was the second puppy. They had a nice voice, deeper than I would've imagined for the orange puppy.

"Eli, they/them." Eli had been half hidden behind María.

They had a latex suit similar to Mistress Erika's, only this one had a fly for easier access to their ass and covered their face too.

Probably into objectification, then.

"Please forgive me if I forget anyone's name," I breathed out.

I was usually good with names, but I could feel my anxiety rising.

Thankfully they just laughed.

"It's fine," María said. "You really only have to remember my name. Both Cece and Jaime will respond to pup, and Eli is just a slut for attention."

"María is also a mean switch who will betray you if you lower your guard," Sergio half-whispered, half-shouted for dramatic effect.

I spluttered, but María just laughed at him.

"Wanna sit down? I love your harness, by the way."

"I know!" Sergio enthused, pulling me down to sit cross-legged next to him. "It's so shiny!"

Everyone bobbed their heads up and down. My eyes stayed on María. Switches were… She would be fine, right? I felt some apprehension, but it wasn't the same fear Mistress Erika, or a Domm in general, instilled. Switches knew about being vulnerable. It was different.

"May I touch?" María asked, already on her knees.

My throat dried up, which meant I had to chug half of my water before I could face her, but I nodded.

I knew the harness wasn't the highest quality out there, but it was still quite a few steps above something from AliExpress, which made me happy.

I felt more than saw Sergio scoot backwards while María scooted closer to me. Her hands wrapped around the straps, dangling casually close to my half-covered breast. My heart kicked up, my throat bobbing up and down, pupils wide. I couldn't move, but I didn't find myself *wanting* to move.

"What do you say we kiss?" María gave me a sly smirk. It showed off her dimples, creating a dichotomy between her sweet appearance and the implication of her words. "In the spirit of breaking the ice and all that."

I was…

There was no way I could say no.

"I'd like that."

María grinned. There was some more scooting, but I was anchored to my spot. It didn't matter. Her hand cupped my cheek, and it was soft and gentle. I shivered. I hadn't had soft and gentle in so long, I could feel tears brimming up. Her lips were on mine before she could notice or my body betrayed me. I was glad for it. She had some kind of gloss on, but I wasn't sure what it tasted like. I just knew she felt nice against me, warm.

My hands moved to her waist, pulling her closer. I wanted—needed—more of that warmth.

I wasn't sure how it happened, even though I was pretty sure it had been all me. I found myself leaning down until I was lying on my back. María let out a faint laugh as she followed. Her hands roamed down my sides.

"Damn, aren't you gorgeous," she hummed. Her eyes glinted above me. I whimpered. Being vocal was hard for me once I got into the throes of it, but I tried to express things how I could. "Needy, too?"

I whimpered again. I tried not to smile in glee, but I liked how she tested the kind of talk I'd respond to. I bit my lip. I didn't want to waste time pondering whether or not I should try to sit up to discuss everything properly. I just nodded.

Sergio was there. People were monitoring the scene. I was safe.

I *felt* safe.

María didn't move, her body covering mine. I relished the weight pinning me down as she nibbled around my jaw and touched everywhere. Shivers ran through me. It felt silly—we were barely doing anything—but she didn't draw attention to it.

"We are basically the queer group here," María murmured against my ear. Another shiver ran down my spine. Her voice had a sultry quality to it I couldn't get over. "Sergio just plays with Jaime if he plays at all, but everyone else is fair game."

I nodded, my head tilting back, my spine arching. One of her hands trailed up and down my hip bone, making it damn hard to concentrate.

It wasn't fair.

"What about you?" she asked eventually.

To be fair, I couldn't really tell how long it had been.

"Fair game," I mouthed.

"Good girl," María teased.

She looked back. I thought one of the pups—maybe both—were saying something. My thighs clenched, need building and pooling.

Her hair brushed against my face when she focused her attention back on me. It smelled nice—like coconut. I breathed it in before I pushed myself to focus on the words coming out of her mouth.

"What do you say we get you out of these clothes and I eat you out, hmm?"

I was bucking my hips up before she'd finished talking. Nodding frantically, too.

"I was tested." I cleared my throat, some clarity pushing through the haze in my brain that came with group play. "A few months after I broke up with my ex. Haven't been with anyone since."

María nodded. "We all get tested regularly," she said, "but we still use dams and condoms every time. Is that all right?"

I nodded. Eli appeared in my periphery, handing María one of the dams I hadn't noticed earlier without a word. I loved that they had these dynamics between them. I just hoped I could join them, too. I liked sex without the pressure of power exchanges and protocols.

María seemed to understand it, too.

She peppered my body with kisses as she got rid of the harness and lowered the mesh down my body. My breath hitched a couple of times. There was no way she wasn't thinking I was little more than a blushing virgin, and I wanted to explain myself to her, but not now. Now one of my hands traveled to grab a fistful of her ginger curls and led her down toward my throbbing clit. There were only too many gentle touches I could handle before I lost it.

I groaned with the first flick of her tongue, my thighs clenching before she pinned them down. I moaned, back arching before I settled on the mattress. My head lolled to the side, my lips parted.

My body tensed. I hadn't meant to focus on the people—Domms, mostly—watching from the couches pulled against the wall, but she was there.

Mónica.

Her eyes were on me, unwavering but casual. I'd gotten good at reading what was brewing behind someone's gaze. I was too used to seeing anger. Disgust, too. Mónica wasn't showing that. She was relaxed, but observant.

I prepared myself for the spike of fear to come. There was a hint of it, and my heart raced for a minute, my mouth drying, but it was manageable. Maybe my hand tightened slightly on María's scalp, but she didn't complain.

I might've given my boss a subtle nod, but it was hard to tell. Focusing was hard, and multitasking was so not my thing when I wasn't being paid for it.

9

MÓNICA

I had yet to decide what the best course of action was. Granted, it was hard to think of much with the sights before me.

Everyone in the queer mattress—as they liked to call it—had zeroed in on Kara. I hadn't been sure how she'd feel being the absolute center of attention, but clearly she had no problem with it.

That was evidenced by the scene going on.

Sergio and Kara were being railed into the mattress by Jaime and Cece. Jaime was on Sergio while Cece was on Kara, both of them sporting the biggest strap-ons they could find from the looks of it. Most of the people on the mattresses nearby had stopped what they were doing to watch, too.

It was hard not to.

"You haven't taken your eyes off the new girl all night."

It was Tony. I barely acknowledged him on a good day, and I definitely wasn't planning to change that now. It was bad enough he'd decided to sit down next to me.

"She's off limits." It was acknowledgment, but I wasn't going to function if I didn't put that out there.

I might respect what he had with Jen and Marga, and I might even admit it worked for them. That didn't mean I trusted or liked how he could be with newcomers. He was too forward.

"Why?" He turned toward me. "You've collared her already?"

I scoffed. It was always about whether a sub was collared or not with him. It was one of the reasons I didn't trust him.

"No, I haven't." I didn't stop to wonder why the words made my jaw clench. I'd dropped the habit of gritting my teeth as soon as I finished my MBA. "It's in her profile, no Domms."

Tony rolled his eyes. I caught it from the corner of my eye but refused to acknowledge it. The last thing he needed was an excuse to go off about how fluid human sexuality was. Funny how it only applied to the women around him.

"That boy needs someone to train his hole," he muttered.

"Are you volunteering?"

Tony just sneered.

Case in point.

There was some truth to the statement, though. Sergio often bit off more than he could chew, and he wasn't used to big toys. It was rare that he participated as much as he was doing tonight. I suspected he was doing it for Kara's benefit.

Erika exchanged a glance with me. It wouldn't be the first time we pulled him away if he wasn't thinking clearly. I shook my head in her direction.

As competitive as Jaime got when in pupspace and topping someone next to Cece, he was going softer—slightly, but softer—on Sergio. What I focused on most, though, was Kara. She was squeezing his hand, letting him squeeze back. They were both whispering things to each other between high pitched moans and cries. I doubted they were really hearing the words, but the sentiment was there. I got the feeling that was what mattered, and something Kara had needed. She had been tense all week.

We really needed to have that conversation about boundaries, but after the texts and that phone call… It would've been irresponsible of me to not show up and make sure she was okay. That was the story I was telling myself, at least.

"María."

The ginger came to me quickly enough, Eli following behind. While the pups and the littles were having fun, María had been sitting on Eli's face.

"Yeah?" Her voice sounded wrecked as she fixed her hair. "I didn't know you were coming tonight, Ma'am."

I grinned. I'd never met anyone who switched as effortlessly as her. We joked that she was our club's premium switch for a reason.

"I'm full of surprises," I teased, "but do me a favor and make sure those four stay hydrated, will you?"

Both Kara and Sergio had had bottles of water when I'd arrived, so I wasn't so worried about the thin layer of sweat clinging to their skin. I couldn't say the same for the two pups, and they were still wearing most of their gear. It didn't take a rocket scientist to figure out they had to be drenched by now.

"On it, Ma'am." María winked. "I have it all under control."

"Watch the attitude."

The girl just laughed at me.

I shook my head, deciding to let her go and keep having her fill of Eli.

It was purely selfish of me, really. After all, as much as I could split my attention between the two if needed, I didn't want to. Not when Kara was just right there.

I hadn't been sure about how she'd react when or if she noticed me. There was a world of difference between talking on the phone and sending a few texts, and seeing someone in person. It didn't happen often, but I'd swear I didn't breathe when I caught her noticing me.

Then she'd given me the subtlest of nods. She hadn't glanced in my direction since, but…

"Wanna place bets on which pup gets tired first?" Erika came to my side. She was the Domme I trusted the most here, so I didn't ignore her like I did Tony.

"I think they're both already exhausted." I snorted. They might have stamina, but they had been going for a long while now, and they didn't know the meaning of pacing themselves. "But they're together, and the Littles are not complaining, so…"

"So we're picking them off the floor later."

"Someone should, yeah."

Erika hummed. I knew she had something to say—she hadn't just left her post to joke about the two pups, but I let her bide her time. Sergio might think of her as the big scary Sadist who was mean to him, but I knew she often took her time to word herself just right, or to plan the perfect sequence when flogging someone.

"Do you know what the deal is with the new sub?" If the question had come from someone like Tony, I'd sneer and remind them Kara had a name. I knew Erika was only avoiding it so that Kara wouldn't notice we were talking about her. "Sergio only referred me to her profile and announced himself in charge. His words, not mine."

I shook my head. I really hoped Sergio found someone for himself. "I told him to look after her, but I don't know much of the backstory. I just…"

"Suspect," she finished the sentence for me.

It made sense. We'd known each other long enough.

"Yeah." I cleared my throat. "Just today, it felt like she was going to open up to me, but it's kind of tug of war with her. She gets close one second, and draws back the next. It's the same at work."

"At work?"

Shit.

To be fair, I hadn't meant to say that, but their mattress was the closest to where I was sitting, and Kara's moans and cries were proving too distracting.

"She works for me. I found out when the Littles called me for help last week."

Erika didn't say anything at first, only nodded slowly. I hadn't expected any differently, so I just kept watching. Cece all but collapsed on top of Kara before pulling the dildo out. They were squishing her to the mattress, but Kara didn't complain. I could just imagine how pliant and soft and warm she—

Nope.

Not going there.

I was the one who had talked Kara into staying in our community. I couldn't be the one making things weird at work come Monday.

"I hope it doesn't blow up in her face. Or yours."

I sighed. "That makes two of us."

I KEPT CATCHING up with Erika while the Littles and pups snuggled in a cuddle pile. I should make more of an effort to keep tabs on her—and everyone else in the club—but I admitted I wasn't always the best at doing it. Too bad some of the Littles kept thinking of me as a Mommy. I really wasn't Mommy material, and I wasn't even that into them. I just had a soft spot for them when they regressed.

My plan was to wait for Kara and Sergio to head to the lockers and leave then. It wasn't cowardice, but it didn't take a lot to see Kara was vulnerable, and there was too much we had to talk over before I could feel comfortable around her in that state.

"Mistress Mónica!"

Of course.

Erika and I exchanged a glance before I turned to the voice. Very few people could holler like that after the scene they'd just had.

Sergio was one of them.

I forced my stare blank before I turned to him. "What is it, baby boy?"

He giggled, squirming on his side as he held Kara tighter, pushing her back closer to his chest.

"We need you here."

Did they now?

It was calling for trouble, but I still got up and headed toward the mattress. Cece and Jaime had moved to the opposite end and were frotting against each other. María and Eli were nowhere to be seen. I thought they'd just left to grab more water, but they must've called it a night instead.

"Well?" I raised a brow, knowing it would make Sergio squirm more.

For now, I only focused on him, ignoring his casual use of *we*.

"We're cold." He tried to give me his best pout. He dropped it real quick, though, so it must've been clear it wasn't working. "We need blankie."

"And *I* have to get it?"

Sergio blinked innocently. Population he was fooling with that: zero. "Pretty, pretty please?"

He was really good at using his baby voice, though. It would be annoying if I wasn't so fond of him.

Ugh.

"Fine."

There was a pile of fresh blankets in a closet tucked in the corner. I went there while avoiding disturbing anyone who was either still playing or in the middle of aftercare. It wasn't as easy of a feat as it would've seemed at first glance, but I got there and grabbed the softest blanket I could see.

We should discuss getting more of the good ones. Some were beginning to show their age.

"Here you go."

"You gotta tuck us in, too, Ma'am."

No one talked about the amount of patience one needed to deal with Littles.

"Of course."

It would be downright cruel if I said no, really. Kara wasn't drawing away, either, and she didn't look distressed. I was taking it as a good sign.

I still avoided touching them as much as possible while complying with Sergio's request.

"You have a way to get back home, little one?"

"I'll drive her after a tiny nap, Ma'am."

"Good boy."

"Mónica?" Kara's voice startled me enough I almost stumbled back.

Note to self: squatting down was a bad idea when I wasn't in complete control of my surroundings.

"Yeah?" I cleared my throat.

Honorifics or pet names didn't have a place between the two of us.

Kara met my gaze when she spoke, her eyes more open and awake than I would've expected. "Did you come here tonight to check on me?" I blinked. That wasn't the question I was expecting. I didn't have an answer—I'd just been trying to figure it out myself. She spoke again before I could come up with something to say, "Thank you."

"You're welcome." I answered on autopilot. In reality, my heart was beating as fast as it could, and my throat felt parched. I should've gotten some water for myself, too. "Text me when you get home, okay? Both of you."

I stayed there until they both nodded. I knew before I turned around that Erika would be giving me one of her looks.

I would be too, if the roles were reversed.

"You two need to talk."

"I know."

In hindsight, I should've done something to force that talk, but I... didn't. The more it got postponed, though, the messier it could all get—for everyone.

10

KARA

SERGIO

you can do it !!!!

I reread the text thread with Sergio for the tenth time. After he dropped me off at home, we exchanged numbers so we didn't have to use the kink app all the time. I'd texted him when I woke up, and that had somehow led to texting about Mónica.

To be fair, I'd been thinking about her nonstop. Not last night, after the shock faded. There were too many people, too many touches and stimulation to even remember anything. As things started to slow down, though? My brain started to go on overdrive, making me too aware. I didn't know how I managed to get any sleep.

It must've been all the orgasms.

I shouldn't be thinking about orgasms before I texted Mónica. It had been a really fucking long time, though. It wasn't as if I hadn't masturbated, or played with toys since *Her*, but it was the first time I played with anyone else. The first time in years. And it had been the best fucking night I'd had in a long time.

But it also meant I couldn't ignore what was going on—or wasn't?—with my boss.

Mónica.

I'd texted her as she'd asked when I got home. She'd replied right away. I read it, but I didn't know what to say—hence texting Sergio as soon as he got up.

> MÓNICA
>
> Thank you for texting.
>
> Did Sergio tell you about the brunch we set up the day after a play party? I thought we could talk.

The thing was, I agreed, but I should have been panicking about the idea of spending longer than I needed to in her presence. I wasn't. I wasn't ready to delve too deep into what it meant, but... Maybe I didn't have to run away from it. Maybe I could just talk with her, and it wouldn't be the end of the world.

> KARA
>
> i've never been a big fan of brunch
>
> (i know, not very American of me)
>
> but i wanted to talk, too
>
> maybe we can just meet for coffee?

> MÓNICA
>
> Of course. Tell me when and where, I don't have anything to do today.

> KARA
>
> i don't know a lot of places here yet, but there's a café near the bus station? they have milkshakes and smoothies and stuff for cheap?
>
> you can choose the time

> MÓNICA
>
> Did you want coffee or a sugar high?

> KARA
>
> but milkshakes are fun?

> MÓNICA
>
> All right, I know the place.
>
> 13:00 works for you?

> KARA
>
> yeah

I bit on my thumbnail as I reread the last texts. I shouldn't have said anything about the milkshakes. It was too close to Little talk.

It wasn't safe.

It had felt natural, though.

I didn't know what to do with that. I was already dressed, and I'd made myself a bowl of cereal and cottage cheese, though, which left few things to distract myself with. I lived relatively close to the bus station, so that left me with an hour and a half of staying home with nothing to do but obsess over everything.

There was no doubt in my mind that I was going to be a mess by the time I reached the café. I was determined, though. That was also new.

"Hey, stranger," Lucas said. He was playing some video game in the living room. He was the only person I'd met so far who actually woke up early on his days off. "Wanna play?"

"No, thanks." I was too jittery to be any good, but I still sat next to him. Watching him race around could be the distraction I needed. "Do you have a day off?"

"I'm on medical leave for the next couple of weeks." He shrugged.

My eyes widened. Why didn't I know?

"What's wrong? Are you sick? Hurt?"

Why didn't I know?

"It's okay." He patted my arm as he spoke. "I just sprained an ankle last night, and I can't be a lot of help in the ER if I have to hobble around."

Oh.

I took in the elevated leg and the cast around his ankle then, along with the crutches resting against his side of the couch. It said a lot about my general state that I hadn't noticed as soon as I walked into the living room.

"Do you need anything? Ice? Or… I'm going to head out in a bit. I could get you something from the pharmacy, or… Cake? Comfort food?"

Lucas just chuckled, which wasn't fair. I was genuinely worried about him. I worried about people, dammit.

"If it'll make you feel better, you can get me one of those sandwiches from the Greek place by the beach."

I nodded. I knew the one because Lucas had insisted I needed to try it on my very first week here.

"Will do."

"I really am okay."

"You promise to call me if you need anything, right?"

"I already have Alex hovering," he complained, "but yeah, I will. Promise."

"Thanks." I leaned against the back of the couch then. "By the way, thanks for sending me the contact info for that therapist."

I only spoke when he'd started a new match. I thought

that would mean the words wouldn't register fully, and he wouldn't make a big deal out of it.

"You called?"

I could feel him studying me, so I avoided glancing in his direction. Very mature behavior over here.

"I sent an email." I swallowed. "I imagine I'll get a call on Monday."

"That's good," he said. "I hope it works out for you."

"Yeah."

I had experience with therapy; it wasn't that. It was just frustrating and embarrassing, to a degree, that I still seemed to need *more* therapy.

"Are you sure you don't want to play?"

"Maybe after I'm back."

"Where are you going, anyway? You've been heading out a lot lately."

I snorted. I didn't know that going out once during the weekends amounted to heading out a lot. Then again, before I dared to go out with Sergio, I'd only been leaving the house to go to work, if I needed to buy something, or if Lucas or Alex dragged me out.

Yeah, there was definitely a need for more hours of therapy.

"I'm meeting up with Mónica."

"Ohh, a girl?" Lucas waggled his eyebrows.

It looked ridiculous on anyone, but it looked even more ridiculous on him. He was a literal giant with the bushiest eyebrows. I wondered if he'd ever gotten them done, or if he'd let me. I'd never done it, but I'd watched videos. It should be fine.

"Shut up!" We weren't going to mention if my voice went too high pitched, or if I was blushing hard. "She's my boss."

Lucas's car crashed into something before he could pause the game.

I winced.

"You're meeting your boss on a Sunday?"

"It's…" I squirmed. Now I was avoiding his glance for real. "Complicated?"

I knew both he and Alex were part of the LGBTQ+ community, but I didn't know if they were kinksters, or what they thought about it. I didn't tend to hide it from people, but I usually wasn't feeling so vulnerable. I wasn't isolated in a country where I didn't know anyone I could run off to if things went wrong.

"You realize I'm going to be pestering you about it now, right?"

"Please don't?" I squealed.

Yeah, there was no way he wouldn't. To be fair, I'd be more judgmental if he didn't pester me or see anything wrong with it.

Lucas snorted.

Thankfully, he was also easily distracted by the screen and the cars coming at him from every angle.

Small mercies.

CAMERON TALKED about tornadoes in his stomach when he was going to meet a new potential Daddy. I'd always teased him and said that made no sense.

If we were still talking, I'd be texting him right about now to apologize. After, I'd complain because he never mentioned tornadoes made you want to throw up. I was genuinely nauseated.

I hid it behind a forced smile when I spotted Mónica. I'd arrived before she did and grabbed a table inside. It had comfortable chairs, and it was hidden near a corner, which suited me.

"Hey!" Mónica spoke first. She was wearing all black, leather boots included. Sergio had mentioned something about it.

It was still weird; her style and the way she carried herself was so different from what I was used to seeing Monday to Friday.

Then again, the clothes I chose for myself versus the clothes I wore when I was working were also different.

"Hi."

I waved. I knew the custom was to stand up and give her two kisses, one on each cheek, but I was frozen. She didn't seem to mind, simply sitting on the chair opposite of mine.

"How're you doing?" Her voice in Spanish was different than it was in English. Her registry was lower, more gravely. "Wait, did you prefer we talked in English?"

"It's fine." I swallowed. We talked in Spanish at the club, so that wasn't the issue. It just wasn't the best start if she was already misinterpreting my silences. "I already ordered something to drink. They said they brought tapas with everything so we should be good. Unless you're hungrier, I mean?"

"I'm not particularly hungry," Mónica said as she took off the leather jacket that hugged her shoulders way too well. "It's windier than I thought outside. Did you live too far from here?"

"No, it's fine." How many times had I said it was fine already? I hoped no one was recording this. "It's just fifteen minutes or so. Uh, but thanks for agreeing to meet up here."

Mónica quirked an eyebrow. "Wasn't I the one who told you to pick a place?"

"Well, yeah, but…" I groaned, rubbing my face with both hands. "Can we start again, please?"

I couldn't lose control like this. It just couldn't happen.

"Sure."

I blinked my eyes open, forced myself to pry my hands away. "Really?"

I'd been expecting her to begrudge me or say something sarcastic—not that I thought that was Mónica's style, but...

Yeah.

"I wouldn't say it if I didn't mean it." She looked like she meant that, too. There was just something about her expression that was relaxed, open. "I want you to feel comfortable. Take your time."

I nodded.

It didn't really answer any of my questions, but I tried to do as she said. I even tried breathing exercises.

By the time I thought I could string two sentences together—probably—the waiter arrived with my milkshake.

They'd called it unicorn-flavored, so there was no way I wouldn't try it.

Even if Mónica was eyeing it as if it was going to spew out an alien or something.

"How many extra toppings did you order?" she asked after asking for a caramel latte without whipped cream for herself.

"None," I protested. Sure, there was a mountain of whipped cream with a shit ton of sprinkles, tiny marshmallows, and fruity pebbles, but for once, it wasn't my doing. "But it looks so pretty! I'm definitely ordering this every time I come here."

There was a hint of a smile on Mónica's lips as she shook her head. "All yours."

Well, yeah. Anxious or not, I wasn't planning on sharing.

Huh.

I squinted my eyes as I unfolded the napkin to reach the tiny spoon. Had she assumed I'd share?

"So..." Monica's latte had just arrived, and I took the

opportunity to start talking while she took her first sip. "You said that we should discuss boundaries and stuff, and I wanted to do that."

"Okay." She nodded. The mug stayed by her mouth, which I actually appreciated. "I wanted to do that, too. Did you have anything in mind, or did you want me to take the lead?"

"I actually did have something in mind." I cleared my throat and didn't say why her taking the lead was not something I could trust. "I saw in the community app that there's this thing where, if someone was under a Domm's protection, Domms couldn't DM them without their permission. I wondered if you'd be open to do that."

Maybe I blurted that out too quickly, but hey. I put it out there.

The fact that Mónica took her time to answer didn't help, though. "You want to be under my protection?"

"Uh… Yeah? I mean, just on paper? It would be pretend. So that Domms can't message me." I glanced down.

I'd thought she'd be open to the idea, but it might've been too much.

"I have to say, it wasn't what I'd been expecting you to say."

Yeah, she was probably thinking more in terms of what she could call me or do to me when we were in the club.

I'd thought about it, too, to be fair. I just wanted to get the protection thing out of the way. I hadn't got too many DMs since I signed up, but I'd still gotten some. Besides, it helped soothe the most paranoid voice in my head that said She could track me and join the app.

Mónica licked her lips. I ignored how my eyes tracked the movement, and how my heartbeat rose. It was just a timing issue, because I'd been thinking about the other thing.

"You can be under my protection," she said slowly, "but I kind of need to know what you need protection against."

"Easy. Domms." It wasn't a question I had to think hard about. The words came out as soon as she stopped talking.

"I'm a Domme," she seemed to feel the need to point out.

Did she always quirk her eyebrow like that when she tried to make a point? I'd caught her using that expression with her brothers at work, too.

"Yeah, but I…" I cleared my throat. Just for the record, I hated Domms and their need to be all thorough and smart. "You're different."

"Do you know me enough to say that?"

My heart stopped before it went back to beating rapidly, my anxiety rising. There wasn't enough air here.

"What do you mean?"

"Nothing bad," Mónica rushed in to say, her head slightly tilted. "Do you need a glass of water?"

I shook my head.

No distractions.

Mónica didn't seem convinced, but she barreled on. "Why don't you want Domms to contact you, Kara?"

I had to barrel on, too, I guessed. "Domms can hurt me."

There was a beat of silence. I couldn't worry too much about reading her face, too worried about getting myself under control first.

"I'm assuming we're not talking about impact play or SM here."

I shook my head, my eyes trained on the floor. I should've prepared more to talk about this. I didn't know what I'd been thinking, believing I could just ask her to list me under her protection. Of course she wouldn't just let it go when I hinted at the trauma I was running from. Was I a rookie now?

"Are there any specific triggers I should know about?"

There was a mile long list of triggers, if I thought really hard about it. I didn't think there were things Mónica was going to do or need to know, in any case.

I shrugged, which was a compromise. She wouldn't have liked it if I said no, I could tell as much.

My hands found the milkshake glass. My fingers trembled, but I managed to take a sip. The cold strawberry flavor coating my mouth helped.

"I can't trust that a Domm won't hurt me like She did. I can't."

"Okay." Mónica leaned closer to the table. "Have you talked to anyone about her?"

"I've been to therapy in the States, and my roommate gave me the details for a trauma therapist here. I sent her an email, so I'm just waiting for her to answer and set an appointment."

"That's great." Mónica's voice had progressively turned softer. I sometimes hated when people did that, but it didn't feel condescending or pitying with her. "Hopefully they can fit you in the evenings, but let me know if you need to go during work hours, okay?"

"You wouldn't mind?"

"I'm sure I'd manage without you for a few hours a week."

I chuckled. It wasn't that funny, but it kind of was, too.

"But your father won't fire me?"

"No, don't worry about it. HR might try to send you a passive aggressive email or two, but let me handle it if it comes to that, okay?"

I nodded. It sounded too good to be true, but I wasn't about to look a gift horse in the mouth.

"Thanks."

"Is that why you searched for a job here?"

"I can apply for dual citizenship down the road because of

my father, so I figured all the bureaucracy would be easier, and I... I needed to get away. I mean, I'd already left—the relationship I mean—but it felt like She could just show up, anywhere, even if I moved cities."

Before I could say anything else, I grabbed a spoonful of whipped cream and toppings. This was the most I'd talked about Her outside of therapy. It was strange, but less strange than I'd thought it would be. Mónica was easy to talk to. It was disturbing. She wasn't reacting like I imagined people would. She was just listening. Silently.

"It's a huge change. Brave, too." I didn't know about that. Thankfully, my mouth was still stuffed with whipped cream. That was my excuse for not saying anything back. "Thank you for trusting me with all of this, by the way. I should've said sooner."

I shrugged. "It's fine."

"I don't know that it is." Mónica took another sip of her latte before continuing, "Is that all you wanted to ask or tell me?"

I cleared my throat. I hadn't realized, but I was already halfway done with my milkshake. The chair scraped against the wooden floor as I pulled it back. I didn't care about building a distance, but I needed to pace myself with the drink.

"I guess not." I didn't particularly like it, but that was an entirely different beast. "I didn't mind you watching while we were in the club, but I... It can't be more than that. I mean, I don't think I can handle discipline, or... commands or anything that's Domm-behavior, really?"

I counted twenty—rapid—heartbeats before Mónica said anything.

"I'd argue there's plenty of Domm-behavior that's not centered on discipline or obedience," she mused. "What if you drop, or you have an anxiety attack like you did the other day? What do you need when that happens?"

Saying that wasn't going to happen would surely not please her. It was on the tip of my tongue, though.

"Sergio can help."

Mónica clicked her tongue. "I am not leaving your well-being in the hands of a Little."

My blood boiled. It was instant, and not a sensation I was familiar with. "What do you mean in the hands of a Little? Just because we're subs doesn't mean we can't—"

"I know Sergio," Mónica stopped my tirade. It felt like the air was knocked out of my lungs. "I know he goes deep in Little-space, and I know that no matter how much he cares and feels responsible for you, if he's deep in that space, and you start struggling, he's going to freak out, and panic himself, and then he's going to be inconsolable."

"I…"

How on Earth was I supposed to respond to that?

It wasn't as if Sergio had agreed to doing anything. I'd just mentioned him because it was the easy thing to say.

"Excuse me." I heard Mónica's voice in the background, but she wasn't talking to me. I hadn't noticed the waiter, but she had. "Can you get us two glasses of water, please? Thank you."

I swallowed, my throat bobbing up and down. I wanted to say I didn't need water, that I was fine, but I couldn't. It was clear that I wasn't, anyway.

"Kara."

"Uh?" My voice cracked.

Dammit.

"I don't know how things worked in other kink clubs you've been to, if you have been to any, but here, we keep each other safe. If you were to apply to become a member, instead of just showing up as Sergio's guest, these are questions you'd have to answer so that Dungeon Masters knew what to do."

"Can't I just go as Sergio's guest, then?"

"You could," Mónica hedged. It was pretty obvious the prospect didn't enthuse her. Too bad. "But do you understand why I'm asking you these things?"

If this was years ago, and being Little felt safe, I'd be huffing and crossing my arms against my chest. Maybe kicking the floor, too, for emphasis. Now I just scowled.

"I guess." If I took myself out of the equation, that was. "It's just... I didn't join the app or the community to find a Domm. I wanna make that clear."

"That's all right. It's not a requisite to join, or to stay, for that matter."

But would we be having this conversation if it really wasn't?

Even I knew I wasn't going to get the answers I wanted from that line of questioning.

"If I am triggered, you can bring me blankies and water," I mumbled. Hopefully she had good hearing because I was not in the mood to repeat any of it. "And maybe talk. Softly. From a distance. No touching."

"Okay." Mónica nodded, so she must've gotten it all—or most of it, at least. "What if I'm not in the club?"

"I only trust you."

"So..." I looked up to watch her lean back on the seat. She had that assessing look on. I'd seen it at work often. I was a problem she was trying to find loopholes through. "I know you're not looking to have rules enforced, and I respect your reasons. That said, I also think that if you're at a point where only I am allowed to help you through a trigger, the only responsible thing is to agree that you can only go to the club when I'm there."

I frowned. My first instinct was to fight it, but I hid it

under a loud slurp of milkshake. As appealing as throwing a tantrum was, I didn't think it would be appreciated or play in my favor.

It made sense, too, as much as it made me squirm and want to run.

"Okay." My shoulders slumped. I should've ordered a hot chocolate or something warm to wrap my hands around. The glass was too cold and not at all comforting anymore. "What about at work?"

The topic was just as anxiety-inducing, but it forced a change in the line of questioning—or so I hoped—and I'd take it.

11

MÓNICA

Deep breaths.

It seemed to be the one thing I had to keep focusing on ever since I'd sat down opposite Kara. I'd counted on her anxiety, and some push and pull. I hadn't counted on anything else.

"Did you want anything at work to change?"

It was a tricky question. We both knew it. Well, I knew it, and she had to, as well. There was no way to compartmentalize that well, even if the arrangement she wanted with me was only about keeping Domms off her back.

Lurkers always caused problems. I knew for a fact none of the regulars had messaged her. There had just been a few questions and a bordering-on-unhealthy dose of curiosity on the group chat, especially after most of them had seen her last night.

"N-no?" She balked. Her hair was loose, blonde strands cupping her heart shaped face. I found it impossible not to notice how much softer she looked. "I don't want things to be awkward, though."

"Like they were last week?"

Kara's eyes widened only for a second before she nodded. "I tried to stay professional."

"I know." I was very aware of it, in fact. "You did good, and I apologize I didn't do more. I already told you, but this is new for me, too. There are going to be some growing pains."

"But my job isn't threatened, right?"

"It's not," I promised. "And even if we ever reached a point where we decided we couldn't work together, I'd help you. I'd keep you on the payroll while you searched for something else, write you a letter of recommendation or anything else you'd need."

I would've done it before I knew about her past, but there was no doubt in my mind about it now. As much as I wanted to say it was Kara's anxiety speaking, and the likelihood of her ex moving across the country to find her was low...

The statistics said otherwise. If Kara had looked at her options and determined she was safest with an ocean between them, I refused to be the reason she lost that protection.

I would also reassure her as many times as she needed. It was bad enough that there was an actual power imbalance between us before there could be a role-play inspired one.

"Can I ask you something?"

I knew Kara didn't want to go back to talking about the club and the scenarios that had happened or could happen there. I understood why. At the same time, it had plagued me all night. I wasn't going to be able to focus all week if I didn't get some kind of explanation.

"Uh, yeah, sure."

Her hands wrapped around the milkshake as she asked. I imagined the waiter had forgotten about our glasses of water. The café kept getting busier, and they were always overworked here. I'd remind him, but she seemed to be doing better. Her face didn't look pale as a ghost, at least. It was a win.

"What happened last night, when Sergio called me over? Was it all him?"

If I'd been worried about the blood circulation going to Kara's face, I didn't have to anymore. Her cheeks flushed as rosy as I'd ever seen them, the color spreading quickly down her neck.

"He asked me first. If we should, I mean," Kara mumbled. She slurped half of the milkshake she had left, the straw suddenly the most interesting object in her periphery. "I was just warm, and happy, and it felt good. I'm sorry."

I bit my tongue. I wanted to press, to ask what it meant when she said it felt good. I'd already pressed her enough for the day, though. I wasn't under any impression that our relationship was now completely solid. It was still new, finding some semblance of balance, and I wasn't planning to tip the scales anytime soon.

"Why are you sorry?"

"I guess because I don't want to send any mixed messages? I don't know."

Her lips wrapped around the straw again, but I didn't think she was sucking.

"Would you have wanted me to say no?"

It would suck to learn that was the case even though there was little I could do about the past. At the same time, it felt crucial that I knew.

Kara stopped, worrying her bottom lip between her teeth. "I think I would've felt quite sad, so… no."

It was a relief. Probably more of a relief than it should've been. It didn't mean anything regardless.

"What if it happens again?" I focused on the issue at hand. "What if you're feeling warm and cozy with Sergio, or anyone else, really, and you agree to their plan to bring me over?"

"Uh…" Kara licked her lips. I definitely didn't focus on the sheen covering them. "I guess you can. If you're okay with it, obviously. It's not like I'm ever going to say yes to anything big, anyway."

I kept my face neutral. I had no business getting hurt because of her casual dismissal. I hadn't come here looking to score a date or an arrangement of any kind. Besides, her words were about her ex. Still, I'd already started to notice last night, how lines were beginning to blur.

"I guess we'll go with the flow then."

I was a big girl. Kara was going through something big. Supporting her was all I could hope to do.

I wanted to, too, complications be damned.

"Yeah."

TONY

I thought you'd said the new girl was off limits, @Mónica?

Under your protection already?

ERIKA

Kara is under your protection?

MARÍA

Ohhhhh is she?

Damn, can I message her? I want deets, Ma'am

MÓNICA

You're all the worst.

> It's just a formality because certain people can't be bothered to read or respect someone's bio.
>
> @María, I'll ask her, but you'd probably have better luck approaching her at the club.

MARÍA

Okay, do you know when she's going to be there next then? We didn't make any plans last night

MÓNICA

> I don't know. Maybe for the next Little playdate?
>
> Check with Sergio.

MARÍA

But that's so far away !!

I LEFT the group chat after that, mainly to double check the club's schedule. I knew Kara only wanted to attend something during the weekends, but the only event we had going on this weekend was a whipping demo. I highly doubted she'd be interested in it, or being anywhere near it, for that matter. I guessed it was up to whether or not Sergio talked her into one of his schemes, though.

Before we'd said goodbye, Kara had admitted she was beginning to worry that my rule was going to restrict her visits to the club or her time with Sergio and the others. I assured her it wouldn't be the case, of course. I truly didn't mind spending more time in the club than I usually did. I already spent most, if not all, weekends there anyway. As far as I was concerned, the rule only meant Kara had to tell me when she wanted to visit Plumas so I knew where to be there.

Speaking of that, though...

> **MÓNICA**
> By the way, Kara is not to be in Plumas without me there.
>
> I don't think she's going to try to go against my word, but just in case, do not approve her for anything unless I've already RSVP'ed.

> **ERIKA**
> Got it
>
> Everything okay?

> **MÓNICA**
> Not my story to tell, but it should be.

I didn't wait to see what Toby had to say. I did send a private text to María so that she didn't go gossiping or trying to get anything out of the other subs. The absolute con to having switches in the group chat for Domms was that they didn't always keep everything to themselves.

> **KARA**
> hi
>
> i'm heading to bed, but i wanted to thank you for today
>
> it went better than i thought

> **MÓNICA**
> I'm glad.
>
> Rest well, Kara.

I responded on autopilot. In my defense, I was getting dinner ready with Prince wreaking havoc around the kitchen. I hadn't thought she'd text, either. In fact, I'd already figured out at least two times when I could corner her if I had to tomorrow at work.

She had said she didn't want things to be awkward, after all. I would've just been keeping my word. Doing my duty, really.

"Prince, stop!"

I left my phone and dinner forgotten on the counter before my devil of a cat managed to open the door to the washing machine. It wasn't the first time he'd succeeded. I'd even tried to google cat-safe washing machines once, but nothing had shown up.

Maybe it was time to try again.

What was it with people texting today, though? I'd just gotten Prince to scurry away from the kitchen, and I moved my dinner to the living room. I only unlocked my phone screen to check that I hadn't gotten any ill-timed emails.

I hadn't. I had a thread of texts from Sergio, but I would check them later. I needed a minute to center myself. I'd barely gotten to do that all day.

12

KARA

Good news: Monday wasn't actually awkward.

Well, it started a bit awkward because I'd been nervous and bought pastries for Mónica, except I'd forgotten she wasn't arriving at the office until later.

Yes, I'd been the one who scheduled that on site meeting that early.

So it was a bit awkward when she showed up and a box of croissants had been on her desk, but we recovered. By the end of the day, I was giving her a rundown of the meetings for the rest of the week like a pro.

I even managed to convince myself it was all under control.

Tuesday proved me wrong.

I'd barely left the elevator when I noticed something amiss.

Mónica's office had the door closed. I knew she was there —because this time I did remember her schedule of the day —but it made no sense. She should be in the break room with a cup of coffee. Or enjoying that coffee in her office, but with the door open.

Was I supposed to check in with her?

"Morning, Kara," Javi jolted me out of my stupor.

Shit.

"Morning." I cleared my throat.

Okay, standing in the middle of the hallway was not an option. At best, I tolerated Javi. I didn't need anyone else trying to make conversation, though. They were either awkward or creepy, and I could barely cope with my own awkwardness on a good day. Creepiness was out of the question, too, for obvious reasons.

I still hesitated by the door to her office, though. I might've been working here less than a month, but saying good morning and talking for a bit before settling in at my own desk had become routine.

There were voices. Iván, I thought. I wouldn't tell Mónica, but most of her brothers sounded the same to me. They all had the same holier-than-thou tone, and it was hard to see past it. Even the youngest one, Iván. He just adorned it a bit with a devil may care attitude.

I didn't eavesdrop, though. Maybe I could reward myself with another milkshake. I could text Sergio to go there. He said he'd be in the whipping demo I had zero interest in, but maybe we could meet during the week. Or before the demo started?

I did, however, linger for a minute or two.

Would Mónica think less of me or something if I went straight to my office? It wasn't as if I had a lot to do, and no one was calling. I'd hear the phone from here.

By the time I'd already decided Mónica could be the one to walk into my office if she needed me, the door opened.

It startled me, making me jump back before I could process it.

Iván froze before giving me a glance over. "You okay?"

"Uh huh."

I ducked my head down and waited for him to leave.

Well, now I definitely had to go see Mónica, right? She would've heard me. It would be even weirder if I didn't.

"Hey." I stopped by the door, though. Mónica hadn't noticed me after all, so I got a first row seat to her scraping the chair back and letting out a soul deep groan. "What happened? Are you okay?"

I closed the door behind me before I finished talking.

She noticed me then, her eyes focusing on me. I wasn't going to lie; it was slightly unnerving, but it didn't stop me from walking toward her. Or from stepping around the desk and kneeling in front of her when words still evaded her.

That didn't fit the image I had of Mónica.

"Mónica?"

Mónica blinked down at me. "I'm okay. Just family drama."

She didn't look like she was okay, or like they'd just been having a sibling squabble over what to buy their parents for their anniversary.

"Are you sure?"

Mónica seemed a bit dazed, that was all. It was normal of me to worry.

"Kara?"

"Yeah?"

I frowned. Maybe I should go check if there were any leftover croissants in the break room fridge. She looked a bit out of it.

"You're kneeling."

"Huh?"

Oh.

Oh.

Yeah, I... was.

And now I was scrambling backwards until I was sitting

down, my back leaning against the desk. "Sorry, I'm just… What did he say to you?"

"Just his regular speech about how to run things. It happens every few months." She sighed. "Do you think you can reschedule everything that's not urgent today?"

"There's only that first interview with the German insurance company. I think the rest can be moved easily."

"Okay." Mónica nodded. Color was coming back to her face, so there was that. "Sorry, Iván has a way to get on my nerves."

"If you need anything…"

"I'm good."

I wasn't so sure, but she sounded more confident now, so there was that. It wasn't as if I could bug her to tell me. We didn't have that kind of relationship, did we?

"Okay, well, I…" I swallowed the lump in my throat. "I'll go reschedule everything."

"Thanks, Kara."

"WHAT DO YOU MEAN, you ran out?" Sergio spluttered.

Loud enough some of the people at the café turned their heads not so discreetly. The place had been emptier when I'd met up with Mónica the other week, but I'd wanted milkshakes.

"I couldn't face her!"

I was still blushing. I knew it was from recounting all the events of the day, but I didn't think I'd stopped blushing since the second I sat down in front of my desk, and I remembered what had happened.

I knew Sergio wanted to laugh at me, or at the very least, tease me. "But why?"

"Because I… I kneeled! At her feet! I didn't even think about it! And then she was so freaked out, I—"

I'd avoided leaving the office every time I knew she'd be in the break room, and I'd rushed out down the stairs. Yes, it was the twelfth floor. Yes, my thighs were killing me. I'd even considered canceling on Sergio, but I'd needed to talk with someone.

Sure, I could've kept Lucas company, and I kind of felt bad that I wasn't. But I wasn't comfortable talking with my roommates about kink yet. So there was that.

"Why would she be freaked out?" Sergio tsked. "Believe me, plenty of people kneel at her feet."

"Yeah, but they weren't me. They didn't sit her down to say me and Domms are never going to happen."

I didn't even know what had been going through my head. I didn't kneel. Ever. It was just not a thing.

"Can I ask you about that?"

Shit.

Today was definitely not my day.

"Do you have to?"

"Are you asking a brat to exercise restraint?" Sergio faked a gasp. "From gossip?"

I shook my head. It should upset me, but I just found it quirky.

"I thought you were just Little."

"I contain multitudes, excuse you very much."

I chuckled. I couldn't help it. I thought there was no way someone could utter those words with a straight face, but Sergio had no problem proving me wrong.

Ugh.

"So…" Sergio cleared his throat after taking a spoonful of

whipped cream. He'd been smart and rationed it—unlike me. "Why the rule against Domms?"

Double ugh.

But talking about it was good. I shouldn't feel ashamed of it. It hadn't been my fault, right? That's what all therapists said. I had work to do to dismantle why I stayed so long, and ignored the red flags, and why I lied to the—admittedly few —people who had worried. But I wasn't at fault. Regardless of everything else, I didn't deserve the fear I lived in. I wasn't responsible for it, and that meant I shouldn't live with the burden. The weight.

"Because my last relationship with a Domme lasted five years, and I spent the last three living in complete fear, twenty-four-seven." The words burned in my throat. Was this the first time I told someone who wasn't a therapist, or more than an online friend? "I can't… I can't lower my guard and let it happen again."

"Shit," Sergio leaned forward. His face was a couple of shades paler. Guilt stabbed me in the stomach. "I'm sorry, I just thought it would be something… not that." He swallowed.

"It's fine," I rasped.

It wasn't fine, but I was rather certain that he got as much.

"Does Mónica know?" Sergio whispered.

His hand was on top of mine. It was warm. I needed it, the way he squeezed and tightened his fingers around my wrist.

"Not all the details, but yeah." I recounted our conversation from Sunday and let the silence settle between us. Surprising absolutely no one, least of all myself, that silence quickly became an itch I had to scratch. I rubbed my face. "I know it's stupid. I know it was just kneeling, for less than two seconds, and I know it doesn't have to mean anything. I mean, I call people Sir or Ma'am when I answer the phone, and it's not kinky, but... But Mónica noticed it enough to point it out, and I... I..."

"You're freaking out because you feel like you lowered your guard?" Sergio gathered after a minute.

My eyes widened. It was stupid, but... Yeah, that was exactly it. I nodded. Words felt tough, but nodding I could do.

"I've never been in a bad relationship like that," Sergio kept talking. I loved that he was as terrible as I was with silences. "Well, I've never been in a relationship, period, so I don't have any advice and I'm not going to tell you how to live your life, but..."

I gnawed at my lip. "But?"

"But I'm in your corner, okay? Even if you lowered your guard, by accident or on purpose, or whatever, I've got you. Hell, we all do. You'll see we're all pretty tight. We look out for one another."

"Right."

The smile on my lips felt too forced. I appreciated the sentiment, but it wasn't more than that, was it? Pretty words I would love to cling to but knew I couldn't.

Thankfully, I had an excuse not to elaborate when my phone buzzed with a text.

> MÓNICA
>
> Hey Kara. I just wanted to check in on you.
> Are you all right?

Then again, I should've realized not many people texted me since I moved here and got a new number, and one of the people who did was the one I didn't know how to face right about now.

> **KARA**
> i'm fine
>
> having milkshakes with Sergio

> **MÓNICA**
> So I should schedule you both a dentist appointment?

I gasped.

The threat of a dentist appointment wasn't the reason for my galloping heart, but still.

The audacity.

"Is that her?" Sergio tried to lean over the table to see the screen. I debated about it for all of two seconds before I let him see. It was worth it when he squealed and then covered his mouth with both hands. "I don't want a dentist appointment!"

Another text came in before I could commiserate.

> **MÓNICA**
> In all seriousness, though, do you think we could talk? I'd feel better if we could clear the air.

"She wants to talk?" I pursed my lips.

"Call her then." Sergio shrugged. Hadn't he been listening to everything I'd said? Maybe he was still reeling from the dentist thing and not thinking clearly. "What? You're going to be worrying about it non-stop, and then you're not going to sleep, and you're going to fuck up at work, and the ball is gonna keep rolling. So you should just do it."

"Who are you and what have you done to my friend?"

Sergio's eyes glistened with some unnamed emotion—and a dash of mirth. "Aww, you called me your friend!"

I blushed. Hard.

That had been a bit too close to Little space where we

pretended making friends as adults wasn't hard or a completely different game altogether.

"Shut up."

"But to answer your question, I was channeling my best Daddy impersonation." He nodded to himself. "I think I did quite well, thanks."

He had.

The realization was disturbing.

"Why would I follow what a Daddy says?" I protested, just because I had to say something, right? "Let alone an imaginary one."

"Because it's me, and you clearly love me already."

"I never said that."

Sergio had the gall to take a hand to his chest as if I'd offended him greatly or something. It was really hard not to snort, or worse, giggle in the middle of the crowded café.

"You said we were friends!"

"Yeah?"

"Same thing."

It was not, but fighting it didn't make me feel warm. Maybe accepting it fully wouldn't happen overnight, but I'd enjoy the building warmth while it lasted.

"So…" My hair was a mess from how much I'd been running my hands through it. And I kept doing it, because I didn't learn from past mistakes, apparently. "I should call Mónica?"

"You're with me!" he pointed out. I'd swear he would've started bouncing on the table if the place wasn't so crowded. "So, yeah, you call her. We can create a signal, and if you need to, you do it, and I grab your phone. Mónica loves me, so I'll keep her distracted just fine."

"I'm not sure that's the solid plan you seem to believe it is."

It helped me breathe easier, though, and wasn't that what mattered?

My eyes veered to the phone screen and the text thread with Mónica. It terrified me, but I did want to talk with her.

Last time we talked, she had helped. Maybe it wasn't a one hit wonder.

"If this goes wrong, you owe me so many milkshakes."

"Deal."

Sergio even stretched his arm to shake hands with me. It was silly.

Exactly what I needed, too.

The phone only rang a couple of times before the call connected. Dread settled in my stomach. Here I'd thought I'd have more time to prepare.

13

MÓNICA

"Kara?"

"Uh, hi." Her voice was raspy. There was some background noise, which I hadn't expected. She'd texted that she was at the café, but I'd assumed she'd call—or text, really—once she was back home. "I'm with Sergio."

"Hello, Ma'am!"

Ah.

"Are you two having fun?"

I'd bet Sergio talked her into calling me. It worked for me, but it was both a blessing and a curse. After all, I wasn't naive. Without Sergio's meddling, chances were Kara wouldn't have called. I didn't like the idea of him bulldozing her like that, though. Things with Kara, and the way she felt around me, felt too fragile, still. Today had proved it.

"Yeah, we're good. Uh, are you okay?"

"Yeah, I'm okay." I sighed. I probably should've thought better of an action plan before I texted her to begin with, but I'd been feeling unsettled. "I wanted to apologize about today."

Silence greeted me. Couldn't say I hadn't expected it.

"Apologize?"

"I didn't handle myself well."

An audible swallow. I thought there was some rustling. Maybe she was leaning closer to Sergio? Or the other way around?

"Because I kneeled?"

I shut my eyes, wincing. It was a good thing I hadn't wanted to wait until tomorrow. I'd known, even before Kara left my office, that she was going to be reading a million different meanings into what had happened—whatever it was. I was still trying to figure it out myself. I mean, I knew what had happened—I just didn't quite get my reaction to it. It should've been nothing.

Meant nothing.

"No." I sighed. Princess was purring on my lap, and I absently petted her while I gathered the words I needed. "You did nothing wrong. I'm sorry that you saw me like that, and I'm sorry about how I reacted."

More silence. I had a feeling she might be holding her breath, perhaps waiting for the other shoe to drop. There was no other shoe.

Some more rustling ensued. "Thank you. I think?"

"What do you mean you think?"

I wanted to tease her, but it was probably too soon for it. We didn't have that kind of trust or rapport with each other.

"Sorry." She swallowed. "I just… I guess I don't quite understand what happened."

And I had an inkling her head was stuck on the fact that a Domme had apologized to her. Sadly, I'd seen it often enough to count on it happening. Too many people loved to call themselves Domms, but not the work and responsibility that came with it.

"Iván is just… he knows where to hit." It was my turn to swallow. If I'd known he was going to pull guilt trips like that, I never would've let him in the building. It wouldn't have been the first time I'd gotten security to lie for me to evade one of them. "I was too on edge. But there was nothing wrong with you checking in on me, and I didn't mean to imply anything, or scold you for it."

That was the last thing that had been in my head.

"Uh, right. Is there anything I can do to help? At work, I mean?"

I didn't have to think hard about it. "Maybe keep Iván off my back if he asks about me. Just tell him I have a meeting or I'm busy waiting for a call."

"Done."

Relief washed over me. I obviously couldn't tell for certain, but I could almost hear the smile on Kara's voice.

That was good.

I'd been beating myself over ruining the progress I'd made with her this past week. I really shouldn't have said anything about her kneeling. Rationally, I one hundred percent knew it had just been her checking on me because I must've looked a mess. For some reason, though, I'd seen her, and my head had gone straight to the club, and the way she looked in a harness and later being drilled into the floor.

Maybe I needed to let out some steam—when Kara wasn't there to pull all my attention her way, that was.

"Ma'am?"

Huh.

I pulled the phone away from my ear for one second but, no, I hadn't somehow hung up on Kara and dialed her self-appointed protector.

"Sergio? What are you doing with Kara's phone?"

"Well, she was going to hang up, but I wanted to ask you something," he paused to catch a breath, "Ma'am."

I snorted. "All right, let's hear it."

"I just wanted to know if you were coming to the whipping sesh," he at least lowered his voice when he said that. "I saw Tony would be there, and Erika might be there, and the usual masos, but I didn't see any other Sadists."

Just as I was thinking about needing a visit to the club... It would feel weird if Sergio didn't bug either Erika or I, or both of us, whenever Tony was involved. I wasn't sure that there was even a story between the two of them—and I certainly wasn't going to encourage it—but as much of a social butterfly as he was with other subs, the boy got strangely anxious around Tony.

It was also another reason for me not to trust the man.

"I'll be there."

"Really?" His voice went ridiculously high pitched. I was sure my ear drums had adapted to it over the years of knowing him. There should be research about it. It was definitely a thing. "Thank you, thank you, thank you! You're the best!"

"Sure," I chuckled. If I was feeling mean, I'd tease him about being so grateful when someone was flogging him. I kept the commentary to myself. "Tell Kara I'll see her tomorrow, okay? Breakfast is on me."

"I want my boss to buy me breakfast, too."

"You need to have a boss first," I teased.

"Maybe I would if they bought me breakfast!"

"I'm sure."

He hung up after that, but it was fine. Sergio did have a way of cheering me up.

HE WASN'T SO good at cheering me up now.

"Sergio!" I hollered.

Erika grabbed my arm before I could show him how frustrated I really was.

This had been the week from Hell.

No matter how much Kara was doing her best to keep Iván off my back, it was hard to avoid someone who had my number and knew where I lived. He'd started bugging Noel, César, and Javi, too, which meant the floor was even more tense than it usually was.

When they weren't on the brink of throwing punches in front of potential clients, they were trying to drag me into it. It was the same childish behavior that went unchecked on them, but the longer it went unchecked, the more it grated on my nerves.

"Why don't you take a break?" Erika whispered. "I'll handle him."

"I'm not planning on doing anything to him."

I wasn't. I didn't have a problem with disciplining him when needed, but I'd never play when I was so unsettled.

"Why does he keep coming to these?"

"I don't know." Erika's lips pursed. "I guess he's more desperate for a Dom than he lets on."

"But he's not a pain slut."

There was a difference between the masos who welcomed a flogging or a spanking as a funishment, and the pain sluts who just wanted the impact without any pretext.

"But he thinks he *has* to be."

That was true.

"I'm going to grab some water. Want anything?"

"I'm good."

"Thanks."

Maybe I shouldn't have come, but being around the people here helped. Most of the time.

Downstairs was quieter, but I could still make out the faint noise from upstairs. Some muffled cries, the whips lashing through the air before connecting with skin. It was soothing.

"Hey, Mónica!" María jumped up from behind the bar. I let her hug me before she hopped back behind it. "Water?"

"Yeah, but give me a sec. I need to check my phone first."

Need was a strong word, but it was in the locker room, and I needed a couple of minutes for myself.

That was what I told myself.

"Sure." She beamed. She was wearing one of her sheer babydoll sets, this one in midnight blue with silver stars. "Everything okay?"

"Yeah. Thanks, María."

I smiled back at her, went through the motions, but the truth was, I didn't breathe until I was alone in the locker room.

The job was catching up to me, I guessed. Too many years of keeping the peace while ignoring every jab and reason why I hated working with my own blood.

I did grab my phone though since I was here.

Might as well check in that no one had tried to reach me.

> KARA
>
> hi!
>
> have fun at the club!
>
> ...
>
> this isn't an awkward thing to text, right?
>
> apologies in advance! my roommate is making me watch VERY bad movies

Huh.

Admittedly, those weren't the texts I was expecting. I couldn't ignore the genuine smile they'd put on my face, though.

MÓNICA

> It's not awkward, but how bad are we talking?

KARA

it started off with Lethal Weapon and has gone down from there

for an ER doctor he really digs violent movies

MÓNICA

> My mother was obsessed with that franchise.
>
> I'm just taking a break from the floor upstairs.

KARA

too many paddles?

MÓNICA

> I wish.
>
> Too much Sergio.

KARA

oh?

MÓNICA

> He's okay. I bet he'll tell you all about it tomorrow.
>
> He can get really loud.

KARA

i think you just don't understand him

MÓNICA

> You think, huh?

There wasn't an immediate response, but it was fine. It shouldn't be, if I tried to look at this objectively. Kara was only an employee, one I happened to have more in common with. I should draw firmer boundaries in my head, not let the warmth spread when we texted and I got to see a more playful side of her. It was good that she trusted me with it, that she was opening up, but it was all it would be. Kara was rebuilding herself.

I respected her for it.

> KARA
>
> yeah
>
> we Littles are just misunderstood beans

I couldn't start nurturing a crush of all things on her because she texted things like that. No, I just had to watch over her and help her heal. That was the responsible thing to do. The only sane thing to do, really.

> MÓNICA
>
> I see.
>
> I'll keep it in mind.
>
> KARA
>
> you do that

Thankfully, Sergio had already mellowed down by the time I made it back upstairs, water in hand. By mellowed down, I meant that someone had gagged him and tied him to a spanking bench.

"Who put him there?" I asked Erika as soon as I spotted her watching over him.

"I did." She didn't take her eyes off him. It didn't surprise me. Her level of focus never wavered. "We need to sit him down and establish some kind of code for when he needs a spanking."

I nodded. It wasn't that he was truly bad when it happened, but he could be a bit of a wild card. That wasn't good for anyone in the club, least of all for him.

However, as much as I agreed with Erika, he wasn't the one I needed—or wanted—to talk about.

"I think I'm biting off more than I can chew with Kara."

It was a whisper, but I knew Erika had heard.

"What do you mean?"

"I may be getting more involved than I'd originally planned."

And more than what she'd asked of me. Kara might feel more comfortable with me than she did with others, and she might have let me list her under my protection in the community app, but that was all. She'd been clear about her boundaries from the start.

I didn't say that out loud.

"Seriously?" Erika arched an eyebrow. "We talk in riddles now?"

Yeah, that kind of answer was to be expected. Before I went on to explain, I grabbed one of the stools nearby and sat down. This was going to take a while.

"I could've told you that last week." She snorted. "Sadly for you, unless you wanna take me up on the offer to hire her for the gym, you're gonna have to buckle up."

She'd texted me about it after I'd first shared my suspicions. I'd thought it was sweet, but dismissed it right away.

"I know." I groaned. I didn't want to take her up on the offer, either. I would if it came down to it, of course. It was selfish, but Kara was a small ray of sunshine in the office. I needed all of those I could get while my brothers tried to sort out their egos. "I'm worried that the reason she trusts me as a Domme is that she's never seen me play as one, and when she does, it will all blow up."

"It's a possibility," Erika mused, "but it's not like you can invite her to watch you have your way with a random sub, is it?"

I *could*, but that would certainly fall under the umbrella of awkward. I wasn't sure she'd recover from it, either.

"I don't want to be asking her to talk every other day. She should have some breathing room to come into her own, too."

"Agreed." Erika nodded. "I honestly think we have to get her to break that no-Domms rule of hers. Maybe not right now, but you and I both know it's not sustainable long term. Don't get me started on how definitely problematic it would be if the two of you…"

"Not going to happen," I cut her off.

It was bad enough that I was being forced to admit—to myself—that some feelings were growing there. Entertaining the idea of the two of us was *not* going to happen.

I wasn't so masochistic.

"Mónica," Erika warned.

"I mean it."

"Sure you do."

14

KARA

"I'm officially losing it."

I even slumped down on the couch to drive my point across. Lucas quirked an eyebrow, but sadly, he'd already heard all my woes the day before—and teased me about it, thank you very much.

"Did therapy go that bad?" Alex asked.

They'd just arrived and were preparing something in the kitchen.

Right. They asked about therapy.

I'd kind of hoped I could forget that happened today, but… No.

Living with people in the health sector sucked big time. Zero out of ten, would not recommend.

"I mean, what do you call it when I spent the entire hour going on and on about how a guy I've only met a couple of weeks ago hasn't texted me all week?"

"That was a mouthful," Alex said as they walked into the living room.

"Didn't you go off about it enough yesterday?"

At times I didn't know if Lucas meant to be teasing or was just plain mean. This was one of those times.

"Well, I'm clearly affected by it!"

My therapist even suggested we leave the assessment for next week. She tried to make me feel better by saying something about how I was in crisis mode and she'd rather help me through it instead of redirecting the session.

It was a nice way to say I had issues, I supposed.

"Are you going to see her again?" Lucas pressed because apparently we were focusing on the important stuff.

Never mind that I'd much rather throw myself a pity party.

"Yeah. Once a week for the first few sessions so she can make her assessment, and we'll see if I need more after that."

I hated it, but the way I was going? I wouldn't be completely opposed to seeing her more than once a week—if she suggested it. I obviously wasn't going to ask for it.

At least, work hadn't been too awful. Iván hadn't showed up a lot, and I was slowly becoming an expert at avoiding the other three. Mónica was all right, too. We went back to having breakfast at the break room, and she didn't lose it when I asked stupid questions. In my defense, we were about to sign on a British bank, and I was supposed to act as a spokesperson of sorts.

It obviously didn't help my general state of anxiety.

"That's good." Alex sat down next to us. The couch was a bit of a tight fit, but I actually didn't mind being between the two of them. "So what is it about the guy? And weren't you gay? Honest question."

"I generally prefer women, but I'm bi," I corrected. Not that it mattered much at the moment. I used to say I was bi and leave it at that, but then I started dating Her and people started assuming, and it was a lot of work to correct them.

Now it felt weird to even talk about it, to be honest. "And I can be hurt by a friend ignoring me, too!"

To be fair, I didn't think Sergio was quite ignoring me. He did respond when I texted him. He just sounded duller. He didn't text me first, either, which was something I'd learned to track with an unhealthy intensity over the years. My potential new therapist said that it sounded like I was just worried about him and projecting my own hangups about the event last weekend, which was... Okay, it might not be completely off base, but it wasn't just me.

Right?

"Don't get her started," Lucas advised. Now I *could* tell he was teasing. "Wanna play a match?"

"Just one, though. I'm exhausted."

"Kara?"

"Start without me." I wasn't as good as them anyway, and that was on a good day.

While they fought over which game to play, I unlocked my phone and scrolled.

I was just considering why it wasn't a good idea to adopt one of those cute tiny foxes when a text came in from Mónica.

No, my heart didn't start beating faster. No, I didn't ignore said adorable foxes to tap on the notification as soon as I saw it.

MÓNICA

Do you have a sec?

KARA

i guess?

what's up?

MÓNICA

I wanted to run something by you.

> KARA
>
> sounds ominous

Mónica didn't text back right away. I started fidgeting, my fingers playing a random rhythm against my phone case. Maybe it wasn't ominous, and it was a language thing? I hadn't gotten hung up on these things in a long while, but it wasn't completely unheard of, either.

MÓNICA

Would you be open to meeting up with others?

I could be there.

> KARA
>
> what do you mean?

MÓNICA

Sorry.

Other Domms.

Oh.

> KARA
>
> uh, why?

"Excuse me, peeps."

I scrambled off the couch and all but ran to the kitchen. The tight fit I hadn't minded five seconds ago was suddenly too much. I needed air. I needed to make sense of the words on my screen.

My stomach tightened. My hands clasped on to the edge of the granite counter in front of me.

It didn't make sense.

She'd said she understood.

MÓNICA

Because I think you need to see that we're all on your side. (At least the people I personally introduce you to).

KARA

what side is that?

MÓNICA

The side of hurting subs is never condoned nor accepted in any way.

I swallowed. I needed something to drink.

Yeah, that was a good idea.

Leaving my phone unattended, I turned toward the fridge and cursed when there was no water in it. The one American thing I hadn't thought I'd miss most.

At least there was Arizona tea. Alex had wanted to try it because the bottle looked pretty, and they offered to share it.

I couldn't remember the last time I'd bought any back in the States, but it was fridge-temperature, and somewhat familiar. Everything I needed.

KARA

what if i said i don't want to?

MÓNICA

I can't force you to do anything.

It would be great if I could just send screenshots of this to Sergio right about now. I obviously couldn't, though, not when I was doubting where I stood with him.

Then again, that gave me an out. I wasn't too ashamed to not take it.

KARA

what happened last weekend? with Sergio

> you said he'd tell me, but he hasn't, and he sounds off

MÓNICA

What do you mean?

Oh, how the tables had turned.

Sure, it was a serious topic, and guilt made my stomach churn, but the attention was off me. Mission accomplished.

KARA

> i don't know him enough
>
> it's just a vibe

I might be willing to embarrass myself by freaking out about it in front of my roommates. It was pointless to try and save appearances with people who were going to see me at my worst one way or another.

Mónica was different.

MÓNICA

Want to come check on him with me?

KARA

> huh?

MÓNICA

If he's off, I want to go and check on him.
Figured you'd want to join.

KARA

> i've never been at his place

MÓNICA

He was doing you a favor. Spoiler alert: it's a mess.

KARA

> hey!!

> i feel like i should be offended on his behalf

MÓNICA

Sure.

So, are you in? I'm finishing dinner, but I could drive by your place and pick you up.

KARA

> okay

I blinked at the screen, but no, the words hadn't changed. I'd just, for some reason, agreed to get in a car with Mónica. The two of us. For reasons that had nothing to do with work.

Right.

I was an idiot.

Then again, it was about Sergio, so… It was about being a good friend. It didn't have anything to do with my boss. She just happened to have a car, and Sergio's address.

Nothing personal.

Lucas was going to skin me alive when he heard the whole story.

KARA

> fair warning, Mónica and i are gonna drop by your place, apparently? so… i don't know, be decent?
>
> i defended the state of your apartment, just fyi

SERGIO

??????????

!!!!!!!!!!

Kara !!!!!!!!!!!!!!!!!!!!!!!!!!!!!!!!!!

KARA

> i KNOW

> don't shoot the messenger???

There.

Just being a good friend.

MENTAL NOTE: do not ever again defend Sergio's apartment. Scratch that, do not doubt Mónica's assessment of anyone's living quarters.

Sergio looked winded as fuck when he opened the door for us, which made sense as we walked into the shoebox studio he'd been in the midst of cleaning. To be fair, though, it didn't look like he'd been cleaning so much as figuring out where to shove... everything.

The result was that the small space looked as if a nursery had exploded inside its four walls, with a dash of bachelor pad and college boy who didn't do his laundry often enough.

For a second, I thought Mónica was going to go off on him. My body froze, drawn taut when she crooked a finger until he was in front of her. They were about the same height, but Mónica still seemed to hover over him.

I wanted to protect him, but what if I couldn't?

"What's going on, little one?" Mónica's tone was softer than I'd ever heard it as she pulled him into a hug.

It was good. I didn't need to protect Sergio from hugs—hugs he returned, too. I could relax. But it made me uncomfortable for other reasons—reasons I didn't want to dig too deep into.

Mónica whispered something in his ear I didn't get while she rubbed his arm. It was intimate, but it was mostly heartwarming.

That wasn't a feeling I wanted to associate with her. With Domms, Mónica included.

"Have you been eating?"

"Yes, Ma'am." Sergio's voice came out grumbly.

"Anything healthy?"

He didn't answer, and Mónica took that as enough of an answer.

"Okay. I'll order us something while you finish cleaning up, yeah?"

"B-but."

"Little one, self-care reasons aside, we're going to need space to sit down and actually eat." There was a strange glint in Mónica's eyes as she spoke. A mix of mirth and affection, perhaps with the tiniest dash of exasperation.

"Oh, yeah."

"I can help!" I chipped in.

A, I could actually help, and I wouldn't mind having something to do. B, I already felt anxious enough about coming here and whatever was going on with my newfound friendship with Sergio. I figured I could earn myself some extra points and stop just standing there.

The subtle nod coming from Mónica and the way it made me all squirmy did not impact my decision-making at all.

Nope.

"Okay." Sergio turned toward me then, running a hand through his hair. Maybe I could talk him into going to a salon with me. It could count as a self-care day. "Thanks."

Cleaning up didn't take as long as I'd thought, probably because of how small the apartment was. The place still needed airing out, but doing that now would only invite all kinds of bugs in. It was a lesson I'd learned the hard way. There were way too many mosquitoes here.

"Are you okay?" I whispered while we were dropping

things in the laundry basket he had in the bathroom. "Did something happen on Saturday?"

Sergio's eyes widened. "Oh gosh, you thought that—? N-no, it's not about Saturday. That was fun."

"Are you sure?" Because if it wasn't about going through sub drop, then I had no idea what it could be about, and the loudest voice screamed in my head that it was about me—as irrational as the thought was. "I was just worried, but then I kept telling myself it was silly, and—"

"Kara?"

Damn.

"Yeah?"

Mónica was standing in the main living area.

"Is he about done?"

"Yeah, we were just going to set the washing machine."

"It's done." Sergio didn't sound as excited as I imagined he'd sound.

Instead, there was almost resignation as he announced it, then headed to the couch.

Mónica studied him for a minute before she was sitting next to him. I sat on his other side. It felt like the least awkward thing to do.

"Wanna talk to us now?" she asked. "You've kept Kara quite worried this week."

"I mean, it's—" I tried, but one look from Mónica had me clamping down.

Sergio's fingers intertwined with mine. It was grounding. I just needed a second.

"I'm sorry," he spoke. One second later, he was repositioning himself so he was wrapped all over me, his head resting above my chest. There was some lingering weirdness, but I still wrapped my arms around him. I was going to be a good friend no matter what. Besides, he was wearing clothes this time, so it could've been weirder. "I didn't mean to worry you."

He was almost mumbling the words against my hoodie, but I managed to understand him.

"It's okay." He was clearly going through something, and it wasn't his fault that I was a mess, anyway. "I just wanna help."

Sergio nodded, so I squeezed him closer to me. Whenever I was with other Littles, I was always the one being squeezed and the one being tended to. That was to say, I was feeling a bit underwater here.

I glanced at Mónica for guidance, but she didn't seem in a rush to take over.

Ugh.

"Ma'am?" Sergio turned his face just enough he could peek in Mónica's direction. "I'm trying to remember if I ever told you of Tony's brother? Or if you met him?"

Mónica pursed her lips. I liked that she was taking her time to answer. Many people would've just shaken their heads, then interrupted him mid-explanation when they remembered.

It was a real pet peeve.

"I don't think I even knew he had a brother."

"Yeah." Sergio cleared his throat. "Jen and Marga were at the brunch on Sunday. I was talking with them, and they told me about him. He's, uh, getting married, apparently."

I frowned. I remembered he'd said he'd never been in a relationship, so maybe he'd had a crush on the brother? I barely remembered Tony or his face, so it was hard to follow along. I was more of a visual person.

"And that's got you out of sorts?"

"It's stupid," he sniffled. I really thought he'd be getting more comfort out of Mónica's lap, despite how that made me feel, but I didn't get the feeling he'd appreciate me moving him now. His fists even clenched around my hoodie. "It's not like I ever had a crush on him."

"Are you sure?" I asked.

It was most likely the wrong thing to say, but it was the only thing I could come up with. We'd already established I wasn't good at standing by the sidelines.

"He made my life a living Hell, so yeah, I'm quite sure." He snorted. "I'm talking, hospital stays kind of Hell, in case that wasn't clear."

Shit.

I might have whimpered as I squeezed him tighter against me. My eyes might also have flashed to Mónica in panic. I was definitely not equipped to make him feel better from this. How could I? I might not have gone to a hospital, but I knew what that kind of Hell felt like.

In a way.

It had to count, right?

"Does Tony know about this?"

Sergio didn't answer Mónica right away. I felt him nod, though.

Mónica cursed something under her breath. It was a good thing, because I'd just started to wonder if I'd get in trouble for doing the same.

"Okay, I'm going to have a few words with him and his subs if you let me, but is there anything you want to tell us?"

Sergio shrugged before he slid down from my lap and let himself sink on the couch.

"I know it's stupid. It's just… He gets to be happy, y'know? And it's tripping me up so bad. He's out there, and I mean, I've always known that, but he's out there, and he's happy, and building a life, and a family, and I'm—" He breathed out, his eyes darting between the two of us before he bit on his lip. "I'm alone."

This wasn't the time for my eyes to start watering. It was

definitely not the time to make it about me and feel like crying because he didn't see me as someone who was there.

Shit.

I really needed to get things moving with therapy.

"You, little one, are not alone, and you know it." Mónica was the one who punctuated the words.

It was a good thing because I wouldn't have been able to without breaking out in tears.

"You know what I mean."

"What I know," Mónica kept talking without raising to his bait, "is that I'm going to go find you one of your blankies, and you're going to share it with Kara until the food arrives. Sounds good?"

Another minute nod.

I nodded, too, just in case Mónica needed my feedback on the plan.

"All right. Stay there."

Sergio nodded again. He waited until she had her back to us to look at me. He just looked so sad. Realistically, I knew I couldn't claim to know him when I'd only seen him a few times over a couple of weeks, but I did. This wasn't like him.

"I'm a mess. Please don't hate me?"

"Why would I hate you?"

He couldn't meet my gaze when he shrugged. "I don't know."

Words stuck to the back of my throat, but I pushed them through. "I just don't like seeing you sad."

I had to be blushing furiously. It was silly, the kind of thing a child would say, and we were adults.

It made him smile, though. I had to double check for a second, but he did smile, so that was good. I'd done something good.

"I'm sorry. I wanted to tell you, but I thought you'd think I was stupid."

"I'd never think that."

I thought he was silly, but never stupid. I definitely wouldn't have thought he was stupid—or silly, or anything else—because of a bully bringing back bad memories or making him feel insecure.

I knew about feeling insecure—about regressing and losing every inch of progress you thought you'd made over the years.

"But you're so put together, and my stuff is high school bullshit. It's not like—"

I was so not put together.

Before I could say it out loud, though, Mónica was back with a giant blankie full of cartoonish tentacles in different colors. I might have held my breath while she tucked us in, but maybe—hopefully—she didn't notice.

The buzzer rang after, which meant my window to protest Sergio's words was shot. It was awkward to say anything after his attention had switched to something else. Besides, Mónica would hear. Well, I was sure she'd heard everything up to this point—it would be impossible not to—but it wasn't the same.

"What did you get, Ma'am?"

"Steamed dumplings and California rolls," Mónica spoke as she moved around the kitchen island. "A ton of both."

Sergio perked up—not at his usual level of over the top perkiness, but it was something. "Finger food?"

"You can't say I don't spoil you," Mónica teased.

"Um, Mónica? Should I help with the plates or something?"

"I've got it," she answered with barely a glance my way. "You can help by keeping Sergio snuggled in and cuddled."

I nodded. I guessed I could do that. It was less nerve-wracking, too. With my luck, if I tried to move around the apartment with Mónica doing the same, I'd end up dropping something.

"Ever ordered from this place?" he asked me. "It's really yummy."

"And they have healthier options," Mónica added.

That *was* a Domme thing to say.

I snorted.

"It's more expensive, though," Sergio whispered, "which is why you wait for Sugar Daddies to invite you. Or Mommies, I mean. I'm not discriminating."

"I didn't know I was your Sugar Mommy now," Mónica said.

She'd finished bringing everything to the table by the couch. She'd even gotten chopsticks, which I personally thought defeated the purpose of finger food. I supposed that was a me thing.

"You buy me things, you're a Domme, and you have more money than I do, Ma'am." Sergio burrowed against me as he spoke. "You might as well be."

"Good to know."

15

MÓNICA

"What do you need, baby boy?"

As expected, Sergio had all but binged on the takeout food. I'd have to remember to ask Kara if she wanted to grab something to eat after we left. I'd already eaten, but I hadn't asked if she had. She'd eaten some now, but not nearly as much as Sergio had.

At least the boy didn't look half-dead anymore. Only a tenth. I'd take it.

I was kicking myself for not checking in on him. He was usually bugging me for one reason or another every other day. When Kara asked about him and mentioned he sounded off, I realized he hadn't said a word all week. I should've noticed earlier.

"I don't know. Find me a Daddy who is into all the same shit I am and actually wants me?"

"Hey!" Kara protested before I could try and scold him for the tone. "Be nice to yourself."

"Did you just pinch me?" Sergio squealed.

"I wouldn't have to if you were nice to yourself!"

"All right, you two." Littles fighting could be adorable, but it was not what either of them needed. "Kara, why don't you come help me clean up for a second?"

I kept my voice as soft and non-threatening as I possibly could. Kara still froze for a second. I kept the grimace to myself. I wouldn't have singled her out, but I needed a second to talk to her if I wanted both of them comfortable tonight.

"Sure." Her voice was slightly clipped, but she got herself out of the bundle they'd made with the blanket.

It was all I could hope for, I guessed.

"I'm gonna go to the bathroom," Sergio muttered.

He was watching Kara closely. I guessed he knew more than he let on. Maybe she'd opened up to him at some point. It would be good if she'd had.

"Should we just load the dishwasher?"

"Turn it on, too." I let her rinse the dishes while I recycled all the containers. "Pick the fast program so we can unload it before we leave."

"Okay." Kara hovered for a second. To be fair, I hadn't used up a lot of plates when I got everything out of the containers, but I doubted he'd been on top of doing the dishes this week. "This is nice, that you're doing this."

"It's what we do." I shrugged. "We take care of each other."

"That's…"

I stopped rustling with the plastic bags so that I could focus on her. It felt more important—my gut feeling proved right when she couldn't meet my gaze.

Her eyes darted downward, too, arms tightly wrapped around her hoodie. "Hard to believe."

It was risky, but I dared to take a step closer. "You don't have to believe it right now. Just let us prove ourselves."

"I don't know that my roommates would appreciate you storming in and taking over the kitchen."

Another step. My heart was starting to beat faster now. I wanted to be in control, but I couldn't lie to myself and say that I was.

"So we'd drag you out."

Kara's fists curled around the fabric of her hoodie, her voice merely more than a thin whisper. "Is it like a Domm thing?"

"It's a community thing," I countered. "If I'd been the one having an off week, I would've had Sergio terrorizing my cats in no time."

Kara wouldn't meet my eyes yet, but there was a hint of a smile on her face. I'd take it.

For now.

"Why did you need my help cleaning up?" she whispered.

"Because I want to baby him for a bit, let him really relax, and I don't know that you'd be comfortable staying in a grown up space if he's not."

"Huh?" That frown, at least, was expected.

Expected reactions meant I could still cling to an ounce of control.

"Can I take care of the two of you? As Littles?"

She looked up then. I hated myself for noticing, but she was beautiful—even when she stared at me with widened eyes and her bottom lip was worried between her teeth.

Erika was going to roast me when we chatted next.

"Okay."

"You sure?"

In hindsight, I could've sounded less surprised. Then again, if I had, Kara wouldn't have looked like she was trying hard not to laugh in my face. One could argue it was a fair tradeoff.

"Yeah, I mean, I like being Little with Sergio."

That was all the endorsement Kara seemed willing to give. It was enough tonight. Truth be told, I just wanted to get Sergio to change and color for a bit so he could get his head off everything. Hopefully, it would lull him to sleep, too. I knew how deep Sergio could regress, though, and I also knew the best way to ensure Kara wasn't uncomfortable was if she looked at it through the lens of Little space.

I wasn't about to go bossing her around or anything else that would require a deeper conversation.

"Do you think I should invest in curtains? For privacy?" Sergio tried to sound innocent, even.

I snorted. "You should invest in an apartment with walls."

"Is that an offer to squat in one of your buildings, Ma'am?"

Well, he was definitely feeling better. Apart from the fact that there was color on his face again, that glint of mischief in his eyes was unmistakable—for better or worse.

"It is not."

He wasn't in such a place financially that he couldn't afford a nicer place. We didn't talk much about it, really, but my understanding was that he was waiting to have a clearer goal in life—whatever that meant—before bothering to invest somewhere else.

To be fair, the place wasn't completely terrible. Just… tiny.

I liked open concepts as much as the next person, but I'd never been a fan of studios where only the bathroom provided some privacy.

"Do you even do residential buildings?" Kara asked as we went back to the living room.

"My father did back when he started the company." I shrugged. I was pretty sure we still had when I was younger, but giving a history lesson into my family's company was not too appealing at the moment. "We don't anymore, though."

"Which makes squatting better!"

"Why are you so focused on squatting today?"

"Eat the rich, Ma'am, is all I'm saying."

Kara giggled. It wasn't the first time I noticed how smoothly she slipped into Little-space. "Weren't you just saying you wanted a Sugar Daddy?"

"Well, yeah?"

Kara giggled again. I shook my head. The thing was, they could get stuck on this for hours. It was up to me to redirect them.

I realized it would annoy some people, but this was the kind of thing that filled me up and let me breathe after the day—week—I'd been having.

I started with Sergio first. Nothing personal; he was just easier to handle. "Sugar Daddies aside, I'm guessing you know what I want you to do next? Since you so helpfully pointed out the lack of privacy in this place?"

Then again…

"Uh…" He just blinked at me, eyes open wide.

It shouldn't be so cute.

"Go and get your Little things."

Sergio's eyes widened even more before he licked his lips. "Even the…?"

I raised an eyebrow.

If he hesitated, he was probably thinking about his diapers.

"Ask Kara."

As much as I'd berate myself for it later, I hadn't really had much of an opportunity to go through everything that playing with Sergio entailed. To begin with, I hadn't known what I was going to find when I first suggested that we check on him. Letting him go on supervised Little-space hadn't been part of the initial plan.

The initial plan lacked a lot of information.

The reminder of Tony and his subs's irresponsibility had a

surge of anger taking hold. I breathed out, hiding the fact that my hands had started to curl into fists.

I wasn't a violent person, but there were things that made me rage. Lately, those things and Tony went hand in hand more often than I was comfortable with.

The conversation with the others—and with him, ultimately—was not one I was looking forward to.

This evening, though… This was different.

I could just sit back and watch as Sergio eventually turned to Kara and whispered something in her ear. He was, of course, using both hands to cover his mouth.

The fondness spreading across my chest was a surefire way to battle those tendrils of anger. So I focused on the two Littles in front of me and let myself smile when Kara gave a small nod and Sergio tried to hide the faint blush that spread through his cheeks.

"Um, I'll be right back, Ma'am."

"Sure."

I didn't stop to think that him leaving—I assumed so that he could change in the bathroom—meant Kara and I would be alone. I'd just been quote-unquote alone with her, but this felt different somehow.

Erika was going to have a field day with me, that was for certain.

"You're a good friend," she all but whispered.

I blinked. Kara was staring at me from the corner of the couch she'd claimed earlier. Her head rested against the pillows, and the way she stared had an owlish quality to it.

"You are, too."

I wasn't just responding to her comment. I meant it, too.

Undeserved praise had never been my style, anyway.

Kara beamed. I hadn't said anything big, but one would've thought I'd just told her she was the best girl to have ever walked on Earth.

"Someone's into praise," I muttered.

It was a tease, I was aware of it. I could only behave too much, and the way happiness radiated out of her? It was contagious.

I wanted to keep it there.

"I don't know what you're talking about," Kara spluttered.

It would've been more believable if she was't blushing—or if she hadn't started playing with her hair.

"I'm sure you don't."

After all, if she wanted me to push more, she'd have to come forward about it. There was no way I'd willingly open the can of worms that would come with anything going further between the two of us. Definitely not right now.

Kara was biting her lip. She didn't look uncomfortable, though—maybe a little shy.

I could work with a shy Little.

"Did you get sucked in by the toilet, baby boy?"

I diverted the attention to the direction where the bathroom was, but I kept an eye on Kara. Her whole body relaxed as soon as I'd looked away. It was the confirmation I needed —nothing could happen beyond what had already transpired.

Truthfully, I'd thought the realization would hurt. I even stopped for a second to check inward, expecting some kind of stabbing pain or ache in my gut.

It didn't happen.

I liked that I was reading her right, that I was giving her what she wanted and nothing more.

It calmed me down.

"You know, Ma'am, that could absolutely happen, and it's not nice that you're laughing about it so willy-nilly!"

I'd bet half the neighborhood heard Sergio's huffing and puffing.

Kara chuckled, the sound taking a softer tonality. She

really was fast at switching between different headspaces—the kind of fast I had a weak spot for.

I shook my head. Those thoughts were leading nowhere good. "Well, I'm pretty sure you don't want me to go in there, so hurry up."

There was no way I'd go into the bathroom, but neither of them needed to know that tidbit of information.

16

KARA

What were people supposed to do with their hands? I wasn't going to faint, was I? I would hate to faint, today of all days. I was here to cheer up a friend, dammit, not make it all about me.

It wasn't fair.

I blamed Mónica, of course. She just…

I knew what she was doing. She was pretending to focus on Sergio, teasing him about how long he was taking in the bathroom and whatnot, but I knew she was keeping an eye on me.

It should terrify me.

It didn't, which in turn happened to be more terrifying, but in a way I didn't want to stop. I clearly had issues—more issues than the ones I was already aware of, I mean.

Ugh.

Where was Sergio, anyway? He really was taking his sweet time there. I guessed he was nervous about wearing a diaper in front of me. I got it, but I still thought he was being silly.

I'd seen him naked more times than I could count already, and he said he wasn't going to use it; it was just comforting.

I was all about comfort items.

That made me realize…

I should've brought one of my stuffies with me. Stuffies were comforting, and I needed the extra cuddliness.

Huh.

Sergio's blankie was extra soft—almost as soft as my favorite teddy bear, actually. It would work; and if Mónica had any thoughts about my sudden urge to burrow into it, she'd save it to herself.

I was just cold. It was perfectly reasonable and not at all a sign that I was hiding.

Dammit, I'd agreed to this.

I *wanted* this.

When was the last time I had even dared to want something that involved relinquishing an ounce of control?

I was in danger.

I was in imminent danger, and Sergio was still locked in the bathroom.

Next time I was going to demand that he give me something to entertain myself with. I was sure he had coloring books somewhere, but I'd take anything at this point.

"Coming out now!" he hollered.

"Finally," I grumbled.

It may have come out kind of bratty, too.

Mónica raised an eyebrow. I pretended that I didn't see it.

I'd never welcomed someone's loudness so happily, but Sergio all but crashing into every piece of furniture on his way to the couch was the perfect distraction. It even made me giggle, and I'd feared the sound would be stuck deep down my throat.

Nope, my voice was working fine.

Both a blessing and a curse, though.

If I couldn't speak, I couldn't blurt out something I regretted. I'd learned that one early on.

"Owwwww!"

An *ow* was fine—especially when it was warranted. I would say I was very much in my right to protest. I was beginning to realize the last two times I saw Sergio as a Little, he'd been behaving himself. The real one was a brute—one who apparently thought it was fine to jump on people and half squish them to death.

"Little one."

It was a warning, but it didn't scare me. There was no... anger or bad things behind them.

I knew because...

I knew because I trusted Mónica—because she didn't scare me.

That shouldn't hit me the way it did.

"What?" Sergio squealed, probably because he couldn't hear my inner monologue.

"Be careful, will you?"

There was fondness in Mónica's tone. It was wild. I knew it shouldn't be, and it was the *normal* thing, but... Damn. I hadn't realized how far away from normal I'd been all this time. I didn't even remember the last time I'd been around someone who had a normal reaction.

Funny, I'd never liked the word normal, but maybe there was something to it.

"I'm careful!" Sergio kept arguing with Mónica. "Kara loves me anyway, she told me!"

My name brought me back to the conversation. I laughed while I tried to push him aside—he was still more than half on top of me, even though I'd complained very loudly.

Tsk.

"I said we were friends!"

"Same thing!"

"Okay, you two." Mónica chuckled. "Sergio, apologize to your *friend* for hurting her."

There was a pause for all of two seconds. I timed it.

"Fiiiiiiiiiine," Sergio huffed. The attitude evaporated as soon as he turned back to me. I liked that. Soon we were both giggling while I tried to wrestle him out of me because he was doing kissy faces at me. "Ma'am, Kara doesn't let me kiss her cheek!"

"So?"

"So you said to apologize to her!"

"And…" Mónica started to talk slower. It was very funny. "Apologizing involves slobbering all over her?"

"That's so rude."

"You'll survive," she drawled.

"Are you sure about that, huh?"

"Yeah," I spoke up. It was good—I'd wanted to do it for a while—but it still had my heart beating way too fast. "Being rude is mean."

Mónica's eyes widened for a second. She tried to hide it, to sober up her expression, but I caught it regardless. There was little I missed.

It turned out that trait wasn't only useful to survive.

"I see. You think you two can gang up on me now?"

"Uh…" Sergio turned to look at me, hesitant.

I didn't have to think about it. I shook my head—frantically, and right away.

Just because I was beginning to make peace with my feelings toward Mónica didn't mean I was going to…

No. No, I couldn't, no matter what.

"It's okay," she said. Her voice somehow penetrated through the mist in my head. "No one's getting punished today. I just want you two to have fun."

Sergio recovered first.

Well, there wasn't anything in what Mónica had said he'd

need to recover from, so that was probably why.

"Fun how, Ma'am?"

"I'm sure you have a lot of things to have fun with," Mónica said.

She was so patient.

I… was not, but maybe I could learn. It seemed to be working on Sergio. I hadn't thought that would be possible. I loved how easily he gained so much energy, but the problem with the really energetic Littles was that they didn't know when to stop. I was a very good Little, obviously, so I didn't speak from experience here.

I was being serious, dammit!

The point was, I was noticing the things Mónica did. I didn't like it. I liked that she was so good at directing Sergio's energy, which I didn't even think was possible. I liked that she was gentle while still being sharp and attentive.

I didn't like that I was cataloging these things now in my head. I didn't like any of it, any of the feelings I was *so* not entertaining now. It was stupid. It didn't mean anything. I wasn't going to do anything about it. I couldn't, no matter what, so what was happening?

"I have coloring books." Sergio didn't sound as confident as he would have if this had happened one week ago. He still sounded much better than when we first arrived, though.

Warmth spread across my chest. It felt good to see proof that I'd made a difference. I'd cheered him up enough that he was relaxing.

"Coloring is good."

"And we can watch TV, too?" Sergio bounced on the seat.

It was the first time he'd done it since we'd arrived. I wouldn't have noticed with anyone else, but he was the kind of person who was always bouncing.

"Yeah, can we?"

Shit.

The words left my mouth before I could think them through.

There was no mistaking who I'd asked, either.

Mónica.

"Under one condition," Mónica—who clearly recovered faster than I did—said. "You two pick either one movie, or two episodes, and it's bedtime right after."

"But!" Sergio started to protest.

I was still wrapping my brain around the fact that I'd asked a Domme for permission and hadn't thought twice about it.

A small voice at the back of my head pointed out the world hadn't imploded, either. The internal snide wasn't appreciated. I ignored it.

A lot was happening tonight.

Lots of realizations, and feelings, and resolutions. Those weren't part of the plan. I didn't come here—to a relatively isolated town in the north of Spain, or to Sergio's house in particular—to go back to square one. Square one meant falling for a Domme and ending up trapped, obviously.

This was supposed to be a chance to breathe, and maybe play but... Play was just that.

It was pretend. It wasn't real or difficult or something that would send me into a frenzy.

"Kara?"

"Huh?"

Damn.

I swallowed. Mónica was the one who'd called my name, but they were both staring at me.

Note to self: ask therapist to do something about getting lost in my head and losing track of time.

"Yeah?" My voice was croaky. I hated it.

They didn't mention it.

I hated that, too. Then again, I probably would've hated it

even more if they had. Or, maybe I wouldn't have hated it, but I wasn't ready to offer an answer.

Maybe they knew.

I was a stupidly open book.

"Are you okay with watching Frozen 2?" Mónica kept her voice level, her eyes gentle. It was unnerving and soothing at the same time. I wanted to scream. "Sergio was saying he hasn't watched it."

"Oh." I blinked. "Yeah, sure, but it's a sad movie."

"But it's Disney!"

"Disney has sad movies, too." I snorted. Sergio looked genuinely distressed, though. "Do not watch Togo. Ever."

He pursed his lips. It looked as if he was deep in thought. It was funny.

"But it has a happy ending, right? Elsa doesn't die or anything?"

"N-no!" I gasped. "Of course it has a happy ending, silly."

I was just a goner for the sad song Anna sang. It might be a good excuse for him to let it all out, though.

"Have you watched it, Ma'am?"

If Mónica had watched it and she deemed it acceptable, then I didn't have to worry. If I used a honorific to refer to her, it was just because of the roles we were in. Nothing to see here, folks.

"I have," she confirmed. There might have been a few beats of silence where she was doing her best to keep a poker face. I wasn't watching her like a hawk or anything. "My nieces cried a lot, but they also insist on watching it again and again. They love Kristoff's song."

Huh.

I supposed I did, too. It was a good song.

"Kristoff sings?" Sergio nearly yelled and destroyed my eardrums in the process. I might have squealed in protest. It was something I did now. "We *have* to watch it now, Ma'am. Please?"

Mónica gave him a look. For a second, I wasn't sure what it meant, but then she was chuckling, so I relaxed.

"Sergio here has a massive crush on Jonathan Groff."

"Ooh."

That made sense.

17

MÓNICA

"You didn't have to drive me, M'— " Kara cut herself off abruptly, way too abruptly. "I mean, yeah, you didn't have to drive me. Sergio said I could've spent the night."

I kept an eye on her while I took the turn to her street. She had been slipping more and more as the night progressed. I was itching to confront her, to ask her to sit on my lap while I was in charge, for *real* this time. It wouldn't be okay, though. I couldn't be certain where her head was, if she was too deep in Little space to really know what she was doing and what it meant.

But that also meant I couldn't not watch over her. It would be irresponsible of me, and that was something I didn't know how to be.

"You still have work tomorrow, and the buses take much longer from Sergio's place," I reasoned. It was the same thing I'd told Sergio when he'd frowned at me and tried to get in the way. "I'm sure you can have a sleepover with him over the weekend if you two want."

She seemed to mull it over for a few seconds, her cheeks puffing as she shifted air from one side to another. It was adorable, but I kept any reaction to it to myself.

"It's not about having a sleepover. I just don't wanna put you out, and I worry about Sergio, too."

"I'll pass by his place on my lunch break tomorrow," I assured her, "and you can text him, too. He can get on these spells, when something happens, but he gets back on his feet pretty fast, too."

It was true. I was still going to have a few words with Tony—and Marga and Jen—but the boy was resilient.

"Okay." She nodded. Her hair was messy from how much she'd been playing around with it throughout the night. I knew because my eyes kept straying to her every time it happened. I just hadn't thought it was my place to say or do anything about it. "Do you want me to get you something for lunch with him? Or breakfast?" Her voice started rising in pitch.

I was ninety-nine percent sure we'd already talked about her bringing me breakfast, and what it meant when I said she was my secretary and not my maid. Any other day, I would've —jokingly—scolded her about it.

I got the impression she just needed some order, or just something to do, to know where she stood.

"What if we have breakfast in the place you like down the street?"

Her eyes lit up. It happened before something else clouded them and she started nibbling on her lip.

I still counted it as a win. I wanted her first, instinctual response to me to be positive, regardless of everything else.

"Yeah, sure." Kara nodded twice, then three times. "Sounds good."

I wanted to keep monitoring her, but I needed to take my

eyes off her to focus on finding a parking spot. It didn't look like there were any.

I hated killing the engine in the middle of the road. I would hate making Kara walk at one a.m. even more, though. One look through the rearview mirror showed there weren't any cars around, at least.

"All right." I sighed. "I'll see you tomorrow, then. Text me if anything happens."

"Of course."

There was no chance for silence to settle. Kara was already unlocking the door. I didn't mention it when she all but tripped on thin air. She didn't look back, either, so I just waited there until she was safely inside her house, and drove off.

I didn't think I was going to sleep much. Another day, I would've seen if Erika or one of the others was awake; maybe they'd had a night shift, or they were at the club. I knew I needed the sleep, though. I wasn't good when I hadn't gotten any rest.

At least both cats were happy to snuggle with me in bed. Their soft fur and purring always helped lull me to sleep. They also woke me up when they started growing antsy, which was why I didn't always let them in the room at night, but tonight was worth it.

I'd made plans to wake up early anyway.

SOMETHING WAS GOING on with Kara. It didn't come as a full surprise after last night, but it still bothered me. There was too much up in the air, too much uncertainty and too many questions and confessions I probably shouldn't voice out loud. I *could* confront her, or open up myself, but I didn't know where that would leave us. I didn't even know how she'd react to the news that I could read her silences, the pauses before she answered a simple question, or the way her cheeks turned pink every time she caught someone's gaze.

I was beginning to realize she was *precious*.

My second realization of the day was that I didn't know how to face someone precious. I didn't know how much I could lead or push before it broke. My fingers itched to try, though. Pictures of Kara on her knees, a leash attached to a nondescript collar between my fingers didn't help.

It was too much, anyway. I had no business picturing it.

"How do you wanna go about the Zoom call this afternoon?"

The question took me out of my rambling thoughts. The mere fact that I had wandering thoughts felt foreign, yet it was quickly becoming my new reality—at least when it came to everything Kara.

"Did you have any questions about it?"

It was a big client, but we'd been preparing all week—all month, really—for it. Kara didn't catch all the technicalities too quickly, but she made up for it with sheer determination. I'd been worried the first two weeks, when I had to go through the basics over and over.

I wasn't now.

"No, I don't think so." It was easy to tell she was keeping herself from swallowing. A poker face was not something Kara had or knew how to use. "Sorry, I'm… I'm sure I'll feel better after I go through my notes again."

I studied her. I knew I wasn't being subtle about it, either. Regardless of what I felt toward her, my instincts to protect and take her out of any situation that caused her discomfort…

This was business. I couldn't excuse her on the basis that she was my anxious little sub if she stumbled. I couldn't lose this account, either.

"What do you need, Kara?" I leaned forward. "Be honest, here. What are you after?"

Kara's eyes widened, the sunlight making them look a brighter shade of blue. "Huh?"

I could've let her have a breather.

I didn't.

Erika was going to give me hell.

"Do you even know?"

Her body drew taut. Her hands began to curl into fists before she relaxed them. "I…"

I wanted to say that I was ready. I was ready for her to lash out, to snap, or to look lost and plead for some guidance. I could take it.

Hindsight was a bitch.

I might have been able to take that. I wasn't ready for the way her eyes watered in a matter of seconds. I wasn't ready for the way her body began to tremble, imperceptibly but oh so clearly for anyone really watching.

It took effort not to acknowledge the tightness in my chest, the way my mouth dried.

"Kara?"

Her eyes snapped back to me. She got lost in her head a lot. It was something I would give anything to help her with.

"I…" she mouthed, again. Her chair scraped against the floor, the sound jarring to us both. "Sorry. I, I don't know, but I—"

"Yes?"

It was a teetering balance—a thread of gentleness intertwined with the firmness she responded to more than she probably wanted.

"Can we talk about it later? This weekend?"

"Depends." I sighed, because every instinct wanted me to agree, to soothe her anxiety and wrap her up in a hug she hadn't consented to yet.

"On?"

"Are you good for the call today?"

Kara paused to think about it. Seconds passed by. Her body slowly deflated. She pushed the chair closer to the table, where it had originally been.

"Yeah."

"Good." I wouldn't count it as praise, but I took note of the way her eyes lit up and her cheeks flushed. "We'll talk on Saturday, then. I'm doing a demo at the club. We can meet there, or around lunchtime."

I didn't expect a response—definitely not when I hadn't even volunteered what the demo was about. No, what I would've expected was that she'd ask Sergio about it and text me later that evening. She wouldn't have chosen the safe route right away. I knew that. For as much as Kara insisted she wanted nothing to do with Domms, that wasn't how she behaved around me. She wanted to please—she just didn't know how to go around it. Didn't remember, maybe. I doubted an abuser would give her much praise, or make her feel like she was doing things right.

"We can meet at the club." Her voice was small, but unwavering.

For a second, I convinced myself I hadn't heard her right, but the delusion didn't even last that long. "I'll write you down."

"Thanks."

Sadly, work awaited us. It didn't mean I didn't spend much of the day wondering. What would've happened if I'd pushed harder? If I'd had more time to decipher the resolution that shone bright in her eyes? If I'd hinted at the theme of the demo?

Not even Sergio's usual self and brattiness during lunch distracted me enough. At least he was doing better, even if it didn't fix everything. It didn't fix that he'd been hurting, that he'd probably still hurt for a while longer.

18

KARA

I was stupid.

Then again, maybe I wasn't so stupid?

There had to be some redeeming quality or something to this.

Sergio promised it wasn't stalking behavior. My therapist hadn't said it with those words, but she hadn't looked like she was planning to report me, so I guessed it was the same thing.

I still felt very much like a stalker. A very sweaty and very clumsy one.

"Hey." I clasped my hands together when Erika spoke. I didn't think it helped, but I didn't know what to do with them, either. "Kara, right? I'm Erika."

"I know." What I didn't know was how I managed to speak without my voice completely breaking. Erika looked very different when she wasn't wearing gear, but she was still hard to miss. Her thighs looked like she could crush me, for one. "Sergio introduced us."

"True." She watched me too intently as she finished

placing a bunch of dumbbells back in their racks. "Are you joining the gym?"

"I should, shouldn't I?" I half-joked, half-questioned.

Erika gave me a look over. She wasn't shy about it, but it didn't feel like she was trying to be mean about it. "Did you want to speak somewhere quieter?"

It wasn't too loud on the floor. There was music playing through the speakers, but it was softer than in most gyms I'd been to, and there weren't many people working out. There was no reason to put myself in a position where I'd be alone with her, but I still nodded.

"Please," I said.

I had manners. I wasn't sure what it said about me, but Erika could figure it out.

"Let's go to the office," she suggested. "I have a class in twenty, though."

"It's fine." At least, I hoped it was fine. To be honest, I hadn't planned this as much as I should have—let alone timed it. "I'm sorry to bother you at your workplace. Sergio said it would be okay, but I know sometimes he says things like that."

"He asked me," Erika revealed. If I hadn't been so nervous, I would've gasped, because betrayal was apparently a thing we did now. "Probably after he'd already told you, but I figured I'd let it be."

Still.

"Did he tell you anything else?"

Maybe I could forgive him for the betrayal if he also did the hard work for me while he was at it.

Seemed reasonable.

"No, but I can take a guess."

Erika opened the door to an office then, and walked in first before holding it open for me. It was a small, standard office that looked more like a cubicle than a proper office. I didn't let myself flinch when the door shut behind us.

"A guess?"

My heart began to race, but I focused. There was a ficus plant against the corner. It didn't look too alive, but it was a good place to start grounding myself.

A few deep breaths later, I could look at Erika again.

She hadn't moved, but she hadn't spoken, either.

"Take your time."

"I'm good." I would be. I was never going to be good if I didn't push myself. My therapist hadn't used those words, and I didn't think she'd approve of them either, but the meaning was the same. "Mónica said she wanted to introduce me to others, and I didn't react well when she did, but… Here I am?"

"I see." Erika was harder to read than Mónica. For example, her eyes had glinted when I spoke, but I couldn't tell if she was amused, teasing, intrigued, or something about what I'd said made her want to challenge me. "I don't know if Sergio has told you, but I'm not too interested in small talk."

"Oh."

No, he hadn't told me. I wasn't going to lie; it left me a bit unmoored.

I couldn't say I was too interested in small talk myself, but I was anxious, and cutting to the chase was not something I was too good at.

"Mónica thinks very highly of you." Erika pulled out one of the chairs by the desk for me before she pulled a second one and placed it facing me. "We usually tread more carefully when someone's been a victim of abuse."

Her words felt like a slap, or a bucket of cold water. I didn't want anyone to tread carefully. I hadn't realized they'd been doing it, either.

"What do you mean?"

"There's more of a process, to make sure no one ends up retraumatized."

"I'm okay." I clamped down. That came out more defensive, more biting, than I would've wanted. "I'm going to Mónica's demo later today."

"So I've heard." Erika squinted her eyes. "Is that why you're here?"

Partially.

I swallowed. "I haven't seen her as a Domme yet. Not really."

"I'm aware," she hummed. "Mónica said she was worried about it, too, but that was a while ago."

"She was?"

"Does that make you feel better?"

Erika's arched eyebrow was telling. The question had some kind of trap, some kind of double meaning that didn't make it as innocent as it sounded the first time.

I didn't answer.

I knew when not to take a risk with someone like… like her.

"What if I can't do it? See her as a Domme?"

"Then I suggest you don't hang out with her within the club walls."

Erika leaned back on the chair. The almost slouched position didn't quite suit her.

"That easy?" I swallowed.

It felt anything but.

Erika's chuckle surprised me.

I met her gaze. I didn't think she'd taken hers off me ever since I stepped into the gym.

"I never claimed it would be easy," she said. She didn't elaborate, not for several excruciatingly long seconds. "But I don't think that's the question you should be worrying about."

"What should I be worrying about?"

"Why it matters that you see her as a Domme."

I didn't breathe, didn't move. It didn't matter, right?

But it did.

It mattered so much I was pushing so far past my comfort zone it wasn't funny anymore.

An alarm made me jump on the seat.

It wasn't the most comfortable seat, and I was suddenly aware of the steel bars biting into my skin.

The alarm had come from Erika's phone. She silenced it quickly and went back to watching me.

"Got to prepare for class. You can stay here if you want. There's a mini fridge with water and shakes under the desk."

"I can just go."

Erika's eyes darted down and up again. "I'd rather you didn't."

"Why?"

"We take care of each other." She shrugged. Mónica had said something like that, too, and it still felt surreal—the kind of empty statement people made to feel better about themselves. I wasn't sure it sounded more believable now, but there was something to be said about strength in numbers. "No offense, but you don't look too hot right now."

"I'm fine."

I didn't want her to see me as the victim she had to tread carefully around.

Yeah, that might have stung a bit.

"Do it for me, then," she said. She was already by the door, but didn't open it yet. "Or because Mónica will kill me if I'm the reason you chicken out and are a no-show today."

"I…" I wasn't going to chicken out, was what I'd wanted to say. The words stuck to my throat, though. I swallowed down bile. I couldn't tell for sure I wouldn't. "Okay."

"Atta girl." Erika gave a mock salute before she left.

I frowned once I was alone. Having an hour to myself inside a random gym office hadn't been in my plans for the day.

I noticed she hadn't locked the door, but I suspected going outside would be more daunting. Gyms had never been my favorite places, and I wasn't even dressed in attire that meant I could pretend to be using one of the machines.

KARA

i talked with Erika

well, kinda

i think she wants to talk more before i leave

ugh

SERGIO

heh

you'll warm up to her

i promise

Erika's scary but she's the best

KARA

she's very different to Mónica

SERGIO

well yeah

KARA

...

do you think i'm a mess?

SERGIO

we're all a mess

KARA

you know what i mean

He was going to make me spell it out, though, by the looks of it.

> **KARA**
> Erika asked why it mattered that i saw Mónica as a Domme

SERGIO

ooooooh

what did you say?

> **KARA**
> nothing
>
> i don't know what to say
>
> i'm terrified

SERGIO

why?

i mean, other than the obvious "last time you trusted someone they fucked you over"

> **KARA**
> do i need more reasons?

SERGIO

i suppose not

sorry

i didn't mean to be insensitive

> **KARA**
> it's fine

SERGIO

i'm also sorry i won't be at the club today

> **KARA**
> i know
>
> you should feel ashamed

> it's your second betrayal of the day

SERGIO

second???

i did nothing!!!

> KARA
>
> you told Erika i was coming !!!

SERGIO

...

well fine yeah BUT in my defense

she would've punished me and she's been threatening me with her whip for WEEKS now

WHIPS ARE SCARY, KARA

> KARA
>
> you wouldn't take a whipping for me??

SERGIO

don't pull that when i don't know if you're joking???

i mean

i would if it was a life or death thing

i think??

possibly

you have a 60% chance

65% maybe

> KARA
>
> fine
>
> now keep me busy till Erika's class is over

"YOU LOOK BETTER."

Shit.

I squealed. I might've also thrown the chair back and almost face-planted the floor in the most pathetic display of aerobics known to mankind. Thankfully Erika didn't get to witness any of it. She just took some mild damage to her eardrums, which seemed like a fair turnabout for keeping me here, to be fair.

I'd been so engrossed with texting I hadn't heard the door open.

"You shouldn't threaten Sergio with whips," I blurted out. That was a thing I did now. "It's not nice."

My heart skipped a beat, sure, but I said it. There.

Erika snorted. "Are you aiming for something here, Kara?"

"What?!" I jumped up. "N-no? Of course not! Never ever ever ever."

That was one ever too many, but I didn't care.

Erika didn't seem to care, either. "Wanna grab something to eat? We can carpool to the club after."

"I could eat, I guess?"

"Are you asking me?" Erika quirked an eyebrow. She did it a lot. It was annoying—I mean, I could acknowledge it was hot too, but annoying nonetheless. "How do you feel about Ethiopian?"

"I didn't know there were any here."

"My neighbors opened it last month. It's good."

I believed her. I was just still processing that someone was inviting me out for lunch because I'd stumbled upon a community that took care of each other, whatever that meant.

"If you feel obligated—"

"I don't." Erika shrugged as she leaned against the door. "I have a feeling we might've started off on the wrong foot, though, and I'd like to fix it."

"There's nothing to fix," I said—mostly because it was the proper thing to do.

Besides, it wasn't as if I thought Erika was evil or something. I gathered she was just bigger on protocol and old school kink, maybe. I didn't have a lot of experience with that particular scene.

It was hard being a Little when there were so many rules about honorifics, posture, and eye contact to remember. Littles weren't good at that kind of stuff, and it wasn't a me thing.

"Is it because of your rule against Domms?"

I opened my mouth before I processed what she meant. No sound came out, though. I frowned.

It should be about that rule.

I'd placed it for a reason. I'd made a vow—to myself—to follow it.

I couldn't quite remember when the last time was that I'd actively endorsed it. Granted, most of my interactions involved Mónica, but…

No, I hadn't been thinking about my rule all week. I definitely wasn't thinking about it now.

"No." I could've lied, but I didn't like lying. There was no point. "It's not that."

"What is it, then? Walk me through it."

"Why?"

Was it petulant?

Kind of.

I didn't care.

"Because it's important to me."

I reared back—slightly. There was arrogance in that statement, but there was more to it. If it was only arrogance, I'd lash out, snap something she'd label as bratty, and get the hell out.

There was something like vulnerability too, though.

"Okay."

It wouldn't be so bad, right? I hadn't had Ethiopian food in ages, but I liked it, and I doubted it would be too different here. Besides, I *was* kind of hungry, even if I wasn't the one who had been working out all morning.

And I thought Mónica would appreciate it if I made a genuine effort.

Why my brain was stuck on *let's please Mónica at all costs* was not something worth delving into.

Not right now, at least. I had to take things one at a time.

"How long have you known Mónica?" I asked as we got into her car.

It was black, a BMW, but recognizing the logo on the back was about as far as my knowledge went. I used to know more about cars—well, trucks—but that was back when I'd had a resemblance of closeness with my father.

There was a pack of water bottles in the back, along with a first-aid kit and a couple of towels. I wanted to ask about them, but I didn't. Besides, I'd just asked a question, and Erika hadn't answered yet. It would be weird.

"Eight years or so, I think?" she said after starting the engine. There were quite a few cars on the road, so I guessed there was going to be some traffic. The streets were pretty narrow around here. "I'd just started working at another gym, and she was in one of my kickboxing classes."

I imagined I would take up kickboxing too if I had to spend my days with her brothers. I didn't say it out loud. I also didn't stop to think about the kind of stuff people learned to do in those classes.

Mónica was safe, period.

"I thought you would've met at the club."

"We helped found it, but no." She smiled as she spoke. I guessed I could see the appeal when she wasn't threatening violence or trying to taunt me. "We probably would've met there, though, if she hadn't gone to my gym. The community here is really small."

"Did you know you were Dommes already, then? Eight years ago?"

Mónica was only three years older than I was—the siblings' birthdays were on the company website for some reason—so eight years ago, she would've been in her early twenties. Twenty-three or so.

"I did," Erika said. Her fingers drummed against the wheel. "I started advertising myself as a pro Domme when I was eighteen and needed the money, and it snowballed from there. I think Mónica stumbled upon it more organically."

"What does that mean?"

"I'm sure she'll love to tell you the story."

"It's nothing dark, though, right?"

I couldn't think of an organic way to enter into the scene, but that was me.

Erika spared me a glance. She was playing nice—nicer than she'd been in the gym. "You have nothing to worry about."

"Okay." I nodded, bobbed my head up and down until there was no question she'd caught the movement. "So what is she into? Her profile just talks about leather, and I know what the demo today is about, but—"

"You haven't spoken about it?" Erika frowned. We were waiting for the light to turn green, so she could turn her gaze to me. Her eyes were really dark—great for sucking someone in, not that I knew what I was talking about. "I swear I'm gonna strangle the woman."

I giggled.

I felt really self-conscious about it, but… That was another new thing. Domms threatening violence on other Domms was now hilarious to me.

Erika's lip tilted up in a smirk before she was shaking her head.

"I knew you were going to be trouble." The light turned green, then, giving a natural pause to our strangely civilized conversation. "She's hard to explain as a Domme, honestly. She's… more of a classic Domme than she would like to admit, with a dash of Mommy vibes, and a streak of an infuriating disregard for rules and protocols."

"That's hilarious."

I giggled again, but… seriously? Infuriating disregard for rules and protocols?

That was a mouthful.

"You laugh now," Erika half-grumbled.

"How are you two friends, if you're so different?"

"We just clicked at first." Erika paused while she checked the street for a parking spot. "And then we stuck close while we navigated all the icky parts of running a community."

"Right."

I got a feeling there was more to it, but I wasn't going to press someone into disclosing their deep feelings.

Boundaries, and all that.

"The restaurant is just two blocks down if we park here," Erika said after driving slowly for a while. "Is that okay?"

"Sure." I kept myself from scoffing, but I probably pouted a bit. Controlling one's face wasn't as easy as people made it out to be. "Y'know, just because I don't go to the gym doesn't mean I'm completely out of shape."

"I know." Erika laughed. "I've seen you get a proper workout, remember?"

Oh.

Right.

She'd been there, too.

KARA

it's your fault if i die today

SERGIO

you're gonna have so much fun !!!

and then you're gonna tell me everything
because that's what besties do

KARA

it's not my fault you got a last minute gig thing

whatever it is you're doing

SERGIO

well sorry if i wanna afford my apartment

KARA

so secretive

19

MÓNICA

María was going to be the death of me, and I was *this* close to backing out of the demo.

"Remind me again why I agreed to this?"

"Because I'm a lot of fun, and you adore me." She didn't even blink, let alone stutter. The brat. "*And* I was the only one available when you blacklisted Jen last minute."

"Yeah, with good reason."

"I'm not complaining, Ma'am." María leaned closer. We were in one of the more private rooms upstairs while we waited for everyone else to arrive. "You're the one all grumpy."

"Try and call me grumpy again."

María just laughed.

I huffed. Today was not my day.

"If you want to cancel, I'm sure we can improvise something."

"You just want another orgy."

She laughed again. "I do. Even more so if you're letting me play with your sub again."

"Kara's not my sub." I glowered. María had been referring to her as mine all week. It was getting old. "Do I have to turn today into a punishment?"

"I already signed up for one," she scoffed. "When is bastinado not a punishment?"

I paused. "Are you the one who wants to cancel?"

I'd played with María before. I hadn't caned her feet myself, but I knew she enjoyed pain, and I'd watched Erika do it. The only reason I was the one doing the demo and not her was that I was less hardcore, and that meant less intimidating to the newer subs.

"Nope, I'm good," she said. "I'm just saying, I can be good to go and still think you Dommes into this are evil."

"Weren't you the one who asked Erika the other day to teach you?"

It was María's turn to glower. "That's different, obviously."

"Because you're a switch?"

"Exactly."

Of course.

I sighed. I'd brought a bottle of water with me, and I chugged it down. I knew my problem wasn't with María or the fact that she'd decided to test the waters a bit.

No, my problem was Erika's text telling me she was arriving with Kara.

There was a story there, and it didn't help that I'd already been anxious about Kara being here today.

I should've made more of an effort to talk with her *before* the demo.

The chances that this would all blow up in my face were high.

"Ma'am?"

I thought I'd just closed my eyes for a second, but that

didn't explain how María had moved until she was straddling me. My eyes darted down for a second. She had a stupidly perfect body, with all her curves and that cleavage.

"Yeah?" I cleared my throat. It was a good thing that she liked it when we objectified her just the tiniest bit.

"It's going to be all right. I even promise not to curse you out too much on stage."

I raised an eyebrow. "I'll believe that when I see it."

For as docile as María could be, and as good as she could be bordering the line between sub and Domme, she had a mouth on her. We'd all learned that one pretty quickly.

"I take offense to that, just so you know."

"Sure."

María scrunched up her nose. Her hair was tied up in one of those buns that gymnasts wore. It was kind of disappointing. Her curls always bounced around her face when she scrunched up her nose like that. She'd had some family thing earlier, though.

"Ma'am?"

"Yeah?"

"Can I help distract you, maybe?"

I thought about it. In the end, I shook my head. I didn't think I'd be able to focus on anything until I could spot Kara and see that she wasn't about to implode.

Erika had said they were good, but Erika wasn't the best at relaying information through text, so it wasn't the most soothing.

"I'll be fine, and you know my safe words."

María winked as she leaned closer. "And you mine, Ma'am."

Her voice against my ear sent a shiver down my spine. She didn't kiss me, but her lips still ghosted against my cheekbones before lowering toward my jaw.

My hand gripped her side, the skin soft against my fingers. I knew she'd probably bruise, but I also knew she'd like it.

"Come on, let's start setting up."

"You mean the bench and your collection of canes?" María snorted. "Yeah, that's gonna take hours."

"They're Erika's, not mine."

I had two canes at my place, but Erika was the true Sadist in our midst, and it showed in her toy collection. Most of the time I caned someone, I did it here just so that I could use Erika's.

"Don't remind me," she grumbled.

It was my turn to laugh.

"Come on, feisty girl. There's kinksters to educate."

"Yeah, yeah." María rolled her eyes, but she was smiling.

I squeezed her ass cheek before I patted it and she was off me.

Maybe I could go back to her initial offer if things did blow up.

I hoped they didn't.

"HISTORICALLY, bastinado was a form of punishment for criminals, slaves and, more often than it's probably recorded, women, too." There were about a dozen people sitting on the floor, Kara among them. She was close to Erika, but not too close. She hadn't been able to hold my gaze for more than three seconds at a time. "You could force someone to be completely dependent on you if they couldn't stand up on their own, or you could force them to work on their feet while their skin was flayed open.

"Now the context has changed, but I'd say it's important to bear that past in mind. You may not take things as far as they used to do, but I still like to make sure I understand how far I can go with someone."

I turned to María, then. She was sitting cross-legged against the bench. We'd considered setting her up from the beginning, lying on her back with her feet on the rest holds, but in the end decided against it. It was going to be distracting for too many people.

"Questions I like to ask have to do with what they need to be able to do right after the scene ends, and how much they need to be on their feet. So, María?"

María grinned. She didn't take her eyes off me as she answered.

"I need to either be able to get to my bed, or I need arrangements for someone to take me." Her voice didn't falter as she spoke. I loved that about her. "I work from home, so I can take more than most, but if I'm not going to be able to stand comfortably, or skin breaks, I need someone to check on me, in person, at least twice during the first few days."

"This is the kind of response someone experienced will give you," I summarized. "It doesn't mean you can't play with someone inexperienced, of course, but you have to keep in mind they're probably not realizing how sensitive the skin in their soles actually is. It is easy to not sit too much if they've had a hard pain session and their ass is bruised, but it's not so easy to be off their feet, and it can be mentally taxing when the pain lasts longer than a day or two."

I caught a couple of subs squirm, the determination they'd probably felt when they first walked in the room gone.

"It's another reason why, same as with most impact play, it is common to keep it at a surface level. Your feet have lots of nerve endings, and you can get a lot out of a scene by just playing with that threshold between tickling and actually caning and causing pain."

"Can you do actual damage, Ma'am?" Eli asked.

They were sitting by the corner, alone from what I could see. I wondered if they hadn't realized there were people they knew here, or they just wanted to keep to themselves today. María would probably check on them after the demo was over. She always did.

"As with most kinks, yeah, it is a possibility. As I said, there are many nerve endings there, and they are quite exposed, along with tendons, joints, etc. As a rule of thumb, stay away from the top and sides of the feet."

María shivered as I showed the areas I was talking about. She was probably going to get Erika or someone else to give her a harder pain session before the night was over.

"As you'll see, I like to stick to the fleshy bottom of the feet, and use light fast motions. You don't wanna go heavy and end up fucking up the connective tissue underneath." I tapped María's foot until she straightened her leg. "The fleshy part of the toes is a good area to play with, too."

The club's favorite ginger gasped when I demonstrated. I snorted. I'd gone *extremely* light for that one.

"Color?"

I knew what she was going to say, but it didn't make it less important—or fun.

"Green."

"Good girl." I ran a hand down her hair. "We're going to keep it light for the demo, okay?"

We'd already discussed this, but I liked to repeat the conversation once we were on stage. For one thing, it gave beginners an opportunity to see people negotiate a scene. For another, it gave the other person the chance to change their mind about something if the pressure of being exposed became too much.

"Yes, Ma'am." María's eyes drifted close for a second. "May I get in position now?"

"You may." I nodded before I turned to the people watching once more. "We're using a bench here with footholds, but you can use any position where their feet are exposed. Just make sure that they're not going to be at a weird angle for you. Try to have them as straight as possible, too, or you're going to have less area to work with, and less control over where you're hitting."

People nodded. Even Kara did. I tried to not focus on her or the way she was now half-hidden behind Erika. I wasn't sure if she'd noticed, but Erika sure had. Little went past her.

My attention had to be on María now, however. I'd deal with everyone and everything else later.

"As with most impact play, you wanna make sure your partner is aroused," I droned on, my hand ghosting up María's inner thighs.

She wasn't wearing underwear, and had shaved completely. The sight of the glistening skin before me had me fighting a wolfish grin. The perusal made her squirm, mouth half open in a silent gasp.

I let my thumb slide through her folds, then casually press against her clit. María's thighs clenched, her body shivering.

She was aroused, all right.

"Keep in mind that your sub may not be as quick to respond as María here," I teased, getting a few snickers in response and a moan from my willing slut. "I think we can start now, don't you?"

"Yes, Ma'am."

"Twenty on each foot?"

María bit on her lip, hard. She nodded just as frantically. "Shall I count them?"

"And thank me for each one."

I waited until she nodded again, and moved to the side.

The caning was fast. María was used to taking harder than this, so she didn't put up a fight or struggle too much. She just shivered and whimpered and cried a little. There were a few screams too.

It was a good thing that I wasn't a hardcore Sadist. I didn't get in the zone or lose myself in pleasure when I was caning or flogging or spanking someone. I liked doing it, but my enjoyment came from the servitude of it, from having that evidence of what my sub was willing to put themselves through because I said so.

"Did anyone have any questions?" I wiped a thin layer of sweat from my forehead.

When I hosted other demos, I liked asking for questions before the actual scene. In my experience, though, some kinks needed to be witnessed before the questions started flowing.

I wasn't wrong. I kept close to María as I answered questions about aftercare and safety measures, my hand lightly threading through her hair and scratching her scalp the way she liked.

"Ready to move?" I asked her when people started to disperse, no more hands raised.

"Yeah," she mouthed. Her eyes looked a bit glazed over, but she didn't seem too out of it.

I still helped her out of the bench and wrapped an arm around her waist while lowering her to the ground.

"Other than water, do you need anything?"

"Just water. Thanks."

"Of course."

"You know, I could probably stand on my feet. You didn't have to lower me."

"Humor me." I grinned. I knew she'd be able to walk

home, but that didn't mean it wasn't going to sting for the time being. "I'll be back in a second."

I didn't even have to leave the room. We'd placed a bunch of water bottles by the entrance earlier, so I just grabbed a couple and uncapped one.

María didn't complain about it and chugged the liquid down. "Do you know if Erika is open to play tonight?"

I spared my friend a glance. She was whispering something in Kara's ear, but I had no way to decipher what it was.

"You can ask her."

Erika was open to play more often than not, but she might not want to take her eyes off Kara if something was worrying her. I wouldn't know if something was until I figured out why they were hanging out together in the first place.

"Yeah, but I can't move." María pouted, a mischievous glint in her eyes.

"Weren't you just saying you could stand on your own two seconds ago?" I shook my head. The bravado of some people. "Besides, you can crawl, can't you?"

Instead of answering, María batted her eyelashes at me. It looked ridiculous, but I didn't need to spell that part out loud. Instead, I squatted down, placed a soft kiss on her forehead, and leaned back.

"You need more, don't you?"

"I only realized when I was telling you earlier. When you asked me what I could take and I said I didn't need to be on my feet. It doesn't have to be more caning, but I kind of want to be… dependent on a Domme for a couple of days, maybe?"

"Are you in the right mindset to negotiate that, or do you need me there?"

I trusted Erika if she was the one María ended up propositioning, but I couldn't say the same about everyone else.

"I'm good. But…" María squirmed again. "Maybe just make sure she doesn't leave or something? I need a minute."

"Done."

María's smile was completely unfiltered, one hundred percent unguarded. "You're the best."

"I try."

20

KARA

"You good?"

I blinked. Erika had been watching me throughout the whole demo like a hawk. I'd gotten squinted eyes, arched eyebrows of all kinds, and lately more frowns.

It was unnerving, but weird, too, because I couldn't get mad about it. I understood why. I could appreciate it even... from a distance.

"Yeah. Sure. Why wouldn't I be?"

Mónica had been squatting down next to María. I hadn't taken my eyes off her, but Maria looked happy. Not scared at all. I didn't think she felt tiny or vulnerable in a way that had ants running up her arms.

That was how I used to feel after a scene with Her.

It was hard not to draw comparisons, even when I knew anything that had to do with acknowledging Her existence was bad. It never ended in a happy place.

"Go talk to Mónica, then." Erika arched her eyebrow again.

I supposed it made sense that she'd pose it as a challenge.

Deep breaths. I needed deep breaths.

Mónica was there before I'd finished the stupid exercise. My eyes were closed, but I could feel her presence. I knew the way she walked.

It was her.

"Kara?"

Her voice was a jolt to my system. Not a bad one, just a neutral one.

I looked up. She wasn't giving anything away, which sucked. I wished more people were like me. My life would be ten times easier.

"I'll go check on María," Erika announced.

I shrugged, the information barely registering.

"Can we talk?" I blurted out. "Just the two of us?"

Mónica frowned. "Are you okay?"

I nodded.

I didn't know that I was, but that had little to do with the demo, and she was surely just asking about that. Miscommunication wasn't hot, so I was trying to avoid it.

Trying was the keyword here.

"We can go to one of the empty rooms," she suggested. She was too calm. It was eerie. "Are you comfortable with that?"

"Yeah."

Mónica watched me for a few seconds. Something must've given away that I wasn't a complete basket case, because she nodded. I thought she'd wait for me to stand up, but she just led the way. I liked it, oddly enough. She didn't see me as incapable.

It was a lame boost to my self-confidence, but hey, I wasn't about to complain.

"I went to see Erika today."

Did I mention patience wasn't my strongest suit? We hadn't even reached a door, dammit.

If Mónica noticed my lack of filter, she didn't mention it. "You did?"

"You said you wanted to introduce me, so…" I squirmed. "Sergio told me where she worked, so I went there and basically ambushed her? Well, except I didn't because the traitor also told *her* I was going, but… In my mind I was ambushing her?"

Mónica chuckled. "It's a good thing he did. Does Erika look like the type of Domme who enjoys ambushes?"

Huh.

No, I didn't go ten shades paler.

Nope, not me.

"Whatever," I managed to get out. "I did it, so… yeah."

"I see," she hummed. People hummed a lot. It was distracting and not that helpful. The door opening was more helpful. "And you did it, because I'd suggested you should?"

The room was pretty sparse. I'd thought there would be a giant bed and it would be awkward, but there were just random chairs, benches, tables, and tons of rope everywhere.

A rigging room, I supposed.

"Well, yeah, because…" Note to self: prepare what you want to say beforehand once and for all. Thanks. *"I-might-want-to-please-you-and-don't-know-what-to-do-about-all-the-stupid-feels-and-shit-and-it's-annoying-and-very-anxiety-inducing-if-you-were-wondering."*

There.

…

Not there.

Did I speak too fast?

I did, didn't I?

"Uh, what?" Mónica blinked.

"What, what?" I blinked too.

"I'm sorry, that was way too fast and jumbled," she said. At least she looked embarrassed about it. Ugh. It wasn't fair.

"Care to take a deep breath for me, sit down, and try again?"

Anyone would've nodded and done that, right? It was the sensible thing to do. It made sense.

Well, my stupid hormones—I was going to blame PMS here simply out of not having anything else to blame—decided otherwise. They decided the sensible thing to do was send water to my tear ducts until they overflowed.

Why, yes, bawling my eyes out when I'd come here to share my feelings—or something—was a great look.

"Hey, hey, it's okay." At least Mónica didn't bat an eye when I all but tackled her into a hug. No, she was being all perfect, rubbing my back and making soothing sounds against my ear. "It's okay. I'm here."

"I'm sorry," I sobbed. My hands clenched around fistfuls of fabric. I was pretty sure I'd managed to pull her shirt out of her pants, but oh well. "I'm sorry, I'm sorry, I'm sorry."

I wished I could, but getting a grip wasn't in the cards for me today. Shaking like a leaf was, though.

"It's okay," she repeated. "There's nothing to apologize for, baby girl."

I gasped.

The nickname shouldn't have registered, right?

Well, it did.

"I'm a mess."

"That's fine." Mónica chuckled. Her nose nuzzled the side of my head. It felt absurdly nice. "Let it all out, and then I'll get you some water, and we can talk, yeah?"

"I can talk now." Was I speaking out of sheer stubbornness? Partly. "Uh, how do you feel about trauma-dumping?"

Mónica took a second to answer. The only reason I wasn't freaking out was that she tightened her grip on my waist. I wondered if she'd let me be on her lap, but that was probably too much, too soon.

I bet it was soothing, though.

"I don't generally like the term," she admitted. "I understand it's a bad thing when it's used to get out of a fight or to come out on top, but in any other occasion, I don't think it's so much trauma dumping as just… people have gone through shitty things in life."

I nodded.

Way too many people had run for the hills because of it. I didn't know that I agreed with her and it was all good and dandy, but I wasn't going to tell her she should hate me for doing it, either.

So I started talking. I told her everything, probably way more than was necessary.

"Her friends thought I was a bad sub," I admitted. "She had charisma, I guess. And more friends than I ever did. When I dropped after a scene, or when I broke down and cried and went into full hysterics because I thought I'd gotten in trouble… They didn't do anything."

I took a shuddering breath, angrily wiping the tears away.

"I'm not saying I was perfect. I know I wasn't and I fucked up too and I didn't speak up enough and I—"

"You're not there anymore," Mónica said.

She could've just said I didn't do anything wrong. Everyone did that. This felt better.

Images assaulted me, but I pushed through. I could be stubborn. "I knew things were wrong, I knew Dommes weren't supposed to *do that*, that I wasn't supposed to live in complete fear, but… But it wasn't as if she'd isolated me from everyone and everything. We went to clubs. She invited people over all the time, and no one said what she did was wrong, so… How could I trust myself? What if it was me who didn't know better?"

"What made you realize it wasn't you?"

I paused. I'd talked about this before, but it had been a while. I didn't want to just say something easy or dismissive.

"I don't know that I realized right away." My voice came out thinner than it had before. "I just realized that staying would kill me, and whether it was my fault or not was irrelevant."

Mónica hummed. Her fingers threaded through my hair. She'd done the same thing to María earlier while she answered questions. I'd noticed.

"And then you came here?"

"Not right away." I wished. Then again, if I'd come here right after everything went down, I wouldn't have this. The beginning of a community. Mónica. Hell, I wouldn't even have roommates that seemed to genuinely like me when I wasn't mothering them too much. "It all went down a year and a half ago. At first, I tried to stay. I genuinely liked life in Rhode Island, you know, and I wanted to prove that I was strong enough to rebuild my life there."

"I'd say you're plenty strong."

Again, I wished.

Maybe Mónica wouldn't notice—or wouldn't comment—on the snort I couldn't keep to myself.

"I'd started going to therapy, before the big break up, and I kept going, but I don't know that I have the… the skills to keep it from happening again." I closed my eyes. I didn't think I could see the expression on her face, but I had to say the words. "And I know it's kind of an asshole thing to say, to imply that you could be an abusive piece of shit sometime down the road, but—"

"It's not." Mónica sighed. "Do you reckon we could sit down for this?"

"Sure."

After I wiped my cheeks some more so I didn't look like a bigger mess than I already was.

Mónica didn't let go right away. That was nice. I wasn't too confident about my steadiness at the moment.

I didn't think anyone could blame me, really. It was bad enough that I was already panicking about where to sit, and she hadn't even let go of me yet.

"Anything you want?"

Oh.

She had actually moved.

I really had to get out of my head.

"Why am I so easy to read?" I moaned, because priorities.

Mónica just shrugged. "I like that about you."

It wasn't fair; she wasn't the one who couldn't keep her meltdowns to herself. Anyway.

"I don't."

"Uh huh." I might've gone a bit too far with the pouting if I was getting the raised eyebrow treatment. "So, what is it you want?"

There was no way to ask her to sit on her lap, was there? Because I was kind of itching to do that and let go of every self-imposed rule that had kept me sane for the past year or so, but…

"This is your fault," I mumbled.

Deflection was totally a thing. Plus, if I talked and ranted and so on, I didn't have time to worry about what to do about the seating situation.

"*What* is my fault?"

Now she was definitely holding back laughter.

Ugh.

"Because!" My fists curled at my sides. I knew it wouldn't look threatening at all, but that was not the point. "I… I had things together, kind of, and I had a plan for today, but then you did the demo, and—"

"And?" Mónica leaned forward.

She should wear her hair pulled back like that more often.

It was hot—not that it wasn't hot too when we were in the office and she leaned over to check a document and strands fell over her face.

I needed to get out more.

And breathe, too.

"And part of me thought seeing you would prove that this was only a stupid infatuation and we couldn't go anywhere because I'd react the way I react to all Dommes."

Silence ensued. Mónica wouldn't take her eyes off me. It was unnerving. Arousing, too—unnecessarily so. I could tell myself it was just that I'd stopped being used to having someone's attention on me like that.

It wasn't, though.

Well, it was, but there was more to it. My stomach clenched.

"What about the other part?"

"The other part…" I breathed in. Deep. "The other part knew I wouldn't be scared."

More silence.

Was it me, or was my heart beating very loud today?

If she kept it up with the silences and the stares, I was going to start sweating too.

I really was out of practice. No one told you that when you went on a healing journey, or whatever I was doing.

"Sit down, Kara."

Huh?

I tilted my head to the side. I was expecting some line about how it was the same for her, not… whatever that was. How was I supposed to interpret that answer?

Maybe I could sneak out and text Sergio real quick. Sure, he was on the road or whatever, but he could have his phone read the message or something.

"Where?"

Did I mention I hated when Dommes were super observant? Like, she could've just pointed at one of the benches next to hers and thought it was a silly quirk of mine.

Noooo, she had to pull that thinking face and get that glint in her eye.

"Where did you want to sit, little one?"

"Uh…" I swallowed. The stakes were different, higher, when I was certain she knew what I wanted. "M-maybe, I—"

My throat tightened, the words there but unable to come out.

This wasn't how it was supposed to go. I wasn't supposed to look like an absolute mess.

I could be confident, dammit.

I was confident.

Before.

Double shit.

Comparing the before and afters never bode well.

"Want me to say what I think?"

I could've cried.

I didn't, thankfully, but I did nod.

"I think you want to sit on my lap." Mónica's tone was almost reverent as she spoke, gaze fixed on mine. "I think you want to surrender completely, and you want someone to remind you how to do it."

"I hate you," was my very understandable initial response.

I wiped my cheeks. Another tear struck down my cheek, but at least I didn't break down sobbing again.

Progress.

"Sure you do." Mónica chuckled.

There was a lightness in her face I wasn't used to seeing. Maybe it was about being in her Dom-space? I did notice she looked happier here than in the office, more relaxed even if she exuded more control. It was a weird combination. It probably shouldn't do it for me—or anyone—but my thighs clenching said otherwise.

Of course Mónica's eyes flickered down.

"What do I get?" I forced the words out. I could be confident, and I could be playful, even if I was going to need a giant bucket of ice cream to recover. "If I sit on your lap, I mean."

"You get to know that you've pleased me," Mónica murmured. "You get snuggles, too, and a hiding spot if you want it."

I groaned. "That's not playing fair."

Mónica started laughing, but I was already—clumsily—burying my face in her neck. Turned out I only needed to be told once when I was promised anything warm.

"There you go." She sighed, breathing down on my neck. It sent shivers down my spine. It felt good. Too good. Good enough I almost started crying again. "Much better, isn't it?"

"Shut up," I mumbled while squirming to hide deeper.

To be fair, she'd said I could. One could say I was just following orders—being a good girl and all that.

"You're going to be one hell of a brat, aren't you?"

"I'm an angel."

It was true.

Mostly.

To be fair, I didn't remember the last time I'd been relaxed enough to let go and have fun like that. It wasn't something I had to think about when I was with other Littles, but... Domms? It was easier and better for everyone to play it nice—even when nice wasn't always the most fun.

Still better.

"I'm sure you *can* be an angel," Mónica mused. "I'm also pretty sure you don't always want to be one. And that's okay."

"You know, it would be nice if you stopped reading my mind," I huffed.

It really wasn't fair.

I was at a clear disadvantage!

"It would be even nicer if you came over with me tonight," she hummed. Her hand drifted down my back. Her fingers ran circles there, softly, slowly. It was maddening in the best of ways. "You meet my cats, get more snuggles, I make sure you get some rest, and then we can have a lazy morning."

I blinked. "That's too fast."

The idea didn't throw me into a total panic attack—which I'd thought it would—but it was still too much. Right? I couldn't go from zero to a hundred. Even I knew that was a recipe for disaster, regardless of what other instincts were trying to say.

Mónica sighed. She squeezed me, though, so it was okay. "You're right."

I gnawed on my lip. Compromise was important, wasn't it? "Maybe you can drive me home? Like the other night?"

No one could say I wasn't trying here.

"Yeah." Her voice sounded perkier, for lack of a better word. "I'd like that."

21

MÓNICA

Tonight, there was a free parking spot almost in front of her house. Small mercies.

"You know, you didn't tell me what you thought of Erika. Or the demo." I spoke while I parked. I'd considered waiting until I killed the engine, but I didn't want her to run out of the car the second it stopped.

It seemed that every time we spoke, the mountain of things unsaid between us only grew larger and larger.

Kara eyed me warily, but she didn't move for the door.

Warmth spread down my belly.

"Is this a 'pick your fight' kind of scenario?"

I snorted. That wasn't the response I'd expected, but I should have. She had a way of using humor when trying to buy herself time or deflect.

"If you wanna see it that way."

She stood silent for a few seconds. Her brows furrowed as she lost herself in thought. I noticed her eyes shifted as if she was trying to track down the words.

"I didn't want to get anywhere near any event that involved pain or impact," she said, "so it was… shocking, but

I wanted to see you, and test myself, maybe. Does that make sense?"

"It does." I was certain that if someone asked her, she'd berate herself about staying stuck. Yet all I saw her do was push herself outside of her comfort zone with every choice she made. "I wish you'd told me about your limits, though."

"I don't know if they're limits, exactly." She scrunched up her nose, her fingers twirling around a strand of hair. "I mean, I've never been big into masochism, so I doubt that's going to be any different now, but I liked some of it under the guise of discipline, I guess."

I was sure there was more she had to say on the topic, but she drew silent. For a few seconds, I debated the merits of letting her find her words. In the end, though, she'd been doing that every time we talked.

"But discipline turned into something ugly?"

A sharp intake of breath met my words.

"Yeah." Kara swallowed. "I mean, it wasn't like I ever had to go to the hospital or like there were any visible bruises… which I know sounds really bad and you're going to go off about how that doesn't matter and it was still abuse, and I agree? I just mean, it… yeah, I just couldn't *trust* Her to just keep it as a funishment."

I didn't say anything. I didn't think there was much to be said. I hurt for her, for the Little who felt trapped and scared with the person she was meant to trust. I hurt for Kara, too, for the woman who should've never been forced to pick up her pieces like this.

"The last time, she had a flogger, and we were with some of her friends in a club. It's all a bit foggy, I don't fully remember what I'd done, but suddenly I was tied up to one of the whipping posts, and she was flogging me, and s-s-she broke skin? And that was always a limit for me, and I was crying and safe wording but they all just… shushed me? A-

and I-I didn't know what to do, but I vowed that we'd never do anything impact related again."

"Shit," I cursed. I couldn't help it. Kara was shaking in the passenger seat. I wanted to reach her, but I didn't want her to link the touch to the memories. "I'm so sorry."

Kara nodded, chewing on her lip. She was doing that a lot. When she turned toward me, her eyes were glassy. I didn't know how she had more tears in her.

"I kept a closer eye on María than I did you," she said as if it was a confession that could get her in trouble. "She never felt scared, or small, or jumpy."

I thought I heard what she was saying, but I wouldn't be too presumptuous. I'd try, at least.

"I would never keep a scene going if I even suspected my play partner felt like that."

"I believe you." Kara only whispered them, but the words still cascaded down my body. "It's just hard."

"It's okay." I let my head fall against the headrest for a second. "What about Erika? How did it go with her?"

Kara let out a big puff of breath before she answered. I imagined she appreciated the change in topic—or maybe she felt conflicted about it. I knew I did.

"She's… blunt."

"She is."

"She raised some good points, though."

"About?" I turned so I could face her again.

Kara squirmed. I pretended I didn't want to put a hand on her thigh and keep her still.

"You." She breathed out without making eye contact. "What I'm doing here, in general, I guess."

I nodded. "Did you know she's had plans to hire you for weeks now?"

The question got the response I wanted. Kara's alert gaze snapped up to meet mine. "Huh?"

"Since she first saw you and I told her you worked for me."

"I…" Kara tilted her head to the side, brow furrowed. "I don't know anything about gyms."

"You didn't know anything about construction, either," I rebuked.

I remembered she'd worked as a receptionist before from her resumé, not that I was too enthusiastic about the idea of Erika poaching her from me. Everything else aside, Kara did good work, and more selfishly, I liked having her around the office.

"But why?"

I sighed. "I've told you we take care of each other."

"Yeah, she said that, too." Kara huffed. "It's annoying."

It was less annoying now that I had a bigger picture. I could barely picture any scenario where Tony had a good reason to not disclose his connection with Sergio. There was no way I could rationalize how several people would just stand there while a safe word was ignored.

I didn't know how I would trust a community that did that, either, or how I could take it at face value that another one wouldn't do the same.

"It's true." I shrugged. It didn't feel like a shrugging matter, but pushing the issue might only drive her farther away. "Did she tell you she used to be a pro Domme?"

It wasn't a secret, but I had no idea how much they'd talked, or what they'd talked about.

"Yeah." Kara cleared her throat. "I asked her how you met, and then if you'd both been Dommes all that time."

It wasn't the time, but the fact that she'd asked about me? As juvenile as it was, it had me feeling ten inches taller.

I never said I was too level headed when I started something with someone—or even when I recognized the possibility was there.

"So, Erika is not only the most stern person when it comes to consent and establishing boundaries, she is the most educated person I know on everything that has to do with power structures and imbalances."

"Okay?"

I bit the inside of my cheek. I had an idea of the point I was trying to make. I just wasn't confident of how to get there.

"You said she was blunt, right?"

"Yeah." Kara gulped. "It's not an insult, obviously, I mean, in case you tell her something, I don't want to—"

I raised my hand, palm up, before she could keep going down that spiral.

"With what I've told you, and the impression you've got of her... Do you think she's someone who would stand by and not say something if she even suspected someone was taking advantage?"

Kara gnawed on her lip while she considered my question. "You want me to say no, don't you?"

"I want you to say what you think, or feel."

"I don't know what I think," she admitted after a slight pause. "It scares me, everything."

"Everything?"

"The idea of submitting again, of being someone's sub." She cleared her throat before chancing a glance my way. "Of being your sub."

Her eyes shone with vulnerability as they studied me.

"I realize this won't mean as much to you with your experience, but if you chose to be my sub, Kara? You wouldn't be just mine. You'd belong to the club, to our community."

Kara took a sharp breath. Her lips parted. I wished I could read her mind, know what she was thinking exactly.

"That's... a lot." She gulped. "Too soon."

"But do you want it?" I was going to figure out a way to

tell Erika so she didn't carve my eyes out before I was even done with it.

"I shouldn't," she insisted.

I should've left it there, but something stopped me. Her body language. There was desire there, but I could ignore desire. I couldn't ignore *need*. Kara *needed*.

"But?"

"But…" Kara kept torturing her bottom lip. It was starting to give me anxiety. "But if I say I do want some resemblance of what you've said… What does that say about me? That I don't know how to be alone?"

I sighed. "How long since you broke up with your ex?"

"A year and a half since I left?" Kara kept her gaze downward.

I itched to lift her chin with two fingers.

"And since you started checking out of the relationship?"

"Uh… a few months before that, for sure? It wasn't so linear, for the last couple of years. I kept going back and forth between thinking I had to leave and thinking I wanted to stay and make it work."

"That's still almost two years of grieving your relationship."

"You're assuming I was actually doing the work."

I quirked an eyebrow. That wasn't the Kara I'd come to know, but there were only too many assumptions I'd be comfortable with. "Weren't you?"

"I don't know," she said. "I think on paper I did, but… If I'd actually done the work, would I still be so messed up?"

"After years of trauma? Sure."

Kara groaned. "Did I mention I hate when you Dommes go and decide to be all logical about things? It's annoying."

"Is it?" I retorted. She groaned again. Under other circumstances, I would be teasing her about it. Instead, I did another thing Erika wouldn't let me live down. "Close your eyes for me."

"Huh?" Kara squirmed on her seat as she positioned herself to watch me better.

It was the thing that prompted me to push. The more I watched her, the more convinced I was that Kara had been waiting for that push for a long time now. She'd been ready for it, too.

"Close your eyes."

Her lips parted again, but I didn't have time to hesitate. She complied beautifully, her features smoothing out as she took a few breaths.

I let her center herself.

"Picture yourself in the club, in one of the events." I kept my voice even, didn't make a move, either. "Picture me there, if having you under my supervision was more than pretend to keep others off your back."

"Okay." Kara bit the inside of her cheek for a second before she relaxed again.

The temperature in the car seemed to rise. I ignored it. This wasn't meant to be part of a scene, foreplay into something else.

"Imagine a perfect scenario," I said. "What am I doing?"

For a minute, everything remained still. I didn't mind the stillness. Stillness didn't equate tension, it didn't equate fear or anxiety.

Kara's head lolled back, the soft thud it made against the leather the only sound in the vehicle.

"You're there." She swallowed before she kept talking. "The others too. You… you talk to me, tell me I'm doing good. You tell me what to do, too. Who to touch, and how. You tell others what they can do to me. You… pet me?"

My voice caught in the back of my throat. It came out broken, but I couldn't help it. "Sounds like a fun scene."

Kara's voice had taken a breathier quality, too. "You're sweet. You tease me a bit, but you're mostly… you're proud of me, and everyone knows it."

"I worship you."

The words left my mouth before I'd processed them. I wouldn't take them back, though. It felt right. Kara begged to be worshiped without words—needed it, too, most likely.

Kara didn't answer. I didn't think she'd know how.

"But it's… it's not real." She gulped down quickly. Her eyes opened, darting to my face. "Erika… Well, it was funny then, because she said you disregard rules and protocol, but she also said you're a classic Domme, and that… That's about discipline."

"Hmmm." Well, at least I was going to have some sort of ammo if Erika went too far on her high horse when we talked. "Kara, breathe."

She hesitated for a second, but she did, slowly settling then.

"I don't know what she told you, or what she meant, and I *do* enjoy discipline, but discipline doesn't have to be impact play. It doesn't have to be public humiliation."

I was certain Kara had stopped breathing despite obeying less than a minute earlier. I didn't point it out, though, not yet.

"So what is… What does discipline mean for you?"

"Depends on my partner." Even before she groaned, I knew it wasn't a helpful answer. It was an honest one, though. "It can be anything from time out, to acts of service, to—"

"Acts of service?"

"Interruptions get disciplined," I teased—lightly—but I set to elaborate after I cleared my throat. "The way I see it, discipline is about getting a sub to think about what they've done or haven't done. So, impact play helps some, and so do time outs, but other times… Say that I grab all my leather boots and ask you to polish them. That's what I mean with an act of service."

"Oh."

"Do you think that's something you'd be comfortable with?"

It was my turn to hold my breath. In an ideal, romanticized world, I supposed I could've told her I'd give up all my core kinks for her. That wasn't real life, though, and it wouldn't do us any favors.

It didn't mean it didn't cross my mind as I watched Kara chew on her lip as if she was genuinely trying to tear skin.

"M-maybe?" Her throat bobbed up and down visibly. "I don't know."

I breathed out. I could work with that. It was better than a non-response, which was what I'd been expecting. And dreading.

"Are you willing to try?"

More silence filled the car. The walls closed in as I watched her eyes dart all over my face.

I wish I could know what she was seeing, what she was thinking.

Kara squirmed, breaking that simmering eye contact.

"I think so."

"Good."

22

KARA

> KARA
>
> i wanted to kiss you
>
> in the car

In case there was someone wondering, the award to dumbest person alive went to me.

No doubt about it.

The screen glared, too bright, mocking me.

Granted, I'd been in a bit of a haze last night, especially after all but running out of Mónica's car. After I'd told her I thought I could try, my eyes had kept drifting down to her mouth.

It wouldn't have been terrible, but I knew she'd noticed. I knew she was going to say something, maybe to ask if she could kiss me. Maybe she would've teasingly said I could kiss her.

I'd freaked out, because that was my coping mechanism now. Well, I'd held it together long enough to say I should head inside because it had been a long day and there was a lot of thinking to do.

It hadn't been a complete lie, either.

It would've worked, too. I could've headed to bed, managed some sleep, and then text about meeting up somewhere—like a normal person.

But no. After spending a stupid amount of time twirling around in the bathroom, I texted her that and plopped down on bed.

Sergio was going to kill me. He was going to laugh at me, first. A lot. Notice he wouldn't be laughing along with me. No, it would be one hundred percent one-directional.

And well-deserved, honestly.

That was all if I hadn't just ruined all my chances with Mónica—also known as the first and only Domme I could somehow find myself trusting and opening up with.

She'd read the message, about the time I'd sent it, but she hadn't answered.

It was almost noon now, and I knew she wasn't a late sleeper—not in a creepy way; she'd said that once while we had breakfast in the office.

Oh, shit.

If she didn't text back, I'd have to face her tomorrow.

We had a long day of meetings, too, and I'd already proven I didn't work well when I was anxious.

Maybe I should text Erika about that offer to work at her gym—just in case. It couldn't be so hard, right?

KARA

> ... i should've waited to say that until we talked to HR, shouldn't i?

> because i'm guessing we have to do that, right?

> or not?

> i don't know

> please tell me things won't be weird on Monday?
>
> that's all i need
>
> i'll stop bugging you

By "I'll stop bugging you," I meant I literally forced my hands to leave my phone on the kitchen counter. I'd planned to cook something, but my nerves were too fired up for it now.

Alex was in the living room, though I had no idea about Lucas. They weren't as aware of all my drama, so I hesitated a bit, but it was better than scratching my arms raw, which was where my intrusive thoughts were taking me.

Or it would've been.

Why did phones buzz so loudly?

MÓNICA

We should let HR know.

The company doesn't have strong policies on this kind of thing, though, I checked.

Is there any specific reason why things would be weird?

Truthfully, I didn't know if I wanted to laugh or cry, but there was something lodged in my throat waiting for my brain to decide.

It was a good thing I could text in the meantime without anyone being the wiser.

KARA

> i said i wanted to kiss you and you didn't respond
>
> not that you have to

> that sounds really bad
>
> i'm sorry
>
> i'm...
>
> ugh

MÓNICA

Remember how you said yesterday was a lot for you?

It was a lot for me too. I didn't want to say something reckless.

More reckless, I mean.

KARA

> what's wrong with reckless?

MÓNICA

Many things, little one.

Did you want us to meet before we see each other at the office?

I stilled.

Shit.

Stupid Dommes being forward and not letting you talk yourself in circles.

It was an art. A forgotten, unappreciated art.

Ugh.

KARA

> okay
>
> i mean, if you insist *angel face*

MÓNICA

Here I was, about to invite you to one of those milkshakes you like.

PLAY PRETEND

> KARA
>
> don't play with my feelings like that
>
> that's mean

MÓNICA

When can you be ready?

> KARA
>
> i don't know
>
> for what?
>
> are we having milkshakes or going to some fancy restaurant with a dress code that means i have to fight for a last minute salon appointment?
>
> honest question

MÓNICA

I'll book us a table for that some other time. Today I was thinking we could meet at the club. It should be pretty quiet.

My palms felt sweaty. They weren't, not really, but I still sat down. Just in case.

My head felt heavy, too. I didn't know if that was normal. Maybe I should ask Alex. But Alex was intense for all things medical. I only had to see them around Lucas to know, and I didn't see them so often.

"You okay?"

"Eep!"

Shit. The stool scratched against the linoleum floor. The sound made me wince, too loud and high pitched.

"Didn't mean to scare you." Alex remained frozen by the entrance to the kitchen. It felt silly, and I felt like dirt. I didn't want my roommates to tiptoe around me. "Is everything okay?"

I frowned. My gaze darted down to the phone, but there

were no new messages. Sure, it made sense because I hadn't texted her back yet, but that didn't stop me.

Rationality was not my forte here.

"Yeah, I was just texting with my…" I froze there. My Domme? My boss? I didn't know what I could say, or what I wanted to say. I still didn't know where my roommates stood when it came to kinky shit. "A woman. Possibly date? It's complicated."

It was also the perfect timing for Lucas to hop through the entrance, too.

"You're going on a date with your boss?"

Alex had already chastised him for not using his crutches enough. If I was meaner, I'd point it out to get them off my case.

Alas, I couldn't live with the unspoken guilt trips, so I just blushed furiously and proceeded to hide my face.

"It's not like that."

"You're dating your boss?" Alex kept their voice even.

Too even.

"Kinky, right?" Lucas teased.

It was probably nothing more than that, but my head snapped up.

They both noticed.

Health professionals were way too observant.

"Kara?"

"Yes?" No, no, my voice didn't go an octave higher. Lucas' brows didn't raise, either. "I mean, no? Well, yes, but it's not…"

"Kara." Alex cleared their throat. "You're not making any sense."

"Oops?"

MÓNICA

Kara?

> If it's too much, we can reassess. So long as we're talking, it's all good.

Oh no.

Hell no.

I ignored clammy hands and the way my heart was picking up speed. "Give me a sec."

KARA

> no
>
> i mean, sorry
>
> it's not too much
>
> i've just been ambushed by my roommates
>
> (in a good way)
>
> we can meet up at the club if you want
>
> just tell me when
>
> and, uh, what should i wear?

MÓNICA

> Are you asking because you genuinely don't know, or because you want me to make that choice?

Triple shit.

My cheeks couldn't get any hotter, my brain was going to explode, and Lucas and Alex were still there and waiting.

"So…" I chewed on my lower lip. If I thought about it, it was as good a time as any to open up, wasn't it? Sure, they could kick me out, but it was different now that I was here. I could squat with Sergio while I searched for a new place, and I had all my papers now. I didn't want to live in a place where I had to hide. I hadn't done that since I moved out of my parents'. "When you said kinky…"

"Yes?"

"Uh..."

I paused when Alex muttered something under their breath. My confusion only lasted for two seconds, before they were grabbing a stool and all but pushing Lucas into it.

"Aren't you supposed to know how rehab works?" Lucas grumbled. "I'm supposed to exercise it."

"You do that enough when I'm not looking," Alex snapped.

I didn't know what Lucas did when I wasn't around, but what I saw him do was play video games. I'd learned not to get in the middle of those two, though.

"So, as I was *trying to say*," I emphasized. I knew that was going to get their attention. They'd once mentioned my voice was too soft and they were scared to miss me when I spoke sometimes. It worked, as both sets of brown eyes returned to me. "You might've been up to something with the kinky comment."

"*Ooohhh*," Lucas teased. He didn't grumble about sitting down anymore. Instead, he now watched me with his head tilted to the side until I started squirming. "Yeah, I see it."

"Behave," Alex warned, moving to Lucas' side to elbow him.

"What?" Lucas blinked, pretending to rub at the spot Alex had hit. "Look at her."

"*And* now you're going to be offensive, too?"

"I didn't mean it in an offensive way, and you know it."

"But Kara doesn't, you asshole."

I was just watching them as if it was a weirdly enticing volleyball match. My name jolted me back to the present, though, and yeah, the fact that Alex was right and I did *not* know. Well, I could connect some dots now.

It was better than nothing.

"Okay, so what do I do about this?" I asked.

Might as well get something out of their bickering. It wasn't as if I was going to get a nude while they read through the last couple of texts between Mónica and I.

"Oh, I ambush you now?" Lucas huffed.

"Lucas!" Alex hit him in the back of the head. "Forgive him, he's clearly not housetrained and it's a miracle he kept up the pretense for your first month here."

"Mean," he mumbled. "Ohh, so you're going to Plumas?"

"You've…" I blinked. "You know it?"

"Do I know the only kink club in a hundred mile radius?" Lucas pinned me with one of those glances I wasn't always too confident about how to interpret. "Yes, Kara, I know it."

"Who's the mean one now?" I pouted.

Did I look like someone who could take some teasing now, lighthearted or not?

Maybe I should get my phone back, dart to my room, and bother Sergio. At least he wouldn't tease me because he was learning anything new.

"What, am I supposed to tell you what to tell your Domme? Because I'm not sure that's right without some negotiating first."

I opened my mouth. I was going to protest, or say something, but no sound came out.

"I hate you" worked.

"Nah." Lucas winked. "Seriously, though, go with your gut."

Alex had remained too quiet. That should've alarmed me, but I was easily distracted.

"You don't know what to say because of your ex?" they finally asked.

Shit.

Nope, not talking about Her today. I was shaking my head frantically and grabbing back my phone before I could realize that I was up and moving back from the kitchen island.

"Mónica is not Her."

The words flowed out of my mouth almost instinctively. They still hit me hard, my knees nearly buckling.

It wasn't the first time I'd had the thought, but... She wasn't Her, I knew that, it was the main reason why I was going through with this in the first place, so I should start acting like that, right?

The thought was terrifying, but it was... I needed to follow it.

KARA

> is that something you'd like to add to our dynamic?

> choosing what i wear at the club?

I kept one eye on my phone and another on my roommates as I typed. They kept watching me, in an eerily similar way to how they'd watched me before they suggested I saw a therapist. It was fine, though. It would be.

MÓNICA

> Not all of the time, but from time to time, I would.

KARA

> today one of those times?

MÓNICA

> Just wear something comfortable. Like the clothes you wore for the playdate with Sergio and the other girls.

KARA

> will do

> thanks

It shouldn't have surprised me. It shouldn't have caught

me off guard that Mónica hadn't asked me to wear a harness or go nude or wearing anything that would be too revealing or make me too vulnerable.

But…

I stopped by the door to my room, taking stock.

Determination fueled me.

I truly believed Mónica wasn't Her, and… That meant behaving like it.

23

MÓNICA

KARA

so… how much trouble am i in for disobeying you already?

ps: i'm downstairs, you have to come let me in

i mean, Sergio said a member had to do it

he usually did it himself but…

MÓNICA

I'll be right there.

Remind me to get you a key to the door.

KARA

but i'm not a member yet

MÓNICA

Think of it as a homecoming present.

KARA

a bit late for a homecoming present, no?

MÓNICA

Are you complaining?

I didn't wait to see what she was going to text back. I'd soon realized if I left it up to her, we could spend the entire day texting.

It wasn't terrible, but texting wasn't what I wanted today. I reread the short exchange before I brought the phone to the locker room, though.

I didn't stop to ask her what she meant by disobeying me. I wasn't sure I wanted to know. Without seeing her, I couldn't tell where her mind was.

Just because I'd managed to arrive here relatively calm didn't mean I wasn't aware of the pressure. There was a weight lingering. I knew I had to thread carefully. More than that, I wanted to be careful.

Kara deserved it. I wanted to give that to her, if nothing else.

Being in my head wasn't going to help matters. That was a lesson I'd learned early on. Instead, I squared my shoulders, stored my phone in the locker room by the entrance I always used, and headed outside.

The weather wasn't too bad for April—incredibly enough, it wasn't raining—but the shift in temperature when I opened the doors was still quite noticeable. My skin broke in goosebumps easily, and that was before I got an eye on Kara.

Kara, who all but barreled past me in a flurry. I had to blink to make sure I wasn't imagining things, but there was a fire under her step I hadn't seen before.

"Hi. Hello. Hi! I'll meet you upstairs? Okay, good," she rushed out, barely acknowledging me.

Truthfully, I didn't know how to react.

"May I ask what's gotten into you?"

"Sure, but later. Dress protocols to abide by and all that."

She met my gaze then, her eyes glinting with resolution.

I took a deep breath. I might not know what was going on, but I knew when someone was on a mission.

"Shall I get you something to drink while you change?"

I didn't know why she had to change, either. I would've expected her to wear her clothes underneath a coat, but… She seemed full of surprises today. The long black coat wasn't really helping me to figure it out, either.

"Just water? With a slice of lemon, maybe, if there's any."

"I'm sure there is."

I hoped so, at least. Tony was in charge of stocking up the bar, and the last thing I wanted was to get into it with him about slacking off. We hadn't really ended on good terms, and I didn't care too much to make up with him just yet.

The lounge area upstairs was empty. I knew there was a small group of riggers in one of the rooms, but there was nothing else planned. One or two people might show up unannounced, but there would be no bigger groups to distract us or overwhelm Kara. She'd done well during the group play night, but there hadn't been so much at stake—if I could even say there was anything at stake here. I kept wondering if I was reading too much into this, which was unnerving. It wasn't something that ever happened.

Kara was rushing up the stairs before I could talk myself in circles too much.

My mouth opened.

It was a good thing I had enough reflexes to cover it with my glass. I'd been nursing the same iced tea since I arrived at the club earlier.

Kara stood there, past the entrance to the lounge but not quite near me. She was wearing a babydoll dress in pale yellow, her hair loose and cascading down to her breasts. The tulle fabric flowed when she moved, the sheer puff sleeves adding up to that soft glow that emanated from her.

"Is it okay? I know it doesn't exactly adhere to the dress code, but it is a bit transparent, and it's just what… What I would wear to a date, I guess?"

"Aren't you freezing?" was what I decided to blurt out.

I did that, apparently.

It was a good thing the area was empty.

Kara blinked, seemingly frozen for a second or two. Then the most stupidly cute giggle came out of her.

"Well, I had a coat and tights on, and there are blankets here. I think I'll survive."

I nodded, almost petrified. "Right." Truth be told, I had no idea what I was doing or what was going on, or why I had the sneaking suspicion that my hands would start feeling clammy anytime soon. "I can drive you home, too. So you don't get cold."

"Yeah, sure."

I widened my eyes. That easy acceptance had nothing on the hesitation from the day before.

"Is this…" Thankfully, my brain began to—slowly—start up as I eyed her down. "Is this what you meant about disobeying me?"

"Well, yeah." Kara chewed on her lower lip. There *was* a hint of hesitation, but it was obliterated by playfulness I'd only really seen when she spent time with Sergio, or with the other subs. "You said to wear clothes like what I wore for the Littles' playdate."

"I did," I hummed. "So why the change?"

Kara sighed, her body slouching down against the couch. She hadn't taken a sip of her drink yet. I wanted to remind her—hydration was important—but I didn't want to break whatever spell we were under.

"I had a bit of a realization earlier." Her eyes drifted from me to stare right ahead. I let her find her words and the confidence I was only getting sneak peeks of. "Long story short, if I'm not scared of you, I should start acting like it, right?"

My heart thumped in my chest. I didn't want to read too much into her words, though, to move too fast.

"It's okay if you need time or a slower pace."

She just shrugged. Her eyes drifted back to mine. There was a lightness about her. I didn't know if it was the dress or something else, but I was drawn to it, my body leaning closer as if it was a nectar I couldn't quite resist.

"I know," she said, "and I know I'm not gonna be able to go at my usual speed with all things, but... This I can do."

I itched to praise her for that, the bravery it must take. "I get that."

Despite Erika's opinions, I did have restraint and I knew how to exert it. I just hadn't had many reasons to actually do it before.

There was so much more I would do for her.

The thought slipped into my mind with no warning. It gave me pause as I digested what it meant—as I processed the fact that it wasn't a lie, or an exaggeration.

Huh.

"I'm sorry," Kara rushed out. "I mean, here I am babbling about things to do with you even though it's a terrible idea, and we don't know yet if we work, and you're my boss, and I'm not even past my probationary period, and I told myself I wouldn't go down this road, but..."

"Breathe," I murmured. "Are you okay with touch?"

I wanted to soothe her, and I couldn't do it just with words. Her unblemished skin was enticing, alluring to caress and touch.

"Yeah." Kara cleared her throat. Her eyes were slightly widened, as if she hadn't counted on the line of questioning. "I mean, anywhere that's covered by clothes is fine."

That left a lot of skin to touch. I didn't mention it. I just placed my hand over hers. At some point during her jumbled speech, she'd curled them into fists, tried to dig them into the fabric of the couch.

She relaxed them under my coaxing. Slowly. I wouldn't say the simple move didn't melt something in me.

"Do you want to tackle the office stuff first?"

Her voice came out warbled. "I think we have to?"

I agreed.

"My plan was to talk to HR and the legal department on Monday, depending on how today went," I explained. "As I said, I checked, and we don't have a strong policy when it comes to relationships in the office, but I want Legal to write up something that protects you no matter what happens."

"What do you mean?" Her eyebrows furrowed.

"I won't have the details until I talk with them, but I was thinking that if you ever wanted to quit, because you were uncomfortable with me for any reason, we'd keep you on payroll for six months, maybe? And then we'd keep you on paper so that you're never in danger of losing your visa." I paused to take a deep breath. I was getting too ahead of myself. The way her eyes widened proved my worry. "I wanted to add something about how we'll always give you good referrals, and maybe Legal has more ideas."

"That's… a lot." Kara swallowed. "No business is going to cover my salary for six months just because."

"My family has the money." I shrugged. They owed me, too, but there was no point getting into it with Kara now. Maybe later down the road. It would depend on what Legal said, too—and the call I'd probably get from my father. "And it's important for me that you feel safe."

"I do. Feel safe, I mean." A weight lifted off my shoulders. There was sincerity in every syllable coming out of Kara's mouth. I clung to it. "I still think we're going too fast."

"Feel free to set the pace."

Kara gnawed on her lower lip. "I just mean… I know it's been a while since I started something, but there was usually a lot more talk about kinks, limits, and all that compatibility stuff."

So that was what worried her. "I wanna talk about kinks and limits, too, don't get me wrong."

Kara just nodded. I didn't think she was fully processing my words.

"The day before…" Her voice came out raspy. She swallowed it down. "You asked me about what I pictured, when I thought about the two of us."

My heartbeat picked up speed. "I did."

"So…" Kara shifted so she was facing me straight on. It did things to me that would make me sound incredibly stupid. "I wanted to ask you the same, how you picture us… together."

I leaned back on the couch. Of course, I'd thought about it—more than once. It was strange, though. When I fantasized about people, it was usually about specific scenes.

It was different with Kara. I wasn't sure how to put it in words, but when I pictured Kara… It wasn't about whether I was tying her up, watching her, sharing her, or using one toy or another on her. It was more about what she evoked and what I evoked in her.

"I picture us in the club," I said. "I'm sitting with other Domms, and you're kneeling by my side. My hand is carding through your hair. You are relaxed. Trusting."

Kara scrunched up her nose. I didn't think she wanted me to see the gesture, but it looked too adorable on her to give me time to wonder.

"What if I was coloring on the floor? Instead of kneeling?" she tested. "Or I can be snuggling with a blankie. And stuffies? I like the hair thing, though."

I chuckled. I couldn't help it.

"Yeah, we can do that." There was slightly more behind her words, though—or maybe it was my nerves on overdrive. "Honestly? I've never been with a Little, outside of maybe spanking Sergio or one of the others for fun."

"But…" Kara wiggled on her spot, her head tilting to the side. "I thought… But I'm a Little."

"Believe me, I am well aware." I shook my head. She was looking at me with an owlish kind of expression. I couldn't say I wasn't already imagining ways to put that awaiting look on her face—if she'd be into it. "The truth is, Littles have never done it for me before. I mean, I do have a soft spot for the lot of you when you're in Little space, but Littles have never done it for me, sexually."

"Oh."

Kara blinked. She seemed so confused, biting the inside of her check. It was killing me.

"I do want to play with you, Kara." I sighed. "I just thought I'd tell you because I'm new at this. Being with Littles, I mean, for real."

"Okay." She swallowed again. "But you… I mean, I like more things, but age play has always been there for me. I don't want to give it up."

"I don't want you to." There was no way in Hell I'd ever consider that acceptable. "But I know there's stuff, like the kneeling, where you'll have to tell me if it doesn't work for you. I expect you to."

Kara nodded, slowly. She inched forward, though, before I could worry about what the gesture meant.

"So I have to call you out when you don't understand Little things."

"Sure, you can put it that way."

My acquiescence made her giggle. It was a nice, tilting sound. Gosh, how could anyone not have a soft spot for this kind of shit?

"But…" Kara nibbled on her lower lip. I was dying for the time when I could free her lip from there. "What's in it for you then?"

"We'll have to figure it out, won't we?"

It wasn't the most convincing thing I could've told her. I was aware. It was honest, however. We couldn't build anything without that honesty. It wouldn't be fair.

"Y-yeah." Kara breathed out. "But how do we know it's worth it? To go through all the stuff with HR?"

"I don't care if it is or it isn't, but I do care that you have options." I stopped her right there. "I mean, even if we never did anything, the two of us, we're both kinksters, and we're both going to be here often. It's more than enough for me."

Someone started playing music, probably from the riggers' room. It was faint, but the beat of the drums still flowed through the lounge area. It elevated the atmosphere, the sensual hints of bass clinging to the space between us.

"I have another question."

I ignored the way my heart thumped in my chest, on beat with the drums in the background. "Shoot."

24

KARA

My palms felt way too clammy. I thought of hiding them, but I had the feeling that Mónica would just grab them. She'd be gentle about it, of course, but still. I had the feeling that I'd explode the moment she touched me for more than the lightest of caresses. And that had already been tough.

And I had no problem with exploding, but maybe not so soon. That would be embarrassing.

"Kara?"

Damn.

Yeah, I'd said I had a question.

I blinked, once, twice, pulling her back into focus. I should ask my therapist if maybe I should see her more than once a week. I shook my head. Ugh. No one talked about how frustrating it was to keep getting distracted without wanting to.

"Right. Yeah, the question." I licked my lips. "So, basically, it's just... Last night, I got the feeling that if I'd stayed a minute longer in the car, you would've asked me to kiss you. Or something that led to the same end result? Or maybe I just have an overactive imagination, but I don't know, so that's why I'm… asking?"

"Kara."

Her tone was different when she said my name this time. More commanding. It didn't make me recoil, but it made me hyperaware. The air around us felt denser with every second that passed. I couldn't take my eyes off her. I was holding my breath, every ounce of my existence tethered to hers.

It was what happened when I got involved with someone. Fear should be gripping every fiber of my being. It didn't.

Trepidation did.

"Yeah?" I breathed.

"Do you want that?" Mónica kept doing this thing. She leaned forward, brought goosebumps to my skin, but she didn't corner me. I didn't feel cornered, rather. "Do you want me to order you to kiss me?"

"I…"

Mónica moved closer. It was less than an inch, but it felt like ten times that. "Does it turn you on?"

I had to be gaping like a fool, but… Fuck. I didn't think this was going to happen. I would've worn something less exposed, maybe. I clenched my thighs together, too aware of the bare skin and the wetness building there.

"I…" I tried again, my voice an octave higher. "Maybe?"

"Brat." Mónica teased, fondly—and no, it wasn't contradictory. "Come on then. Kiss me, little one."

Ugh. Her calling me little one didn't help. And why did she have to wear so much leather? It looked so buttery soft and shiny.

For a terrifying second, I thought I'd become paralyzed. I thought I'd look like the mess that I felt inside.

That didn't happen. I wasn't sure how I got my legs to work, or how I didn't fumble and fall on the floor, but I moved until I was straddling her hips. I clenched and unclenched my fists. I didn't know what to do with them.

Mónica noticed. She noticed everything. She intertwined her hands with mine, then shifted them to her shoulders. I noticed myself begin to tremble, but I didn't move away.

I stayed.

"You're so good at following directions, aren't you?"

"Huh?" I couldn't string more than two words together if I tried, every synapse misfiring.

"Kiss me," she repeated. "You want to, don't you?"

I bobbed my head up and down, probably a lot. There was no further thinking involved, or needed. Of course I wanted to kiss her. Her lips looked so rosy and soft and fucking *kissable*, dammit. The way her chest rose up and down mesmerized me, had me catching my breath and wanting to sync with her.

"Yeah." It was probably redundant, but putting it out there, into words… There was a sense of freedom attached to it. "I want to."

One breath later, my lips were on hers. The touch was probably clumsy. I didn't care. Couldn't care. Couldn't change it, either.

I wouldn't redo it, anyway. She tasted like fire and ice mixed together. She felt like a warm blanket and a shivering touch down my spine, even before she took control.

Mónica's hand slipped to the back of my neck. She squeezed, just once, gently, but there was no question it was there. Suddenly, I was wrapped up in her. Everywhere I turned, there she was, her breath mingling with mine, her lips on mine, exploring. She didn't demand, but she didn't leave, either. She was firm, solid, reliable when I felt like the gentlest breeze would send me to the floor. Not while we were touching, though, while she was holding me. Her other hand was on my waist, her fingers burning my skin through the admittedly thin fabric.

"Good girl," she whispered.

The words echoed, settling some itch down my very core, but I couldn't focus on them. Her speaking meant she was far from me, and now that I'd tasted her, that I was letting myself be in this liminal space where things felt too sharp and not sharp at all, I couldn't let go of it.

"You're doing so good, little one," she hummed. "Feel so good, too."

I whimpered. The words were too much, but not enough. I needed more.

I tried to lean closer, to let her feel the way my skin was burning up. What was the point of distance, anyway?

Mónica's grip on me tightened, though. She kept me steady. It was grounding and frustrating at the same time.

I panted, blinking her back into focus. My cheeks felt like they were burning up.

"I… Sorry."

Mónica chuckled. It was the way she chuckled when Sergio and I were in Little space. There was a softness to her edges that wasn't there any other time, like she was indulging in a way she usually wasn't. It felt like something to treasure.

"Nothing to apologize for, little one." The hand on my neck shifted to my face. Mónica tucked a strand of hair behind my ear. My hair was always getting in the way. "I could kiss you all day, did you know that?"

"I could kiss you all day, too." I wanted to giggle, but the sound got lodged in the back of my throat. "We should do that."

"We *could* do that," Mónica said, "but I think we had more talking to do."

I chewed the inside of my cheek. "But…"

"But?" Mónica cocked her head to the side.

It was unfair. There was no way she didn't know what I wanted, right?

"I like this."

"I'm glad." She nodded. "What do you like about this?"

Giving her the stink eye wouldn't give me any points, but whatever.

"You," I mumbled. "And it's warm, and safe, and it feels... Good. Right."

They were the most inadequate words to describe how I felt. They were the only ones I could find, though.

My heart beat loudly. I needed her to understand, to see the words I wasn't saying.

"Being on my lap does?" Mónica guessed eventually.

It wasn't all of it, but I nodded anyway. It was a start.

"Yeah."

"You can stay here." Her hands moved to my hips, holding me there. It felt like a weight off, like another layer of pressure taken off me.

"Really?"

"Really." Mónica smiled. "So long as you can speak, you can stay wherever you like."

"Okay." I swallowed.

I could talk—even if it sounded a tiny bit scary.

"So, you already told me about not liking discipline, or the idea of me being too commanding."

I thought she'd say more, but silence set between us instead.

I sighed.

"I can't picture myself liking anything painful or humiliating," I admitted. It felt like a shameful secret to divulge, but I knew that was leftovers from Her. I couldn't let them win. "But I think I can trust you to tell me to do things—like now with the kissing or maybe with others, too."

Was the air in the room more suffocating? I knew I'd only said two sentences, but I felt out of breath. It was disorienting.

It made me dizzy.

"All right." Mónica's hands rubbed up and down my sides. It helped. "So we can play that by ear, yeah? Go slow and check in often?"

"Okay."

"Is there anything else you don't feel confident about?"

"I don't know." I supposed I did, but there was no way I could think that far. "I just want to be Little, and to have fun, with others. And I guess I want to have someone to keep me in check, I guess, but in a fun way."

"Okay." Mónica seemed to mull it over. "One thing I really like when I'm with a sub for more than a night, is have them help with my leather boots."

"Ooh." My eyes darted down to said boots. They were the almost knee high, laced kind. "Like putting them on?"

"And taking them off. Shining them, too."

My breath caught, my heart thumping loudly. "I've never done that before."

"That's okay." Mónica shrugged. "Are you open to trying?"

"Y-yeah," I all but stammered. Flashbacks came to me—the first day I'd seen her boots and my initial reaction. The fear that had coursed down my veins. "She wore boots once."

I wasn't sure how I managed to get the words out, but Mónica didn't rush me, didn't waver.

"Your ex?"

"Yeah." My ears were ringing now. A part of me wanted to retreat, but… No, I couldn't do it. "She made me lick them in front of her friends. Threatened to kick me if I didn't."

I closed my eyes. I couldn't look at Mónica's face, couldn't see the disgust, or annoyance, or apprehension. It would be too much. I knew it was ridiculous, that no one would understand why I'd stayed, why I'd gone through any of it when the thought made me want to barf.

"I'm so fucking glad you're away now."

Her words, the finality of them, pushed my eyes open. Steel determination greeted me. I sucked in a lungful of air. I couldn't look away. It was a different kind of entrapment, but I was trapped nonetheless.

Only, I didn't want to be free.

It probably said many things about me, but I didn't care enough to delve into them.

Not now.

"Me too," I breathed out.

"My boot fetish has to do with worship and service," she explained. "It's not about humiliation."

"I believe you." I did. The acknowledgement had a wave of relief wash through me. "I just… You should know those things, right?"

A voice popped up in my head, saying I was wrong, dumping all my trauma on her, that I should save it—that she didn't want to hear it, and I was fucking everything up already by letting her see.

But fear struck. What if I froze when she told me to untie her laces? What if she thought I was disobeying her, when the reality of it was that I couldn't make my arms work?

Mónica's hand reached my cheek, cupping it, her thumb stroking down my jawline.

I chased after it, burrowing into it.

"I should definitely know about things that may trigger you," she confirmed. "You're doing really good, little one."

For a few moments, I didn't say anything. I let the words, the praise, flow through me. I felt my muscles unclench, relax under her touch.

"You submit so easily, don't you?"

A few months ago, the mere suggestion would've made me run away. Submitting easily had been part of the problem. It was something to be avoided. A sign of weakness.

She'd said that, though.

Right now, as the subtle touch of her fingertips made me shiver, I didn't feel weak.

I felt capable.

Relieved.

"Please, Ma'am."

Mónica's lips ghosted over my cheek. Her scent—leather with an underpowered floral touch—invaded me, grounded me in the fact that I was hers in this moment. Nothing else mattered except the intensity of it.

"Is that how you wanna call me?"

I let my weight fall on her, a progressive show of trust. I needed her anchor. It was only right.

"Yes."

Later, I'd explain why Ma'am fit her better than Mommy, and why I'd rather use Ma'am anyway. Now I just basked in the glow of letting go for the first time in years.

"All right," Mónica murmured. "Are you okay to talk some more?"

"Yeah."

I wasn't so out that I couldn't follow her words. It was just dizzying to experience subspace again, but I wasn't deep.

I liked that she asked, though.

"It's okay if we need to take a break, okay?"

"I know."

"Good girl." Mónica squeezed my waist. I bit my lip. "And are you going to have more questions for me?"

I shook my head no. I probably should, but the truth was, while getting ready for this, I'd only been worried that Mónica wouldn't get anything out of it. That I wasn't what she wanted.

I didn't feel like I wasn't what she wanted when she held me the way she was.

"No?"

"Not right now, Ma'am."

"I guess I'll allow it this one time," she teased. Was it me, or did she shift her legs so that her thigh brushed against me? It was little more than a touch, but it still had me burning up, on the edge of begging. "Wanna talk to me about what you like during sex, then?"

"Huh?"

Maybe I should've taken the out she'd given me.

Maybe she was doing this because I hadn't, and torture like this was what Domms got off on.

Ngh.

I wasn't in the right headspace to be mad about it.

"I mean, from what I saw last month, I'm guessing you're a bit of a size queen, but what else is there?"

I gulped. I *was* a size queen, but the idea of saying it out loud had all air leaving my lungs. "I like bottoming."

"Clearly," she teased, again.

She had a stupidly sexy smile when she wasn't pretending to be the perfect corporate boss.

"Ma'am!" I pouted. "I don't like fingering or using dildos on others. I like oral, but I prefer it if the person is sitting on my face."

"Noted." Her eyes glinted in a way that screamed trouble. "I know you like dildos used on you, but what about other toys?"

"I… like them, too. I like being overstimulated."

Mónica nodded. I couldn't tell anymore if she did it on purpose or not, but she drew me closer, her warmth drawing shivers out of me.

"What about restraints? Sensory deprivation?"

I sucked in a breath. "Restraints are okay with others

watching, and uh, blindfolds are okay, too, but not headphones."

"I can work with both those things," she said.

"Any other questions, Ma'am?" I might've added a whining tilt to my voice.

I didn't care. I wanted to ask her to get me off, to do more than kissing and touching over my clothes.

Mónica chuckled, keeping me still once more when I tried to grind my hips. "Just one. But it's an important one."

The lowering of her voice was the only thing that kept me from grumbling. Or from proving her point about me being a brat—which was one hundred percent false, of course.

"Just give me a sec?"

"Of course, little one." She even tapped the tip of my nose. Ugh. "You're so good, telling me what you need."

Could I hide now? I took her stupid grin as a yes and burrowed against the crook of her neck. She really smelled good. Her arms enveloped me, holding me even tighter than before.

Did I say I was a sucker for hugs?

"Ma'am?"

"Yeah?"

"Do you think we could go to your house after this? Maybe?"

"We could," she agreed easily.

It just helped relax me further. "I'm not being ridiculous, am I?"

"Never."

"And you're not getting tired of me already?"

"Hey." Mónica's tone grew more terse. I should've guessed. She shifted me until she tucked two fingers under my chin before she kept talking. "You're not going to talk shit about yourself under my watch, okay?"

"I…" I squealed, my voice going way too high as my eyes widened. "Okay?"

She watched me for a moment, scrutinizing me, before nodding again. "Did you need a bit longer? We could head out and continue this at my place. Unless you're allergic to cats. Please tell me you're not allergic?"

"I'm not." The anxiety brimming in the voice of the scary big Domme had me giggling. "But you can ask me now. I'm okay."

"Okay." She took a deep breath, her eyes closing for a second. I couldn't remember if I'd noticed before, but she had really dark, really long eyelashes. I'd thought it was eyeliner the first time I met her. "So I know that Sergio is really into mixing sex with age play, but I also know not all Littles like that. I just don't know where you stand there."

I bit the inside of my cheek. I knew the answer to the unspoken question could make or break arrangements.

"I'm not… entirely opposed to *some* play when I'm Little, if things are lighthearted and… playful, I guess?" I winced. I hated that I felt so insecure talking about it. "But most of the time, when I'm Little, sex is literally the furthest thing from my mind and it can be off-putting if it's all people want."

"Hmm." Mónica sank back into the couch. She was calm, calmer than I would've thought. "I really got lucky with you, didn't I?"

"What do you mean?"

"Remember when I said I have a soft spot for Littles, but they don't do it for me?" she asked—to which I nodded, because it had stung at the time. My memory wasn't that bad. "I can't look at you wearing a dinosaur onesie, or whatever, while coloring and giggling and squealing, and think, *Oh yeah, let me fuck her until she can't walk tomorrow*."

That was way too funny.

Or maybe the visual my brain provided was.

The point was, I couldn't help it—falling off her lap while doubling over in laughter.

"Care to tell me what's so funny?" There was hidden laughter in her voice, too.

"Just…" I wheezed. "You said dinosaur onesie."

"Yes…?"

"I would never wear a dinosaur onesie, Ma'am," I managed to say—once I'd pulled some air. "That's so silly."

"Oh, is it now?" Mónica smirked.

Uh oh.

"Yes?"

"I see how it is."

I didn't, but I still squinted my eyes as if I was one hundred percent seeing through her ploy. Domms could never think they had the upper hand. It was Little Survival 101.

"In all seriousness, though." She recovered faster than I did. "Is it because of the dinosaur part, or the onesie part?"

Huh.

"Well, the dinosaur part is a no. I like pastel colors and clouds and unicorns and soft things when I'm Little," I explained, jutting my chin up. Nothing wrong with liking those things, even if they were cliché. "And I've never really had a onesie, so I don't know."

Mónica's eyes widened. "You haven't?"

I frowned. After everything we've talked about, this couldn't be the thing that surprised her.

Could it?

Dommes.

25

KARA

"If you change your mind at any point, for any reason, I'll drive you home, no hurt feelings," Mónica said for what felt like the hundredth time when she parked in front of a townhouse. "Or I'll get you an Uber."

"I'm not scared." I huffed on the outside, but the shaky part that kept making itself known in the back of my mind heavily appreciated all the reassurances. "Your cats won't hate me, right?"

"I mean…"

"Mónica!"

"No, no!" She laughed. She had the audacity to laugh. "Princess will love you for sure, although she might take a few hours before she lets you touch her. Prince doesn't like anyone? But he won't try to maul you. He'll just run away."

Oh.

Well, that wasn't a complete relief—I didn't deal well with pets who didn't love me back—but at least she wasn't saying it was a dealbreaker. Or mocking me too much.

"Are their names really Prince and Princess? You know you don't have to anglicize their names for me, right?"

She chuckled. "Blame my nieces. They're the ones who named them."

"Oooh, right."

It felt strange to talk about family members, but... In hindsight, every topic would probably feel weird when I just wanted to go back to that headspace I'd been in at the club.

"Kara, are you okay?"

"Yeah." I said it too fast, though. Probably. That happened —sometimes. "Sorry."

"No apologizing," Mónica admonished. "Do I need to make it a rule?"

My heart thumped loudly. Once, twice.

"No, Ma'am."

She might have to do it, but I wasn't going to just tell her. That wasn't how it worked.

"So what do you wanna do? Is there any line you don't wanna cross tonight?"

"I..." I gulped down. An apology was at the back of my throat for sounding pathetic or embarrassing. I swallowed it down. "I trust you. You choose."

"Are you sure?"

"I'm sure." If she chose, I could just sink into the same headspace I'd been before. I could *be*, remember and reconnect with who I'd been, with the parts of kink that made me fly high. "Please."

Mónica's hands tightened around the wheel. One second, two seconds. Then she let go, her focus back on me. Shadows covered half of her face. It made it hard to read her. It should worry me, fill me with fear or apprehension.

It didn't.

It was slightly disconcerting. I'd probably need some time tomorrow to really think it through, and process it, or whatever it was mature, well-functioning adults did.

"All right." She nodded, her hand curling around the door handle. "Food first, though."

"Huh?"

Mónica just glanced at me with mirth in her eyes. "It's almost dinnertime, and you barely drank your water at the club. I won't have you fainting on me, little one."

Damn.

She couldn't just use a nickname and make everything okay.

Well, she totally could as proven by my stupid ass nodding with the energy of a kid on too much sugar, but...

It wasn't fair.

"I'll admit I'm not the best cook," she said while we walked up the couple of steps to the small landing in front of what had to be her house, "so any preferences on where I should order from?"

It was on the tip of my tongue to say I could cook for the two of us, but... It turned out that was one thing I wasn't ready for yet. Images began to arise. I was taking too long to answer, too. I knew because Mónica moved to be standing in front of me, until she was all I could see.

It worked.

"Is there any place that delivers Chicago style pizza?" I kind of felt bad for asking, but it had always been a comfort food. "The real one?"

"I think there's a place," Mónica said. Apparently satisfied that I was back in the moment, she focused on getting the door open and leading me inside. "I've never ordered, but I get ads for it sometimes."

"We can try it."

I'd be very sad if it turned out to be normal pizza with a slightly thicker dough, but I'd survive. Normal pizza was comforting, too.

"Anything else?"

"I don't know."

Translation: I was too distracted by the tawny cat that had rushed in to greet Mónica and was now staring at me without blinking.

"This is Princess," Mónica hummed as she petted her distractedly. "You can let her sniff your hand if you want."

I *so* wanted.

"WAS IT GOOD?"

We'd finished the pizza and Mónica had moved to the kitchen so she could load the dishes we used in the dishwasher. I'd offered to help—I had manners—but she'd said no, so I was just sitting on the kitchen island.

I felt guilty, but it was also nice. I usually grew very anxious when someone was feeding me. This was calm. Quiet. Princess had even rubbed herself against my ankles while we finished dinner, so everything was perfect as far as I was concerned.

"So good." I'd actually been surprised.

When we opened the cardboard box, it hadn't quite looked like the pizzas I was used to. Definitely less oily, but the flavors hit home.

"I'm glad," she hummed. "Do you still wanna spend the night?"

"Uh, yeah." I blinked. "Duh."

"Just checking in." She chuckled. My confusion was hilarious now? Tsk. I might have huffed. Sure, it wasn't the most mature, but it also had Mónica staring at me with that playful glint in her eyes. I was quickly becoming addicted to it.

"Don't think I haven't wanted you naked since you showed up in that dress."

I swallowed. There was something about the way she shifted between a caring, considerate date, and an assertive Domme.

"I can get naked."

"I think I'd rather get you naked."

"Uh, sure." That was fine. I wasn't freaking out or anything. My heart wasn't beating wildly or anything. No, it was all fine. "Can I use the bathroom, though?"

"Sure. Let me show you around."

The bathroom was upstairs, conveniently right in front of the main bedroom. Mónica just happened to mention it, then laughed when my cheeks burned bright red.

It wasn't fair.

My cheeks had always had a mind of their own. It wasn't my fault.

Only Littles understood my struggles, though, so I didn't say it. I did pout, and pretended to do it some more when she tried to kiss it better.

The kissing did make it better, obviously, but it was a matter of principles.

It was the same reason I might've stalled a bit in the bathroom and didn't just rush out. Actually, I was going to need some encouragement before I could head out.

KARA

help??

SERGIO

what's up?

weren't you on a date with Mónica?

oh shit

what happened?

do i go pick you up?

Kara !!!!!!

KARA

GIVE ME TIME TO TYPE, GEE !!

i'm at her place??

and we're going to do stuff, i think??

SERGIO

ooohhhh

wait

why are you texting?

go get it !!

KARA

because i'm terrified??

we made out at the club and it was so hot and good but what if i end up disappointing her or something

SERGIO

you really need to learn how to share things in chronological order, just saying

i have so many questions

i'll go bug you in your lunch break or something

KARA

that's not helping!!

SERGIO

how am *i* supposed to help??

in case you missed it somehow, i'm but a poor lonely gay boy

how am i your go to for lesbian sex advice?

> **KARA**
>
> omg !!
>
> i didn't text you for... that

> **SERGIO**
>
> okay then i'm even more confused
>
> and i was already confused, fyi

> **KARA**
>
> ugh
>
> can you just tell me that she won't hate me and the world won't end if i fuck up?

> **SERGIO**
>
> she won't hate you !!
>
> besides, she's seen you getting fucked already, so she's clearly into your sexual you
>
> that makes sense
>
> ... i can't believe i had to say that
>
> you owe me so many milkshakes

> **KARA**
>
> fiiiiiiiiiine

A knock on the door was the only thing that kept me from keeping the texts going. "Toilet swallowed you down, little one?"

I squeaked. Yeah, it was stupid to be shocked that the person who owned the house was there. Whatever.

"All good... Ma'am."

"Wanna open the door, then?"

I bit my lower lip. "Just one sec!"

I'd already done everything I could possibly do in the small room, but it was important that I looked decent—as opposed to on the verge of yet another panic attack.

Cold water didn't have the magical effect I'd thought it would, and finger brushing didn't make a lot of difference. It still was the tiny boost I needed to open the door, so… Yay, small victories.

Nay, eyes widening and compulsive swallowing when Mónica was right there. She just watched. Then she reached an arm out for me, and I almost forgot how to move. Brain: 0.

"Remember when I told you, after the demo with María, that you'd belong to the club, and not just me?"

My breath caught, the temperature in my body rising. I clenched my thighs, but I nodded. I'd dreamed about those words more times than I cared to admit.

"Yeah?"

"Do you want to know what that's gonna look like right now?"

I nodded. I couldn't say I chose to, but was there a choice? I just knew that I needed her to keep talking, needed her to keep walking and cornering me against the sink. I welcomed the marble digging into my skin, the cold that collided against the burning need that kept building.

Mónica ran her fingers up my arms, all the way to my chin. She had a way of forcing me to keep my eyes on her. I just let her do it.

There was little I wouldn't have let her do.

"I am dying to get you naked. To make you do all those sounds you tried to keep quiet at the club, all those gasps and tiny moans and whimpers." Each word was going to one hundred percent kill me, but I was frozen, couldn't tell her to stop. Wouldn't. "I am dying to make you come, to make you go limp against me. To have you sleeping in my bed, next to me."

I whined then. I wanted all of that too. I could just picture it, smell the sweat in our bodies, feel the rightness of it.

"And I plan to do all that, but there's nothing kinky about what I've just said," she kept talking. I wasn't sure I could take much more of it. She didn't care. I didn't, either. "No, when I really claim you, when I show you what it means to be my sub, it will be at the club, with everyone watching. Until you can't remember what it feels like to not feel protected, and loved, and cared for."

Shit.

"I was doing so well, Ma'am!" I managed to start my complaint before the first tear fell down.

A few others followed, but I'd buried my face on her shoulder by then.

Crisis averted, as they said.

Kind of.

"It's okay." Mónica wrapped her arms around me. Not tight, though. I could've just melted. "We can go slow. Doesn't change any of what's gonna happen tonight."

"I want that," I mumbled, "all of what you said, I mean."

"Good." Her lips brushed against my temple. "Come lie down with me, yeah?"

"I'm cold." I hadn't really registered it until the words were out, but I was.

It happened sometimes.

"More reason to hide under the blankets with me, don't you think?"

26

MÓNICA

Kara was a thing of beauty, sprawled on my bed, the sheets wrinkled and disheveled around her. The girl liked to squirm and, fuck, it did things to me.

"Ma'am?" With her face completely flushed, it was impressive that she managed to hold my stare.

I loved her more for it.

"What is it?"

I'd just grabbed a few things from the drawer I kept by my nightstand. Average sized dildo, harness, bullet vibe. The basics. I'd meant it when I said nothing big would happen outside of the club. It had started out as a fantasy I'd built to help her rebuild her trust and sense of community but I'd be lying if I said there wasn't more to it now. It had soon snowballed from there.

I couldn't say who it was for anymore.

I didn't think it was important.

She needed it as much as I did.

"You're not touching me."

I chuckled. That sweet, tiny pout was turning into my biggest weakness. "Patience, little one."

I did fairly quick work of sliding the harness on and slipping the bullet and the dildo in place. I was going to, but there was no need to nudge Kara's legs apart. She did it easily, for me.

"You do so well for me," I rasped. I ran fingers up her inner thighs, watched as the touch made her shiver, her hips thrust off the bed. "So ready for me."

She was completely shaven, her folds glistening under the bright lights in the room. I'd never been a fan of keeping things in total darkness.

"I-I am. Ma'am, please."

I grinned. I could hear her beg for hours.

Probably too cruel for the first time I sank into her, though.

"That's it," I praised as she shifted while I positioned the tip of the dildo against her entrance. "Such a good little helper."

Kara just let out another grumbling whine.

"You're going to take all of it, are you?" I started sliding in as I spoke, my free hand holding on to a fistful of blonde hair. I didn't pull. I didn't need to; I just needed her to be aware of it. "Does it feel good? To be stretched open?"

"S-so good," she gasped, her head tilting back. Her legs wrapped around my waist. It shifted the angle, sinking me deeper into her. "Ngh, please, please, please, more."

"I'll give you what you need. Don't worry."

I thrust faster, deeper. The way she showed no resistance was enchanting. I trailed kisses down her jawline, her neck, teased her breasts.

Kara was loud, moaning and whimpering and groaning. Sweat was beginning to slide down my forehead. The vibe I almost forgot to turn on had me desperate for more—friction, pressure, anything. Making her scream became a need.

"Turn around, little one." I panted, shifting back. "On all fours."

She was literally shaking when I pulled out, but she nodded. She almost couldn't hold her weight when she turned around. I only gave her a couple of seconds to right herself before I was pushing back into her. Warmth radiated from her flushed skin. It was inviting.

"Fucking hell, little one." I moved one hand to her hip and the other to her shoulder. I didn't want her to end up with any bruises, but… She probably would. "You're really going to take all I give you, huh?"

Kara's voice was wrecked as she tried to respond. I didn't quite make out what she was saying.

"What was that, little one?" I squeezed her hips harder, stilling her for the briefest second. "Take a deep breath for me and try again."

A broken sob came out, mingled with her panted breaths and soft mewls. "Need to come, Ma'am. Please."

"You *need* to, huh?" I cooed, going back to driving into her. Faster, more roughly. "Make yourself come, then. Show me how good you are with your fingers."

She didn't last long after that, her cries becoming my catalyst to let go as well. I let my weight fall on her, helped her to her stomach while she tried to breathe lungfuls of air through the aftershock. I kept thrusting into her, fighting the way my legs wanted to go limp, fighting the remnants of my own orgasm.

Fuck. I was already vibrating with a hundred ideas, everything I could do to her in the club, everything I could put her through.

"You really are the best little sub, aren't you?"

Kara half whimpered, half groaned. "Don't pull out?"

"I won't." I did kiss her temple and shifted so I could switch off the vibe pressed against my clit. I was a fan of having multiple orgasms, but I couldn't always deal with the overstimulation right after riding one. "Keeping you stuffed full is no hardship."

"Mean."

I playfully scoffed.

Of course I had to fall for a tiny little brat.

THE SCRATCHING at the bedroom door when I didn't let the cats in at night worked better than any alarm. However, it wasn't what woke me up today—even if the sound of claws hitting the wood I'd already had to replace twice was there, in the background.

No, what woke me up was Kara. After the dildo had inevitably slipped out—and we woke up a couple of times during the night—I'd wrapped an arm around her waist and spooned her against me. She'd shifted, though, shifted us, to be wrapped around me like an octopus.

Awareness began to creep in. Worried voices in my head telling me how irresponsible it had been of me. I should've waited to bring her here until I could formalize all the stuff with HR. I should've slowed her down, probably.

She was just…

I couldn't. For the first time, I got the impression that I was seeing the real Kara, the one that wasn't riddled with fear or hiding under a wall. I couldn't say no to it.

"Ma'am?"

Glinting blue eyes peered up at me. Her voice—softer and lighter than I would've thought when she'd just woken up—sent shivers down my spine.

"Hey, little one." I knew my voice came out much raspier than hers.

It always took me a little while to sound like a human being in the morning.

She burrowed against my skin, the touch burning and soothing in the same breath. I wrapped an arm around her, pulling her even closer. I hadn't known I had it in me. I usually kept more of a distance, was bigger on protocols. I couldn't not touch her, though.

"Can I ask you something?"

"Sure."

"Uh…" Kara leaned up on one elbow. Her hair fell over me in a small cascade. "Will you, maybe, sit on my face?"

That was not what I expected to hear this early in the morning. "Haven't you just woken up?"

She shook her head. The way her hair brushed against my chest was stupidly distracting. Another thing I hadn't known? I was apparently extra sensitive in the mornings.

"Been for a while." She tried to shrug and play nonchalant, but a flush was creeping up to her cheeks. "I'm horny."

"We have work."

"I'll be quick," she rushed out, eyes slightly bewildered.

Slightly panicked.

I stopped thinking there, stopped trying to be the voice of reason.

Panic was the one thing I never wanted her to feel around me.

"Blame the corniness on my still half-asleep brain, but I'm more than happy to add sitting on your face to my morning routine." It made me cringe inside, but it had Kara relaxing, looking at me with the brightest smile. Which meant it had worked. "Now get comfortable for me, will you?"

Kara was quick to squirm until she was on her back, head on the pillow.

"Three taps if you need me to let up, okay?"

"Yes, Ma'am," she breathed.

Fuck.

It might have sounded incredibly corny, but I would be really considering doing as I said if this was what it looked like.

I didn't usually wake up aroused, but I doubted it would matter.

My moves weren't graceful—I needed coffee before that could happen—but I managed. Some rustling ensued, and my knees sank on the pillow, framing her face. I had one hand grabbing onto the headboard before I slid down.

The second her tongue touched my clit, my thighs quivered, my body shaking as I took a sharp breath. I tightened the grip on the headboard, my other hand moving to her head.

Her licks were tentative, almost shy. I would've counted on more enthusiasm for the person who had asked me to do this. After the shock of it faded, I caressed her scalp, pulling her attention back to me.

"Look at me," I kept my voice low. Her eyes widened as she obeyed, panicked. The idea seeped in that it might have to do with something her ex did. It wasn't something I wanted to spend much time on—definitely not when I was still sitting on her face, and I wanted to enjoy it. "Take a deep breath for me."

I didn't specify it, but she buried her nose between my folds to do it. My whole body tensed. It was primal, like nothing I'd ever seen. Electricity buzzed through me, wanting more, needing to push, to see how far I could take her.

Not now, I reminded myself.

"Good girl," I grunted. "Now I just want you to do as I say, okay? You just do what I say."

I lifted my hips slightly, just enough so I could see her

bob her head up and down. Her stormy blue eyes looked dazed already, half hooded.

Good.

One thing I'd observed was that Kara performed better when she let go and just followed her instincts.

"You're so good to me, little one." My voice was strained, but I pushed through. "I bet you're gonna keep being good, right? And you're going to suck on my clit really nice. You're gonna show me how happy you are that I'm letting you do it, how you know it's a privilege."

I hadn't finished talking when she did exactly that, her lips wrapping around my most sensitive skin.

"That's more like it," I hummed, fingers curling tighter around her hair. "You just keep doing that, and lapping up everything I give you, yeah?"

Time lost meaning after that. Kara didn't need more directions than those, the shy licks quickly turning into desperate ones, into moans coming from both of us, into her fingers digging into my upper thighs, pulling me closer.

I didn't have time to consider she was pulling strings she hadn't been told to pull. It didn't matter. I just let myself get drunk on the pleasure, on the pressure of her tongue, her lips, the almost innocence in her apparent inexperience.

When she let go, Kara was just… Her whole body screamed enthusiasm, and energy. It didn't take me long to reach the point where my body began quivering, convulsing around her, muscles tensing before unclenching and letting go, my lips parted in a not so silent O.

It didn't stop her, her newfound confidence keeping her there, licking up everything until her face from her nose down to her chin was glistening, covered in my fluids.

The image hit me hard enough to push a second orgasm out of me, to keep riding her face until a stupid alarm broke the magic shifting around us.

I really was corny in the mornings.

"Let's get you in the shower," I mumbled.

Still had to be responsible, right? And there was no way I wasn't returning the favor. The shower was just the most logical step.

"Okay." *Now* her voice croaked. Completely wrecked, actually. "Thank you, Ma'am."

The flush in her cheeks hadn't gone down. Later, I'd ask if she was thanking me for letting her eat me out, or for helping her to do it. Right now, my priorities lay elsewhere.

"You are just too perfect for me, little one."

27

KARA

A week had passed by way too fast. I still didn't like the way time ran. Nothing big had happened. Work was quiet. I caught Mónica complaining a couple of times about how long Legal was taking, but that was about all that had changed so far. I just kept attending video call meetings with prospective clients and acting as a liaison on the phone so that international companies felt confident about who they were working for.

I didn't quite like the ethics of a company not trusting Mónica—or her brothers, really—on the basis that their English didn't sound like they were perfect native speakers, but... That was just life and capitalism and all those things at work, I guessed.

That wasn't the problem I was struggling with now, anyway. No, the problem was that every time one of her brothers tried to catch her in her office, or worse, every time they approached me, I had the instant fear that they knew. It was irrational, I knew. It was even more irrational to think that they were going to call me out, shame me for it.

It was happening, though, and it had me jumpier than usual.

I hated it.

I hated that I couldn't quite relax, even if everything else in my life was…

I mean, I was scared of saying perfect, because that was how I ended up in bad situations, but it kind of was. Mónica kept talking me into spending the evening, and some nights, at her place, or she indulged me—her words—with a milkshake after work. She was solid, and warm, and there, and I was even beginning to talk to others in the club. María kept leaving me all flustered, though, which made Mónica all huffy, so I only texted with her if I wanted to laugh at Mónica's expression.

She'd said she didn't mind when I confessed what I was doing.

She low-key threatened with buying less milkshakes, but that was fine.

I could buy my own milkshakes.

Even texting Erika was all right. Sergio had looked so bewildered when I'd said she wasn't as scary as he made her out to be, but it was true. He liked to complain a lot, but Erika was nice, and she always asked if things were okay both before and after.

I liked that.

"Any messages while I was out?" Mónica's voice almost made me jump.

I hadn't seen her for most of the day. She did way too many visits to the sites. It was commendable and I believed in her reasoning, but I could be pouty about it if I wanted, too.

Benefits of being Little.

"They're all on your desk," I still answered promptly because it felt important that I could prove I was professional. "I got a couple calls asking for updates, and then one more asking for a budget. I wrote down all their details and said we'd contact them within the week."

"Any problems?"

"Nope." I shook my head. I really was getting the hang of this quickly. "I also reorganized your calendar to account for the delay with that distributor you said, and Noel mentioned a family trip, so I moved things around for it."

Mónica scrunched up her nose. She did that when there was something in the office she didn't like—and that was a common occurrence.

"I'm guessing something for my parents' anniversary." She sighed. "Did he say where?"

"Lyon. I was going to ask if you wanted me to sort out your plane tickets."

She mulled it over for a few seconds. That involved more nose wrinkling, and some foot tapping while she still leaned against the opened door.

"Yeah." She walked deeper into my office. The door swung closed behind her, which was when she revealed a manila folder from behind her back. "Legal finally sent me something I approved of. There's a copy in your inbox, too, but read it over before we close down, okay?"

Shit.

My heart started beating really wildly, my palms soon feeling sweaty.

"Hey." Mónica moved around the desk, grabbing my chair until the wheels were facing her. "This is not a deal-breaker. I just want you to read it so we can discuss it over a milkshake, and I can go back to harassing them tomorrow, okay?"

"B-but…"

She said she'd approved it, but what if it wasn't as good as what Mónica had promised? I didn't really care about all the financial shit, as I had quite a bit saved up, but I cared about staying here and not having to move back.

"Kara?" She was frowning now. Oh, shit. I was ruining everything already. This was a terrible idea. "Kara, remember what we said? Even if you didn't pass the probationary period, which you will, and even if HR wanted to screw you over here, we'd make sure you had a job before your grace period was over."

"You and Erika," I clarified.

Everything felt muddy, but I could process as much. They'd both said that. Erika would hire me in her gym even if I didn't know anything about how gyms worked and all the machines scared me. Mónica would pimp me to her other business friends, too, if she had to. It would be okay, but it still felt scary.

"Exactly."

I nodded. Mónica rubbed the inside of my wrist with her thumb. It made me shiver. She was really into physical touch as a love language, but not usually while in the building.

"C-can you… Can you tell me what it says?"

She squeezed my wrists before she let go. She stood so close, and part of my heart beating so rapidly was due to her, but not close enough I could really feel her. Not the way I needed.

I shook off that thought. Just before, I was saying I had to prove that I could be professional. Acting needy and Little was not that.

"Long story short?" She licked her lips. She was still squatted down, eyes unwavering from mine. "If anything were to happen between us, and we weren't comfortable working with each other, we'll keep you three months on payroll, and up to a year without your salary so you appear as employed. HR has drafted letters of recommendation already that you'd get access to and could use while searching for a new job, and I'm obligated to give you a positive reference if I were to receive a phone call from a prospective employer."

"Is that even legal?"

"I'm sure they're using some legal loopholes." Mónica chuckled. "But sometimes, that's what they're paid to do."

"Way to make it sound dark," I grumbled.

She just squeezed my wrists again. "Do as I said, okay?"

"Okay." Why was my throat so dry?

Ugh.

"IT'S TOO good to be true, right?" I pouted.

Lucas laughed. Alex had been grumbling all week about him going back to work too soon, but he looked good to me. He was less grouchy than he'd started to be the longer he was stuck inside the house. Today had been his first shift since he'd twisted his ankle, and he looked weirdly happy.

"So what if it is?" he asked.

We were in the kitchen because that was where he'd been when Mónica dropped me off. I'd signed on the papers—because I'd be stupid not to—and had a weird interview with HR today. The world hadn't imploded, so Mónica had asked me to have dinner at her place, and I couldn't have said no if I'd tried.

"I don't know, but… these things don't just happen."

"From what I understand, a boss being into their secretary happens quite a lot."

"Hey!"

Lucas raised his palms in the air. I huffed. "What I was going to say is, the difference here is she has a higher understanding of it, and her company has money to burn. So, take it."

"Well, I already did. It just feels weird."

"So start looking for other jobs." He shrugged. "You have a safety net to fall back on."

I'd thought about it, before Monica had handed me the forms earlier in the week, but it was terrifying. It made me an awful human being, but the idea of starting a new job, where they may not care as much about kicking me out? I might be regaining more confidence as the days passed, but I didn't know if I'd ever be that confident.

"Yeah, I guess," I said regardless. I knew Lucas was the rational one here, not silly old me. It stung a bit, but it was nothing new. "She invited me to an event at the club on Saturday, and I think I'll spend the night and then Sunday at her place."

"So no baking goods for us this weekend?" Lucas teased.

See? The two of them complained about my mothering ways, but the second I left for one weekend, the first thing they thought about was my food.

They thought they had me fooled, but no, sir.

"Sorry."

"Don't sweat it. Just text if you need anything, okay?"

"Okay."

I didn't think much about it. Sure, if something went really wrong, I knew I *could* text him—or Alex—but they wouldn't be my go-to. For one thing, I was pretty sure they were scheduled for a shift at the hospital. For another... what could go so wrong? It was going to be me, Mónica, Sergio, Erika, and the others from the queer mattress. There would be a couple more I hadn't met yet, but Sergio vouched for them, so it was good.

And, before they all arrived, us Littles were going to have a playdate. I was more excited about the latter, to be honest.

Then again, those were probably my nerves talking. A playdate with other Littles was safe. It was predictable, familiar.

Group play was a bit of that, too, but I didn't know what Mónica had planned. When I pushed, she said she thought I deserved a proper welcome into the community. The only thing that came to mind when she said that was that they'd all fuck me as some weird initiation ritual, but... Surely that wouldn't be it, and I hadn't known how to ask nicely, so I'd let it be.

I still trusted her, though, one hundred percent. It would be fine.

28

MÓNICA

"You're not going to tell me I'm in over my head?"

"Nope," Erika said while pinching Eli's nipple through their gimp suit. They'd already arrived when I showed up to drop off Kara for the Littles' playdate, and of course, Erika was not going to miss the chance to toy with them. "I called you out when you were both doing that weird game of will they, won't they. You're in the clear now, and I have a good feeling about it."

"No comments about going too fast, either?"

"Oh, please." She rolled her eyes now, sinking deeper into the couch. Eli followed the movement blindly—I wondered if they realized how in tune they were with her for someone who didn't want anything outside of these walls. "You yourself said it, you've been pretty vanilla with her. How is that going fast?"

"I don't know." I shook my head.

I didn't know what had gotten into me in the past hour. The plan had formed in my head clear as day, and I *knew* I could pull it off. More than that, I knew it was the right plan, the right scene to give Kara—and me—exactly what we needed.

"I don't have to give you a lecture on how kinksters tend to move at different paces, right?"

"I thought you didn't agree with that idea."

"I don't agree with the way people interpret it," she scoffed while pinning me with one of her looks. She'd been perfecting them over the years. It was a pity that there was not a submissive bone in my body. "Doesn't mean I don't agree with the principle of it."

"Yes, ma'am."

Erika scoffed. I rolled my eyes. She'd hate me if I told her, but she could be dramatic when she wanted to.

She was probably about to prove my point, but commotion from the Littles' room stopped us both. They could get loud sometimes, but that was Kara's voice.

Kara didn't get loud.

"Go check it out, and I'll show up if you're not back in five."

I was already on my feet, so I just nodded and stormed to the room. Anxiety took a hold of me. It wouldn't make sense that Kara was having another panic attack if she'd been the one shrieking, but that was the only image my brain was not so helpfully providing.

It didn't get better when I opened the door. Jen and Marga stood to one side of the room, looking sulky, with their arms crossed and exchanging glances.

Kara had her back to me, arms wrapped around… Sergio?

"What's going on here?"

Kara spun around right away. "Ma'am!"

I studied her face before I moved to do anything else. She looked flushed, but there were no tear tracks or any remnants of a panic attack. That helped me breathe easier.

"What's going on, baby girl?"

The nickname fit her even more today. Instead of the fluffy sweatshirt she'd worn for her first playdate, she was wearing a dress similar to the yellow one she'd worn for me. This was pink, though, with glittery fabric and clip-on wings in the back. It was absurd, and yet I'd never seen her so genuinely happy as when she twirled around in it for me.

"Sergio is crying."

Fucking hell. I cursed inwardly but didn't show it, instead moving deeper into the room. Yeah, he was hiding against Kara and crying.

"What happened?"

I didn't touch him, but he looked up then. These two were going to kill me one of these days. Sergio just had a way of looking so fucking sad, like an abandoned puppy.

"She said I'm her best friend and she loves me, Ma'am," he sniffled as he spoke, then he was crying again.

Kara held him tighter, but I didn't miss the panicked look she sent my way.

It was one of those days, then—when emotions ran high and everything could set him off, then.

"What happened before? You were screaming."

"Well, yeah." Kara huffed. If she kept squeezing him any tighter, she was going to cut off his blood flow, but I'd give it a couple of minutes to point it out. "I had to defend him."

It was also one of those days when Littles thought we Domms were born with mind-reading abilities.

I started to see many deep breath exercises in my near future.

"What did you have to defend him from?"

"Because they weren't being nice, Ma'am!" Kara all but vibrated. I could tell she wanted to wave around with her arms, and not being able to was only adding to her frustration. "They just came and said you'd told them they had to apologize to him, and I said that's not how you apologize. It's true, because if you start like that, you're saying you don't believe in what you're saying and you're just doing what you're told and that's not nice. And I said he deserves a proper apology, and they had to start again, but they keep saying they don't understand, and I don't know how to make myself any clearer!"

"Okay." I placed a hand on her arm before I focused on Jen and Marga, who looked confused but like they still wanted to protest. "Why don't you two go grab something to drink and wait for your Dom with Erika? And then the four of you can talk when emotions aren't running so high."

It earned me some scowls, from Kara, too, but they eventually nodded.

"But, Ma'am, I'm right about this, and it's important, even if Sergio tried to stop me because it was fine. It was not fine."

"That's when you told him he was your best friend?"

Kara looked down as she spoke, her cheeks burning bright red. "Well, yeah."

"Seems like it's meant a lot to him," I hummed. "Why don't you two sit down on the mats?"

I thought there would be some grumbling, but... No. They literally just plopped down on the floor. There was no way it hadn't hurt, but they still did it. Quite synchronized, too.

"I don't wanna be their friend anymore, Ma'am." Kara pouted. "I thought I did after our first playdate, but I don't wanna anymore."

"All right," I placated her and withheld a sigh to myself before I sat down in front of them. "You don't have to be friends with everyone, baby girl."

"Well, I know that, but—"

"Ma'am," Sergio interrupted. He'd stopped crying, too,

even if his eyes still looked glassy. "She's going to stay with us, right? Because she's my best friend, too."

Damn.

No, my heart didn't start beating at double the speed. Kara's seemed to be doing the same, her whole body tensing.

"I would like her to."

Sergio chewed the inside of his cheek before nodding. "You need to get her Elsa's dress."

"I… do?"

"Yeah!" The little shit sat up on his knees. "She has her hair, and she's Little! It's in her blood."

"I'm…" It really was hard to take Littles seriously like this. So much whiplash. "Does Kara want to dress up as Elsa?"

He crossed her arms right away. "She lets me braid her hair like hers."

"I see."

My eyes shifted to her, though. What she liked and didn't like to do when she was Little wasn't something we'd spent a lot of time discussing. I suspected it was partly because of her fears that I didn't want a Little, and partly because of my insecurities about not having owned one before.

"I do like it when he braids my hair," she admitted in the tiniest of voices.

"And she'd look so pretty, Ma'am!"

I chuckled. "Are you saying she doesn't always look pretty, boy?"

"W-what?"

"Ha!" Kara stuck out her tongue at him.

They were ridiculous together, but I could see how they'd hit it off so fast to now be each other's best friends—even if it was Little space talk.

"All right, all right." I sighed. "I'm sure we can come up

with a Frozen event at some point, and you can both dress up."

"Ohhh, I can go as the snowman!"

"S-sure, I don't see why not."

My bewilderment had them both break out in giggles, at least.

"You're silly, Ma'am."

"I sure am." I shook my head. "Come here, you two."

They didn't fight this, either, wrapping up around me as if it was a lifeline.

"Okay," I said while patting their backs, "are we still up for playing later tonight?"

"Of course, Ma'am." Sergio scoffed. "I am a big boy."

"You sure about that?" I teased.

Before he could complain—or break out in tears again—though, I gave him a squeeze tight enough to rival Kara's.

"I'm up for playing too, Ma'am," Kara mumbled, "even if you haven't told me much of what's gonna happen, and that's just cruel."

I scoffed. "Do we need to negotiate discipline this early on?"

"W-what?" she squealed, pulling back—or trying to. "But I've done nothing!"

"You just conveniently forget that I explicitly asked you if you wanted a play by play, and you said no."

"I said I trusted you," she protested. "As in, you didn't have to tell me *everything*, but that doesn't mean…"

I shifted—as much as I could—so I had a better read of her. "Do you need me to tell you?"

The wording had the desired effect. Kara quieted, the words she'd had on the tip of her tongue swallowed back.

"No, Ma'am."

"Good girl." I kissed the top of her head. "And you know you'd still be a good girl if you'd said yes, right?"

"Yes, Ma'am."

"And you can change your mind at any time?"

"Yes, Ma'am."

"That's my girl."

There was just something about the way she looked up at me, that blush spreading down her cheeks to her neck. There was a certain kind of worship there, of excitement for life. I couldn't see it ever getting old.

"Hey." Erika's voice had me turning toward the door. "Tony dropped by earlier and grabbed the two subs. Everything okay in here?"

"We're good." I cleared my throat. "Did they say anything?"

"Yeah." With the way she was rolling her eyes, it wouldn't have been anything good. I'd have to ask later. "Remind me again why we're letting cishet people in?"

I chuckled. "Because we need to cover the costs of this building?"

She frowned. "We should get more CEO ice queens like you. Then we charge people's memberships based on income, and we're good."

"I'm not a CEO, but sure. Go find us."

29

KARA

There were too many people. Well, not really, I guessed, but there were more people than I thought there would be. There was Sergio, and Erika, and Mónica, of course, and then there was María, and Eli, and Jaime, and Cece, but there were two other people I didn't know. And I heard Mónica say two other people just canceled last minute.

How many people did she want to fuck me in front of?

Ugh.

I didn't even know if that was what she wanted—although I'd be into it. Maybe I'd ask her.

Later.

After she revealed her surely evil plans.

It was kind of wild. Here I was, thinking about Mónica's surely evil plans, and I was fine with them. I was enjoying it —the attention, the knowledge that she was doing things for me, the safety I felt around her.

There were lots of changes in only a couple of months of knowing her.

One thing that hadn't changed was that patience was not my thing.

"Who are they, Ma'am?"

They looked intimidating. Weirdly similar, too, with all the piercings and tattoos and the shaggy hair.

"Who?" Mónica repeated. Was she really going to play silly games? "Oh, León and Danny. They're sport junkies who double as pain sluts into CNC and primal play."

Well, at least she could follow my gaze and get to the point—but wait.

"Ma'am?" I searched her face. I'd just been thinking about how much I trusted her. She wouldn't have betrayed that, right?

"What?" She frowned, which was a good reaction, I supposed, but also bad, because I wasn't sure how to explain the doubts that were beginning to plague me. "I'm not going to sic you on them, baby girl."

"Oh." I wasn't going to lie; that helped me breathe a little better. "So this is not some initiation ritual where everyone is gonna fuck me or have their way with me, and only then will I be let into the sect?"

Mónica just blinked at me, but to be fair, it wasn't that out there. "Is that what you thought was gonna happen?"

"Maybe?" I hesitated. Surely, this wasn't the most outlandish thing I'd ever said or done. "I mean…"

"So." Uh oh. She got that gleam in her eyes that all Dommes got. Shit. "What you're saying is that you imagined everyone here defiling you, and you still showed up today?"

"Technically, you drove me here, Ma'am. Just saying."

"Don't give me sass when I'm planning to fulfill your fantasies here."

Yeah, I was right to fear that look. "I never said it was a fantasy, Ma'am."

She just shrugged. "Semantics."

Domms.

"So what are we going to do then?"

"Patience."

I huffed. Where was the fun in that? And why was everyone so chill? Everyone except for Sergio and I were just sitting on the giant mattress from the room I'd been in for the group play. They were just so… relaxed, in a circle. Why was no one else squirming? It wasn't fair. I didn't deal well with uncertainty.

The two new guys kept staring at me, too, as if I were prey. It made me swallow and inch closer to Mónica. She had said she wouldn't sic me on them, right? She'd better have meant it. Maybe it was because I was still halfway in Little space, but they looked mean.

"M-Ma'am."

"Okay, okay… Do you know what all these people have in common?"

"Uh…" I stared at her blankly. What kind of question was that? I'd barely had a couple conversations with most of them. I was supposed to play spot the difference now? "They're all kinksters, and part of the alphabet mafia?"

Mónica, along with a few others, chuckled. I didn't have the bandwidth to check who exactly was betraying me. "They are, but there's something else."

"Okay…" I swallowed. "What is it?"

Of course Mónica didn't answer right away—because she was mean like that. No, she shifted closer, and started caressing my cheek in that way that made me shiver. It was really unfair.

"Remember when I asked you to share what you envisioned for us?" I nodded, feeling my body temperature going up, but it didn't stop her from talking. "You said you saw group play, but I was there, telling you what to do, and telling the others what to do."

I kept my eyes closed. There was no way I could see what everyone would be thinking. It wasn't embarrassing, exactly, but it still made me vulnerable. Flayed open.

"Yeah," I croaked out.

"But you also said you didn't trust groups, that other Domms would sit idly while you were hurt."

I nodded. My breathing was picking up. I clenched my fists. Dammit, I wanted to stay in the moment, not get lost in visions of the past, and panic, and…

"Look at me, baby girl."

I gasped, the command feeling like a glass of water when I needed it most. My eyes found her immediately, latching on to the flecks of gold there. She caressed my cheek again, a silent praise that threatened to be more than I could take.

"Every person here, they've all at one point or another either interrupted a scene directly if they saw something they didn't like, or they reached out to a Dungeon Master to intervene."

"O-oh."

I swallowed. I needed a second to process.

"There's not even the tiniest doubt in my mind that they'd stop me right here, right now, if you looked like you weren't enjoying what was going on," she said. "Not one. And no, it doesn't matter that they've known me longer."

"That's true," María spoke from my left. "We stopped Tony plenty of times when he started bringing subs, and he founded the place."

Jen and Marga's Dom? But then, did that mean he wasn't a good Dom? I knew I'd said I didn't want to be their friend, but should I check in on them? I didn't want to—

"Did you have to mention Tony, of all people?" Mónica sighed. "They have an… unconventional arrangement, but I assure you Jen and Marga are all right, and we check in on them."

I'd still feel better doing it myself, but I nodded along. I understood what Mónica was doing. I didn't want to get trapped in my head.

"María's examples aside," it was Erika's voice that broke through the mist beginning to form, "subbies, especially Littles like you, as strong as you are, you make yourselves incredibly vulnerable, too. We are aware that you do, and there's no way we wouldn't keep a closer eye on you, that we wouldn't help keep you safe."

I swallowed. I wanted to believe her so badly. If I thought about it, deep down, I did. Maybe it was too soon to admit it out loud—there was no logical way to explain it, and it was admittedly reckless—but I did. Knowing I did helped.

"Right." I cleared my throat. "I feel bad that you all have to come here because I'm a mess."

"Hey." Mónica's tone and the way her fingers dug into my side had my whole body sitting straighter. "Talk bad about yourself one more time, and we'll have problems."

Shit.

I gulped down. We hadn't talked about what discipline would look like between us. I'd mentioned I was open to time-outs, or lines, or service-related stuff. Speech restriction if I'd fucked up really badly. Mostly, though, I really didn't want to be punished.

"Sorry, Ma'am."

"Good girl," she breathed against the top of my head. It was primitive, as if she wanted to scent me, or mark me as hers. I shouldn't have been into it, but it was doing things to me. "Now, will you just hear what everyone has to say?"

So this was an intervention. I hated that I didn't dislike the idea.

It actually had me feeling all fluttery inside—that these people who barely knew me still cared enough to be here.

"Will I get kisses?"

"Hmm," Mónica teased. There was laughter hidden in her voice. I could tell. "You drive a hard bargain, baby girl."

"I like when you call me that," I whispered.

She'd started doing it more consistently the day before. It was special. She called all the other Littles little ones, which was also a butterfly-inducing nickname, but baby girl felt like it was reserved for me.

"Baby girl?" she hummed, her lips pressing against my neck. "Isn't that what you are?"

I nodded, nibbling on my lip. I was still sure some spicy time was going to happen—we had to be in the room with the mattresses for a reason—but that didn't mean I wanted to start things off because I was a needy mess, on top of being a regular mess.

Thank fuck I knew how to use my inside voice. I wouldn't survive a day as Sergio.

"That's right." Mónica kept peppering soft, teasing kisses down my neck as she spoke. "Now listen to the pups, yeah?"

"Uh…" Jaime spoke first, but they both moved closer, tagging Eli with them. The three of them were the only ones in full gear, I noticed—Jaime and Cece wearing their puppy stuff and Eli their gimp suit. "To be fair, we didn't really prepare anything, but I mean… We were in an orgy together, so you're one of us now."

Cece barked, which was funny. I giggled, then covered my mouth with one hand. Today wasn't supposed to be about having fun, but I liked that there could be silly things like that and no one complained.

"Classy, boy," Erika teased him.

I didn't see her grab anything, but he still jumped back. I didn't say that jump looked more like a cat than a dog jump. A quick glance at Sergio said he thought the same.

"Yeah, yeah." One of the pierced guys said. I didn't know who was León and who was Danny, but this one had lighter hair. "Now can we talk about why you're scared of us?"

"I-I'm not!" I spluttered, sitting back. Everyone chuckled which… It wasn't fair. "I'm a big girl."

"Sure thing."

"León," Mónica warned.

Okay, so Lighter Hair was León. That was a good mnemonic rule; Lighter—León. I wasn't sure how that helped me, but… They said information was power, right?

Without thinking, my fingers grasped around the fabric of Mónica's shirt.

It didn't bring the same comfort of a stuffie, but it was still comforting. We had to talk about her getting softer clothes.

"But it's kind of relevant, isn't it?" he pushed. "What on Earth did you tell her about us?"

Mónica shook her head. She was opening her mouth to answer, but I beat her to it. It wasn't that I was looking forward to it, but I had a point to prove.

"She said that you're pain sluts and into CNC and primal play," I parroted. I might be beaming a bit too much when everyone looked at me with a mix of pride and shock. "And something about being sports junkies, but I don't know how that's important."

León snorted while the one with jet black hair coughed. "We go hiking and like camping out, and we're sports junkies?"

She didn't look too apologetic. "That's more physical activity than you'll ever catch me doing."

"Erika is a goddamn gym trainer!" He waved around. It was kind of funny. Sadists got riled up so easily. "Is she a sports junkie, too?"

"Nah, she's good."

Erika glanced at Mónica with a raised eyebrow, but she

didn't get into it. Probably because she was just shaking her head at both of them for the example they were setting.

That made it really hard not to laugh.

Sergio was literally covering his mouth with both hands not to.

I really shouldn't be checking on him if I didn't want to end up failing.

"Anyway," León rasped, attention back on me. I shivered. I thought I did a good job at covering it, though. "So what about that description scares you?"

"Uh…" I looked around. Everyone was looking at me, waiting. I tried to search for shame or judgment in their faces. There was none, but it didn't help as much as I thought it would. "I don't… have good experience. With pain stuff. Any pain."

The playful Sadist act dropped almost as soon as I started talking, turning serious. Danny looked more subdued, too, less… staring in that intimidating way I wasn't about to admit it was intimidating.

"Do you wanna know how I met Dan?"

"Uh…" I glanced back at Mónica. It defeated the whole *I'm a big girl* speech, but if he was about to go off about whipping someone, I might need to bolt. "Do I?"

She watched me for a moment. "I think you should."

I sighed. So much for reassurance. I still turned back so that I was facing the two new guys. "Fine."

"It was what, six years ago?" He pulled Danny closer as he spoke, arm wrapped around his midsection. "So, for context, my brother was in the Army, and he died overseas. His best friend there brought his body back, and he… basically became my surrogate brother. I genuinely worshiped the land the guy walked on."

There was a pause when Danny turned around to place a

chaste kiss over his chest. It was sweet, and I might have had to blink away tears.

In my defense, it was turning out to be an emotional day.

"Flash forward now to him bringing me here. I'd confessed to him I was interested in SM stuff, and it turned out his best friend was a big time Sadist." He chuckled ruefully, which was enough of a clue to what he thought about that now, I supposed.

Mónica wrapped her arms around me from behind, her lips staying on my shoulder. I liked that she was so affectionate with me. Gave me that extra layer of warmth nothing else did.

"I was stoked at the time. The lounge area was a bit different, stuffier, but we were basically there, having a couple of beers, and I think I'm in paradise, that I really have found my community and I was about to have the time of my life."

He ran a hand through his hair. It brought my attention to his hand tattoos, but I couldn't quite read what they said.

It was silly, but distractions like that helped ground me—if I didn't take it too far.

"You there with me?"

"Y-yeah, sorry." I looked down, heat spreading down my cheeks. "Got distracted."

"That's fine, sweets." I still felt bad he'd noticed, my stomach cramping just slightly, but he sounded genuine, so… That meant I could move on, right? "So now, cue in a sub walking toward the guy. The guy who was talking about showing me the ropes and introducing me to all kinds of masos."

"Was it, uh, Danny?"

Mónica chuckled behind me. "Kara here is everything but patient."

"I mean, I'm aware, Ma'am," I grumbled.

People chuckled, but it wasn't fair. I couldn't control my impatience all of the time, and I was curious.

"He was," León squeezed his sub, I guessed, closer, until Danny got the clue and shifted to sit on his lap. "He'd barely reached our table, and this so-called Sadist got him on his knees, face pressed against the floor with his boot, and is pulling out his belt.

"Now, to be clear, I don't have a problem with that level of SM, and I didn't back then either, but literally nothing in Dan's body said he either wanted or was into any of it." León licked his lips before he continued talking. At this point, I was hyper focused on his every move, counting every breath. It was that or focusing on the dread building up inside of me. "I didn't care about any of it. I didn't care about my brother's best friend, or the fact that this guy was my entry ticket to a community I'd dreamed of for years. I think he got, what, maybe two swats in before I was all up in his face, and was pulling Dan away.

"I didn't speak with those two again, and honestly, it was for the better." He scowled now. "I ruined my most important relationship for a stranger, and no, it wasn't because of love at first sight or any other bullshit. The point is, if I wasn't afraid to ruin the only link I had to my brother, no offense, but I'm not afraid to do the same with any of the people here."

I gulped down. There was steely determination in his face, a fierceness that didn't look so scary anymore. I still turned to Danny—or Dan? Maybe that was just how León called him.

"What did you do?"

"Oh." He cleared his throat. "I acted very rationally and yelled at him. Pretty sure I broke some skin, too."

León rolled his eyes. "Because you're a piece of shit?"

"I was going through a phase," he retorted. "Y'know, the

whole I-need-to-be-punished-hard-and-fuck-everything-else. I went to unsafe Doms because I didn't think the ones who were all about consent and shit would go as hard on me as I wanted."

I nodded. I'd met subs like that back in the States, too.

"And, León helped?"

Danny chuckled. "That's one way of seeing it."

That earned him a pinch on the side, but it was fine. I didn't put conscious thought into it, but I relaxed against Mónica, my heartbeat slowing down. It was fine. They were… Well, they were still intimidating, but they were safe.

"León and Danny run some of the best workshops on impact play, safety, and limits I've ever seen," Erika supplied. "Also the ones where the largest percentage of Doms are kicked out."

León shrugged. "Just getting rid of the bad weeds for all of you."

"Yeah, because you don't enjoy it, Sir," Cece said—while half-hidden behind Jaime.

León just smirked.

And I knew things were going to be all right.

30

MÓNICA

It was clear as day that something had shifted within Kara. After León shared his story, and Sergio felt the need to tackle her to the ground to remind her he was still her appointed protector—his words—the ambience had started to relax.

The pups tried to rile up León while simultaneously hiding away from him—which was the usual. María whispered something that looked a lot like begging to Erika. Eli watched everyone in silence, but their body betrayed them as they relaxed into Erika as well. The woman was sandwiched, not that I thought she minded too much.

Then there was Kara. At first, she'd just slowly—but surely—begun to relax in a similar fashion as Eli. Unlike Eli, though, the Little brat wasn't just happy feeling their Domme's warmth. No, at one point, Kara started to—not so subtly—grind her hips like a puppy against my legs. Her hands moved to the hem of my shirt, too, hesitant.

"What is it, baby girl?"

She looked up with those big eyes, her pupils slightly dilated as her lips parted. "I'm... I know you said this wasn't my initiation ritual like I'd thought, but... You'd still planned for something, right, because we're in *the* room, and I... uh, may be remembering what went down last time, and..."

I raised an eyebrow. I'd figured it would come up, but I hadn't wanted to add pressure by making sex a compulsory part of it. My priority had been that it sank into her that she was safe here.

It didn't mean I hadn't accounted for this, too. After all, I'd witnessed her hunger for more, for everyone and everything.

"Are you horny? Is that what you're trying to say?"

Kara didn't answer—not with words. Instead, she just let out a mewling sound, her spine arching toward me.

"Stay with me, baby girl." I ran a hand down her face, her neck, then her still covered body. "I need you to make a choice."

"Yes, Ma'am," she breathed, her chest rising up and down.

Fuck, I needed to be inside of her, needed to see her fall apart. Over and over and over.

"Do you want me to take you apart? To show everyone what a good girl you are?" My fingers traced back to the straps of her dress, tugging them down. "Or do you want to service them instead? So everyone can see how well you obey me?"

Truth be told, as much as I wanted her all for myself, the second plan had me clenching my thighs, desperate for her to choose it.

There would be time, though.

"C-can I..." Kara blushed, licked her bottom lip. I needed to get her some water before we did anything. "Can I choose both? First service, and then you... finish."

That was what I meant when I noticed the primal player in her. When she got in the headspace, she was a selfish little thing, fighting to get all the pleasure for herself, all the sensation. No thoughts or complex emotions got in the way of it. It was just need.

"That'll be my honor," I said. I meant it. My lips met hers, her supple mouth opening for me without thought. "Why don't you start with María, since we both know she wants to play with you so badly?"

Before Kara could answer, María perked up the second she heard her name. Someone should study the hearing abilities of switches, because I'd swear it was a thing.

"I'm not taking offense to that, Ma'am."

"I don't want you to," I snorted.

I was certain she had more to say to that, but Kara leaned closer to me, squirming until she was all but climbing me. "What do I do, Ma'am?"

"Hmm…" I pretended to think about it, but there was not much thinking to do. "With how much she's talked about your mouth, I think you should eat her out, don't you? Show her how well you can do it?"

My words hit the intended effect, Kara's skin flushing before she nodded, lower lip between her teeth.

"You just have to do what I tell you, remember? No thinking for my baby girl."

Kara squirmed. "Yes, Ma'am."

Her eyes fluttered closed for a second. I gave it to her, my hands on her, caressing. I'd soon noticed she reacted more to touch than she did words. It was not something I foresaw having a problem with.

She settled quickly, too. It wasn't long until she was getting rid of her dress, tying her hair up in a ponytail and pressing herself against María.

The image of the two of them together, the contrast in their bodies—María's ginger hair versus Kara's blonde locks—made for a fucking beautiful picture.

"I'm not feeling very Dommy today," María spoke in her ear, loud enough for me to hear, "but I'm not gonna say no to anything you wanna do to me."

Kara gasped, while María exchanged a look with me. I nodded at her. "You don't have to be Dommy," Kara reassured quickly. It really tugged at my heartstrings how protective she could be—of anyone who wasn't a Domm. "That's what Mónica is for."

María chuckled. "How could I have forgotten?"

I didn't have time to scold her for the tone. I didn't feel inclined to, either, not even when Erika raised an eyebrow in my direction.

I'd always enjoyed a certain level of protocol, of old school BDSM, but that enjoyment, that need for it, wasn't there when Kara was concerned. As I'd told her, I wanted to worship her—to take it one step further and show her she should be worshiped. By everyone.

I'd definitely have to revisit the idea of an initiation ritual. With a few tweaks that had everyone worshiping every pore of her skin. Marking her as theirs, too.

"STILL WANT MORE, BABY GIRL?"

I'd thought she'd be exhausted after León and Danny tag-teamed her. Apparently, Kara was full of surprises. She was all flushed, sweating, eyes half hooded, but still trying to rub herself on me. Still wet.

It had given me so many ideas to watch them—to watch *her*, really. The way she'd squeezed between them, and she'd looked up at León to double check he wouldn't hurt her. That was all it had taken before those two had awakened the primal player in Kara.

Most of her sweat came from playing with them.

"Always, Ma'am."

I had to say, I didn't quite mind ignoring the fact that she sounded half-drunk on lust. My gaze was too zeroed in on the glistening in her folds, the fact that it wasn't just her but her body begging for more, throbbing.

"Fuck." I couldn't help but growl, hoisting her up until her back was pressed against my chest, my fingers pressing against her clit. "Wanna know what I think, baby girl?"

Kara clamped down, her body tensing before succumbing to my touch. "W-what do you think, Ma'am?"

"I think," I hummed, teasing her entrance with the tip of my gloved fingers, "the only way to satisfy a size queen like you is shoving a fist up your pretty pussy."

I paused for a second, enough to note the way Kara froze before growing incessant, pushing against my fingers with an almost sense of desperation. "Please, Mónica, need. Please."

"Sshh." I wiped some stray hairs from her face, kissing the skin there. "I need to get other gloves for that, baby girl. Need you to behave for me."

Erika was already up before I finished talking, though. I hadn't fisted anyone in a while, but she still knew the lube and the nitrile gloves I preferred, quickly returning with both items.

Kara whimpered and squirmed against me. I didn't think she'd even noticed Erika moving. My arm tightened around her middle. "Have you been fisted before?"

She'd hinted she was interested during one of our dinners, but I hadn't asked about her history, then. One day, I would have to, but things had felt too fresh. I didn't want to tarnish everything with ugly memories of abuse and insecurity. I'd rather build new connections for her, to play it by ear while we got to know each other better, deeper.

"N-no." She screwed her eyes shut, the poor thing, almost panting as I kept teasing her most sensitive skin. "I've always wanted to, though. Got off on the idea."

"Yeah? Doesn't surprise me," I teased. "Want Erika to hold you?"

"Huh?"

"Fisting can be overwhelming when you're not used to it," I explained. "Hell, even when you are."

Kara chewed on her lip. I was considering taking it back, switching gloves, and starting to open her up when she nodded.

"Erika?"

I didn't bother looking for her. I just started prepping. She was right there in a second, anyway, easing Kara until her head was resting on Erika's bare thigh.

"Thank you, little one," she murmured. "Means a lot that you trust me like this, you know that?"

Kara nodded through a broken moan. She writhed *a lot*, apparently unable to not chase some kind of pleasure.

It was so stupidly addictive.

"I wanna hold your thighs up and keep you spread open for your Domme," Erika kept talking to her. "Is that okay?"

I held my breath for the two seconds it took Kara to nod.

It was a vulnerable position. I was right there between her legs the second Erika had manhandled her into it.

"You look so fucking pretty, baby girl." I used the hand that didn't have the glove on to tease her outer labia. The way she shivered with that mere touch was like a shot straight to my core. "Exposing yourself so well for me."

Kara's lips parted, small pants of breath coming out. She didn't take her eyes off me.

I didn't want her to.

What I wanted was to be inside of her, to have her writhe and pant and make all those alluring sounds for me. It was possessive, but I wanted to be the one that left her gaping the widest, the one that stretched her farther than anyone else tonight.

I covered the nitrile in lube before teasing her entrance. Kara's eyes widened, her throat bobbing up and down.

"Breathe with me, baby girl," I soothed. "Just tell me when you're ready."

Kara nodded, her eyes closing for a heartbeat. "Ready, Ma'am."

"Use my arms to hold on if you need to, little one," Erika spoke. "You have your safe words with Mónica, but squeeze three times, and everything stops."

This was why I loved playing with Erika. There was no one I'd trust more with a sub's safety.

"Thank you, Mistress."

"We use the color system, is that right, baby girl?"

Kara nodded once again, her back arching off the floor. Erika had to press her back down. She really was needy.

I couldn't deny her much longer.

Everyone had formed a tighter circle around us by the time I slipped two fingers inside her, their breaths mingling, adding more temperature to the room.

Kara keened, her head canted backwards.

"Eyes on me, baby girl. I want you to see everything. Can you do that for me?"

I teased her walls, rubbing against the wrinkled flesh while I waited for an answer, or for her eyes to focus back on me—whatever happened first.

It was the latter.

"You feel so fucking warm, baby girl, even through the glove. They've all really made a mess of you, haven't they?" I cooed, teasing. Some chuckled, some moaned, but they soon became little more than background noise. "Must be aching some, too."

"Yes, Ma'am," Kara cried out, her pants coming harsher.

Probably because I slid back enough to add a third finger.

"And yet you said yes to being fisted?" I whistled. "Your very first time, too. So brave of you."

She just gurgled some nonsense in response. I smirked, pressing my thumb against her clit. It was easy to find a flow, where I added more pressure, more depth, and she let her body adjust before bucking her hips to get more of it.

It was pure instinct. She was the dream sub I didn't know I'd been waiting for.

Four fingers were quickly in. My insides were throbbing, the result of being mesmerized by the way her body clenched around my hand, sucking me in.

"You feel so full already, don't you?"

Kara sniffled, faintly, biting on her lip. "Yes, Ma'am."

"You're so close to taking my fist." I bunched up my fingers, getting ready to pour more lube on the glove. "You want to take it, don't you?"

She nodded again. My poor baby girl looked so flushed, so overwhelmed, eyes darted in all directions, but her body kept begging for this, and she was listening to it. She was trusting.

It was a heady feeling.

"You're so fucking obedient," I hummed.

I slid my fingers out, only enough that I could thrust in again, this time sliding my thumb in. Kara screamed when she felt the increase, her body thrashing.

"Breathe, baby girl," I instructed. "Just breathe and let me play with your hole. Let everyone see what you let me do to you."

Shivers wrecked through her body. I waited her out, exchanging a glance with Erika. I knew she loved that kind of talk, where we told our subs their bodies were ours to do as we pleased. She was smirking, clearly enjoying the show.

Maybe we could organize something more intimate sometime, the three of us. Get Kara over her fears of Dommes once and for all.

"More, Ma'am."

My breath hitched, thighs clenching. If it was only the words, I probably would've still set the pace. But it wasn't just her words. It was the way her inner walls kept clenching around my fingers, the tight squeeze almost painful.

"You want more, huh?" I grinned. "Want my whole hand in you, don't you?"

"Please," she sobbed.

She was looking more and more like a mess with every passing minute. The good kind of mess, the one that belonged around wrinkled sheets and in erotic albums.

"I've got you, baby girl."

It was when she was stretched to the fullest, when I was trying to slide in the thickest part of my fist, right around my thumb's first knuckle, that Kara was the most beautiful. When she looked the wildest, the most driven by the physicality of the act, by the pleasure and the overwhelming sense of fullness that had to eclipse everything else around her.

I had it really fucking bad for her.

Fucking her was as easy, as natural as breathing, after that. Her whimpers, soft cries, the way her lips parted every time my wrist slid inside of her, reaching her deepest parts, silent and not so silent moans and pleas falling off her lips, I noted them all. Tucked them all away in my head, where they'd be safe.

Where she'd be safe.

Always.

31

MÓNICA

"Nervous about your performance review?"

Although I had asked her just that morning, it wasn't me who did it. No, it was Noel, who was strolling inside the break room as if he knew something I didn't. It was always the same thing with him. He just didn't know he had a tell, and I wasn't about to enlighten him.

Kara wasn't as proficient in reading Noel, though. Perhaps because I kept him—and the rest of my brothers—as far away from her as I could. It was already bad enough that their so-called joking that first week after they learned we were together had gone unpunished.

"I asked one of the women in HR last week and she said I had nothing to worry about," she gulped.

Without caring what my dear brother had to say about it, I rested a hand above her knee. I couldn't wait to cash in my summer vacation, but it had felt pointless when she couldn't cash in hers yet.

"Well of course you don't." He chuckled. "You're family, right?"

I glowered. "Was there any reason you came in here while I'm trying to have my coffee?"

"Easy." He raised his palms in the air as if that had ever worked on me. "Just being friendly."

Except there had only been derision in his tone, and he was well aware of it.

After squeezing Kara's leg, I stood up, my movements casual, practiced, as I strode up to him. He'd always been taller, wider, but he'd never known how to use that weight to assert himself.

"Well, I appreciate that. Perhaps I could return the favor too, and pay a friendly visit to the CFO who keeps embellishing your numbers?"

That had him drop the smug facade. I saw fear cover his features—it was a blessing only our hair color and eyes would mark us as siblings. His lips twitched, a slight tremble to his lower lip that had always been another tell I wouldn't warn him about.

"That's what I thought."

"You can't prove that."

"Oh, but I can." I shrugged. "I just don't care too much for having to find another job when those dealings make the company collapse. I'd also rather not break Father's heart like that. Doesn't mean I don't have dirt on each and every one of you."

It was the only way to survive in a family that didn't see past the fact that I was born with a uterus instead of a dick.

It might've been unethical, but their entire existence was. I might as well get something done while I was at it.

Noel didn't stay long after that, spluttering something under his breath while he walked toward the elevator. Despite being the oldest, he was taking more and more after Javi, showing up around the office only when it was convenient.

"He was just talking, right?" Kara's trembling voice pulled me back to the present, to the break room we were still in. Her fingers wrapped around a cup of coffee that looked more like steamed milk after all the creamer she'd added to it. "I mean, he wouldn't have done anything to jeopardize my review, right?"

"He'd need more than two brain cells for that." I scoffed before I was in front of her, fitting right between her thighs. We kept PDA at a minimum in the office, but that was when my brothers didn't decide playing with my sub's feelings was nice entertainment. "But no, I can assure you your performance review is going to go great. You've been an amazing asset to the company, and all the reports show it."

Kara scowled. She was looking especially prim today. She'd spent thirty minutes trying to tame her hair into the perfect ponytail, and that was after obsessing over her wardrobe all weekend. Not that I was complaining about the coordinated outfit and pencil skirt with a length that bordered on inappropriate.

Business attire had never been too strictly enforced around here. It was one of the things I could actually stand about the place.

"It's so hot when you're mean like that," she confessed.

I chuckled, tucking two fingers under her chin. "Imagine saying those words a few months ago, completely unprompted."

Kara scrunched up her nose, heat quickly spreading down her cheeks. "I still prefer it when you're mean to *others*, though, not me."

"I'll make it up to you."

I hadn't made plans at the club for no reason, after all.

"SO WHAT'S THE PLAN?" Kara pretended to huff with the Herculean effort of sliding the knee high boots up my calves.

I could always tell what mood she was in depending on how she went around it. Some days she was docile, almost reverent. Those were the days when she'd beg to be filled, fucked, to service and worship me—or anyone I told her to—in any and every way.

Other days, she made a whole production of it, huffing and playing around and getting distracted by every shiny thing in a ten mile radius, her thoughts scattering in every direction.

Those were the days when I did the servicing, when I wrapped her up in blankets and stuffies and brought out her coloring books. They were the days when I'd pin her to a bed and kiss every inch of skin and give her so much praise my brain forgot other words existed.

"We're celebrating, of course."

Kara snorted. "But you're the one who kept saying it was only a formality."

"Formalities still call for celebration." I shrugged.

It wasn't as if going to the club was such a special occasion. Unless her roommates had roped her into spending time with them—which I was really fucking glad for—that was when we spent most weekends. Evenings depended on a lot of factors, but…

Let's just say she'd spent enough time here, in my space, that Prince didn't run in the opposite direction now when we walked in.

"You're silly."

"You like it when I'm silly, remember?"

She chuckled, nuzzling against my still half-tied boot. She looked so fucking dreamy, so content. Even with all that product still in her hair.

"I really do."

"Good."

"Ma'am?" She looked down before she switched positions, on her knees between my legs.

My hand moved immediately to her cheek. It wasn't a rarity that she got nervous or shy around me, but I still itched to comfort her when it happened.

"Yes, baby girl?"

My whole focus was zeroed in on her—on the way her eyelids fluttered, her breath hitched. She knew it, too.

"I love you."

Fucking hell.

She tended to do this, to find the perfect moment to catch me off guard, to say the words that hit straight to my core. It didn't matter if they were new, or something she told me every day. She had a direct line to my heart, somehow.

The corny part of me believed she'd always had, from day one.

"I love you," I said back.

I pulled her up, enough that I could press my lips to hers, breathe in her scent, get drunk in the way she went completely pliant for me.

"Could we stay here some more?"

The question made me frown. When I pulled back, she was chewing on her lip, cheeks flaming red.

"You don't wanna leave?"

There was some more chewing before I pulled her lip off with my thumb. Before she shivered, letting her body chase after my hand.

"I do, but..." Her fingers found my belt, tugging and letting go softly. "I wanna have Little me-time."

"Okay." I kissed the top of her forehead. If only she knew I'd been counting on it, that I could read what she needed and wanted with little more than a look. "What would you say if my plan was to have you sitting by my side with your favorite blankies and stuffies?"

She perked up right away, those stormy eyes that hadn't looked so stormy in the past couple of months studying me. "And books?"

"And books. Everything else you could possibly want, too."

"Really?"

"Really."

"Hmm…" There was that glint in her eyes, the one I'd associated quickly to her feeling extra playful. Every time, it took weight off my chest. I didn't realize I was carrying it until I saw it there. "Ice cream?"

"Before or after we arrive?"

"Both?"

I shook my head.

I guessed I'd walked right into that one.

Littles.

"Just for today."

Kara turned serious, right away, lips furrowed into a thin line. "Of course, Ma'am. I'm responsible like that."

"You are."

Just not when it came to pesky little things like sugar intake in the shape of milkshakes and ice cream.

"So you'd better not forget it."

"I wouldn't dream of it." I gave her ass a playful swat. That was all the pain I'd ever give her, but I was a sucker for her offended gasps and indignant huffs. "Now finish getting me ready."

"Excuse you!"

"Kara…" I only had to raise an eyebrow.

Punishments weren't a thing between us. Every other Domm at the club gave me a look when they heard me say that, but they just weren't. It didn't mean that I wouldn't tease the line when she gave me sass or let out that tiny brat of hers she kept denying. Just the thrill of the threat was enough for her, though, to slow the rapid fire thinking and settle her.

I couldn't care less that I didn't put her over my knee to spank her every other day. There were always pain sluts at the club if I was craving something, but the truth was that I rarely did. I was just happy watching her settle, watching her rediscover everything she'd loved about kink, and about herself, really.

It was a beautiful thing to see now that all the walls were crumbling down.

EPILOGUE
KARA

"Long day?"

Wow.

I really had to work on my poker face. I'd puff about if I wasn't so emotionally exhausted right now. Instead, I plopped down on the stool by the kitchen and let out the loudest of sighs.

"My therapist hates me."

Alex laughed. They literally laughed. I hated them—and they could say goodbye to the slice of cake I'd saved for them. I'd save it for Sergio now.

"I don't think that's how it works."

That was what they all said. Why did I think that EDMR stuff was going to be a good idea? She'd just made so much sense when she talked about trauma processing and all those studies. I didn't remember her saying anything about how my brain would hurt afterwards.

It hurt a lot—enough that I was considering calling out sick tomorrow. Mónica would not be mad, and no one could say it was preferential treatment because it would be my first sick day in an entire year. Besides, Mónica wasn't in charge of my performance reviews, so there would be no way to exert that preferential treatment. It didn't mean I didn't get paranoid about it from time to time, especially when her brothers were in a "teasing" mood.

"I'm not hungry."

The granite counter felt so nice against my cheek. Maybe I could just fall asleep here until my alarm rang.

"Did I offer you food?"

Oh, right, Alex was still there. Sometimes I thought it would be nice to move in with Mónica—I'd heard her talk about it a couple of times. But then I'd miss these two. And I liked having my own space. My first therapist had said it was good to prioritize that.

I shouldn't have changed therapists.

It had made sense at the time—the one I'd first seen when I moved here had started to be too swamped, and I felt like progress was happening too slowly and it kept frustrating me. But she didn't make my brain hurt with weird machines.

Ugh.

And I wasn't the kind of person who recovered from a headache just like that. My head was going to be throbbing all week, I could just see it.

"Mónica's taking me to dinner," I explained, when I remembered Alex was there, and still waiting for an answer.

"You know you can cancel, right?" They sat down next to me. It was nice. They weren't very physical, I'd noticed, but they made an effort regardless. "I know she's your Domme and all that, but you can still say no to her plans."

Tsk.

Of course I knew that.

"I don't wanna cancel," I whined. "I wanna see her and get cuddles."

Alex didn't say anything. I knew that if I turned to look at them, they'd have that expression they sometimes made when they were trying to figure me out. It was funny. I didn't think I was so weird.

Who didn't want cuddles from their girlfriend, anyway?

"Did you want tea?"

"Hm... If you agree to add a shit-ton of sugar."

It was a good thing Mónica wasn't one of those Dommes who cared about language. Not that I cursed too much.

Maybe that was why?

"I think that defeats the purpose."

Whatever. I didn't have the energy to stick my tongue out, but the sentiment was there.

Instead, I grabbed my phone from where I'd dropped it on the counter and squinted at the screen. The brightness was somehow too loud even though I'd set it to zero.

KARA

hiii

do you not care about subs cursing in general, or do i not curse enough for you to make it a thing?

many Domms make it a thing

MÓNICA

You never curse as a Little.

But, no, I do not care about cursing. Why?

KARA

i just did and realized

nvm

my brain's not working right

MÓNICA

Therapy?

KARA

yeah

> **i want milkshakes**
>
> **and cuddles**

MÓNICA

We can do that.

> KARA
>
> **but dinner!!**

MÓNICA

We can go to dinner any other day.

I'll pick you up around 5, okay? I'm picking up groceries and stuff for the cats.

I didn't need the phone's reflection to realize I was pouting. I did want milkshakes and cuddles, but I'd wanted to go have dinner, too. Valentine's Day was coming soon, and it turned out I was way mushier than I remembered.

We'd already agreed we'd be going to Plumas with everyone else, but I'd thought today's dinner was somewhat of a premature Valentine's date just for the two of us.

I probably should've just asked.

Being so much in my head was exhausting—and it led to forgetting stuff like that. Or not realizing it was important.

It was a good thing my brain fogs were contained to just my personal life, and Mónica didn't mind repeating herself.

Erika would've already thrown me to the curb—probably.

I still liked her, though.

That reminded me I had to text her.

> KARA
>
> **is your friend coming in the end???**
>
> *** Mistress ???**
>
> **sorry**

PLAY PRETEND

> brain hurts

ERIKA

I already told you you don't have to use a honorific every time, especially when we're not at the club

> KARA
>
> and i already told you if i don't i will forget at the club and i'd rather not risk it Ma'am
>
> you're scary
>
> we've been over this

ERIKA

...

Sergio is rubbing off on you in all the wrong ways

But yes, my friend is moving here and he'll be at the club for Valentine's

Anything else?

> KARA
>
> no...?
>
> but just for the record, i'm offended
>
> who says Sergio's the one rubbing off on me and not the other way around?

ERIKA

Tell Mónica I wish her the best

> KARA
>
> ???

ERIKA

She'll know what I mean

Erika texted funny sometimes. I was *not* going to tell

Mónica that, though. It was calling for trouble, and I was not about that life. No, sir. Trouble was overrated. I'd rather snuggle in and play and have fun, and then have her or whoever Mónica said have their way with me.

Things were easy with her, and I'd missed easy. I'd forgotten things could be like that, not muddled in a million layers and mind games I didn't remember having consented to.

Ugh.

I screwed my eyes shut.

My therapist hadn't warned me—or not enough—about the headache, but she had suggested I had things to distract myself with throughout the week. Apparently, EMDR was effective and faster and all the good stuff, but it also brought everything back to the surface in a rawer format.

It sucked.

At least I got enough of a good cry in therapy. I should be good for the week.

The month, really.

Some Domms at the club had started to talk about how I always ended up in tears, and it wasn't fair. I'd even told Mónica, who'd then proceeded to go on about tearing them a new one.

I stopped her, but I liked seeing how much she cared. It still was a bit of a novelty.

"ARE YOU A LITTLE OR A PUPPY?"

Shit.

I jumped at Lucas' voice. The two of them had taken a week off to go to a concert somewhere this weekend. I'd miss how Lucas didn't understand the concept of minding his own business more than half of the time.

"What are you talking about?" I squeaked, and then winced.

The headache had gone down—a teeny tiny bit—but loud voices weren't great yet. Definitely not mine.

"You've been staring through the door's peephole like a puppy waiting for their owner to come home after work."

I scoffed.

I really, really wanted to protest, too, but I'd kind of been doing that. Mónica texted when she got in the car, and I'd already gotten dressed and had nothing to do, so I might've come downstairs to wait until I saw her car.

She had a flashy car, so it wasn't hard to spot.

"Shut up," I grumbled. "But just FYI, puppies are really fun and you can't pit us against each other. Tsk."

I wondered if Jaime and Cece would be at the club for Valentine's. I hadn't seen them in a few months, and it sucked. Besides, when they were around, I somehow managed to end up on all fours—on Mónica's orders—and fucked by one or both of them.

It wasn't my fault that they really knew how to use a strap-on.

That wasn't the train of thought I'd wanted to be riding today, though.

Ugh.

Maybe Erika was right and Sergio was rubbing off on me. I wanted to say my brain used to have more of a filter.

Whatever.

While we were talking, my phone buzzed with a text. I didn't bother checking it out. Instead, I peered through the peephole.

Yep, Mónica was parked in front of the house.

"She here?" Lucas asked.

"Yep!" I winced again. That had been too loud, too. Oops? "I think I'll see you in the morning, but if not, have fun at the concert!"

"Thanks, Kar." I beamed. I loved when he called me that —or anyone else, but Lucas had started it. "Don't do anything I wouldn't do."

"I still don't know what that means!" I teased, but I was already out of the house before he could answer.

One day I'd get him to stop being so tightlipped about his sex life. Quid pro quo was supposed to be a thing, but he knew pretty much all there was to know about mine.

There was a possibility I might actually need to work on having a filter after all. Not today, though. Today I'd just be getting cuddles and all the good things.

It was when I got into the passenger seat that I began to panic. Well, it was when I noticed that Mónica had her hair pulled back, and she was wearing her leather pants and the jacket that I'd said was my favorite of hers because her boobs looked so plump and nice.

And in the meantime, I'd gone for comfort and put on the biggest, most oversized sweatshirt I could find and leggings and boots with all the fluff inside.

"Shit." I licked my lips, my mouth dry. "It's... It's fine, I'll go change, I'm sorry, I was just... I'm so sorry, I swear I won't take long, I—"

"Hey." When I dared to look up, Mónica was frowning. "What's going on, baby girl?"

"You just..." I tried to take a deep breath, but it was hard. It had been a long time since I last panicked over stuff like this, but I couldn't help it. "You look so good and date-ready, and I don't, but I'll just—"

"You look perfect," she interrupted. "I'd already gotten dressed before I went to do groceries, before you texted me, and I wanted to pick you up on time."

"Oh." I nodded, gulping. At least I wasn't bursting into tears? "I'm sorry. I mean, yeah, I know you're gonna call me out for apologizing. I guess it's the EMDR thing?"

For a fleeting second, I pictured images I hadn't wanted to see. Laughter and mockery.

"Come here, baby girl," she said instead.

It took me a second to focus, to process what she was saying. "I don't know if I fit."

"I have faith in you."

I couldn't muster a laugh, but I appreciated the effort.

I didn't appreciate having to squeeze through her not spacious enough car, but being on her lap felt good. Even if the wheel was poking at my back.

Her hands cupping my cheeks made up for the discomfort.

"What did I say when you told me about this new therapist?"

I sighed, the memory of snuggling Princess on her bed replacing the ones that kept me in survival mode. "You said that you thought I was doing better, but you understood if I wanted to give a new therapy a try and you just wanted to be there for me."

"That's it," Mónica hummed before she leaned forward and kissed me. The movement meant my back pressed the wheel harder. I almost leaped when the car honked, but Mónica was there. Holding me tighter. "And what did I say when you told me what your therapist explained about what to expect after the first sessions?"

"Uh…" I scrunched up my nose. There was a slight possibility I hadn't been paying much attention to that one. "That you… were okay with it?"

"I'd like to think I was a bit wordier than that," she teased. Her lips turned up in a soft smirk that gave her a more playful air when she was teasing. "I said that momentary setbacks didn't scare me, that you would be fine because you had people who took care of you, and that I only cared about you growing your confidence back."

"Huh. That rings a bell, I think."

"I'll take it." She shook her head, but it was the soft kind of exasperation. "So, the plan for today is I'm going to go get you your milkshake, and one of the sandwiches you like. And you're going to wait in the car, and then we're going to enjoy a slow day on my couch. Okay?"

"With blankies?"

"With all the blankies you manage to bundle up together."

Huh.

That was a very large number of blankies. I recognized what she was playing at, though. Pulling me into Little space, giving me a challenge of sorts that was just about fun.

I didn't mind it. I loved her more for it, if anything.

"I'm going to build the perfect fort."

"Only if you let me inside the fort."

I grinned. She might be a badass manager at work, but she was also the silliest Domme. "Always."

I moved off her lap—making the honk go off again—after that and just watched her. I understood how others could perceive her—detached, aloof, maybe with a superiority complex, or even cold. I even understood that she had to present that way in front of her family, or at work. But watching her… I'd been trying to listen to my gut instinct more, lately. My gut said Mónica equaled warmth, and joy, and safety, and a net to fall back on. She'd given me a chance. A community. She'd stood up for me, but even more than that, and regardless of how much she'd fight me if she learned to read my mind, she'd given me myself back.

"You're staring awfully hard," she said. I'd barely noticed

she'd stopped the car at a red light. There were too many traffic lights in this town. "Should I be concerned?"

"No, Ma'am." I must have the goofiest smile on my face. I didn't even care. "I'm just really really glad you weren't one of those bosses really set against dating their employees."

I now knew—yay, therapy!—that I would've still made it, still passed my probationary period, even if I hadn't met Mónica. Because I was good at my job.

But it didn't matter. My point stood.

Mónica snorted. "Even when my brothers unload their workload on me, and you end up having to rewrite an email five times?"

I chuckled. "Even then."

Not to say that I enjoyed the pressure or the momentary bouts of imposter syndrome as a result, but... If that was the only bad thing I could think of—and I didn't even think of it as part of our relationship—then I'd say I was doing pretty well for myself.

"I love you, baby girl."

"I love you, Ma'am." I reached out to intertwine our fingers together. "Thank you. For seeing me, and... taking a chance."

The light turned green, but Mónica still spared a glance my way. "Best decision I've ever made."

"Even if you're now a regular buyer of unicorn milkshakes?"

She chuckled before letting go of my hand. If you asked me, responsible driving was overrated—but that was probably the reason why I didn't have a driver's license.

"Even then," she murmured, copying my words.

"I love you."

Yes, I'd just said it, but I was riding on the mushy train today, so I might as well keep it going.

"Love you."

***

Thank you so much for reading *Play Pretend*. Consider leaving a review or telling your friends about it so more people can fall in love with Kara and Mónica, too.

ACKNOWLEDGMENTS

This book wouldn't have been possible—or as fun to write—without the support of my super fans:

- Allie
- Ana
- Giorgia
- Jordyn
- Katy

ABOUT THE AUTHOR

Hi! My name is Emily Alter (she/he/they), and I'm a queer, kinky and polyamorous author of both gay and sapphic romance books. When I'm not writing or being a brat to someone who has consented to it, I do my bit of activism as a social psychologist and licensed sex therapist in Madrid, Spain.

My writing journey began when I was a child who couldn't get enough of *Xena: The Warrior Princess* and decided to take matters into my own hands. Since then, I've become a voracious reader and a self-published author who can talk for hours about my craft, tropes, and the characters who drive all of the stories living rent free in my head.

I write in different sub-genres, and I'm always working on more than one series at a time, but a few things that always stay the same across all of my books and universes are themes of found/chosen family, sex positivity, mental health awareness, and a dash of social justice.

ALSO BY EMILY ALTER

Wanna read more kinky sapphic stuff?

Plumas Universe

Play Pretend

Just One Rule

Home Kinky Home

Mistress: Found

Multi-author series

Temptation at Randy's (Diner Days)

Dare to try adding some gay spice in there? I've got you!

Plumas Universe

Hopes and Dreams

Matching Wounds

Multi-author series

Wrestling with Daddy (Pet Play by the Lake)

Gift for a Demon (Possessive Love)

Printed in Great Britain
by Amazon